# BILLIONAIRE'S PARADISE

# BILLIONAIRE'S PARADISE

*Ecstasy at Sea*

## Peter Antonucci

Willow Street Press  New York

*To my mother, Aida, who taught me to love books
and always dreamed I would develop the
concentration, dedication and enthusiasm to write
them, and my father, Anthony, who taught me that
there are no shortcuts in life.*

# CHAPTER ONE

Eva Gabriella Lampedusa reveled in being the hottest, smartest and most successful woman in her world of women. It came entirely naturally to her.

You know the type. Tall women with flawless skin, perfectly plump lips, pin straight golden hair and deliciously tight Armani navy blue slacks riding below elegant (and slightly unbuttoned) cream-colored blouses, revealing a strand of South Sea pinkish pearls – just enough to draw your attention to their alluring cleavage. These women glide effortlessly along the Manhattan sidewalks with abundant aplomb, making the most intimate secrets of their cell phone conversations audible to anyone within ten feet. Intimate details every man strains to hear.

In Manhattan, they're ubiquitous. It's amazing how many perfect tens there are on any block, in any department store, fitness club, or grocery store. They range from seventeen to seventy, blonde to redhead, adorably short to super-model tall. No matter your taste or preference, Manhattan has an abundance of women who are "perfect." Oh, and smart and rich, too – if you like them smart and rich, that is. You can avail yourself of a senior partner from Skadden Arps who looks like a Hawaiian Tropic model or a managing director at Goldman Sachs who outshines Kate Upton.

Some might turn up their noses at that kind of woman. But the men in their Brooks Brothers suits – or in those dreadful business casual Dockers khaki pants and pastel Ralph Lauren button downs with their sleeves rolled halfway up their hairy forearms – find these captivating prima donnas fascinating. Other women must take notice of these goddesses, too; after all, they need to take constant stock of their competition.

It makes no difference that their breasts are enhanced, their golden hair color acquired from a tube, their skin polished and pinned with the latest techniques that the amazing plastic surgeon, Dr. Arnold Banterman, picked up during his last visit to Brazil; and their somewhat less than flat tummies and decidedly more than flat asses evened out by that modern-day miracle of curve redistribution, Spanx. All that matters to these women is that they are coifed, made up, and dressed impeccably to command the attention of all. They like to think it's their world and we just live in it. And they just may be right.

These women who, loosely, consider themselves the gold standard of society in Manhattan and the Hamptons, and who often behave *loosely* as a means of attracting their prey, profess to never being concerned about mundane matters of appearance, money or status – or at least that's what they want everyone to believe. Truth is, there is nothing that concerns them more. When one member of the self-absorbed housewives club gets invited to sit in Mayor de Blasio's box at Yankee Stadium, or to attend opening night of Fashion Week as a front-row guest of Prada, the others cringe with jealousy and plot their next move. And when one gets Botox or a tuck, the others all tell her how "absolutely maahvelous" she looks, then snipe mercilessly behind her back. "Did you see all the lines he left around her eyes? He's a butcher, but you get what you pay for, you know."

Eva Lampedusa was different, and she knew it. As she strutted purposefully through Manhattan, men couldn't help but stare at her finely sculpted ass, the globes of which undulated rhythmically, attracting the attention of everyone on the block. But Eva had something none of the others had, and they all coveted – she was naturally radiant. Born in Cartagena of a Colombian father and Danish mother, she had dark, olive skin, black hair, and cobalt blue eyes so penetrating everyone assumed their amazing color could only have been achieved by contact lenses. It wasn't. Her 5'11, 128-pound frame didn't hurt things either. Nor did Eva's four sessions a week at the exclusive Upper West Side Equinox gym where she commanded the attention of all her gym mates. Even there, Eva was different. Eva was not the typical Equinox client who was there to tell her friends how often she worked out, chat with her trainer, or meet a handsome investment banker. Eva was there because she had a passion for fitness. And, as a result, everyone had a passion for Eva.

It wasn't just her beauty that was so compelling. She had depth. Having graduated from Vassar, then completing her law degree at New York University (summa cum laude), she was flooded with employment offers by the most prestigious firms in the country. She settled on Wilson Everson, an 1,100-lawyer international firm headquartered in the prestigious General Motors building on 59th Street and Fifth Avenue, directly above the space that had formerly housed FAO Schwartz and then played host to the city's flagship Apple store. Having been there twenty-two years, Eva was now a senior partner in the firm's prominent litigation practice. Her specialty was product liability defense, particularly pharmaceuticals, and she commanded high-profile clients: Pfizer, Allergen, Medtronic, and Glaxo Smith Kline.

Because of her extraordinary billable hours and enviable Rolodex comprising most of the prominent clients of the firm, Eva inhabited a palatial office on the northwest corner of the thirty-ninth floor. Seated at her mahogany desk, with its unique red-leather inlay, Eva looked out her west-facing windows and over the Plaza hotel, a slight turn of her swivel chair revealing the vast expanse of Central Park. Beyond, Eva's view was capped by the unmistakable towers of the Dakota apartment building on the Upper West Side, home to so many stars but most notorious as the site of John Lennon's shooting.

Scanning through the floor-to-ceiling windows on the north side of her office, Eva faced the Sherry-Netherland hotel. The senior partner forced to vacate that office for Eva had kept an antique brass telescope on an oak stand. He claimed it was for observing the changing leaves in the park, but everyone at the firm knew he trained it on the Sherry Netherland in the evening hours. His secretary twice caught him pleasuring himself as he watched couples in the hotel enjoying post-dinner intimacy.

Hence, he was forced to surrender that office, and his partnership interest in the firm.

At forty-seven years old, ridiculously intelligent, with no husband, no children, and the hardest and most physically pleasing body of anyone in the firm, man or woman, Eva commanded the attention of her partners, associates, clients ... everyone she met. In sum, she was a rock star on Manhattan's island of wannabes.

At the firm's annual partner meetings, convened at the Bellagio in Las Vegas because MGM was one of the firm's anchor clients through its Nevada office, all of Eva's 340 partners tirelessly huddled to absorb whatever wisdom she would dispense. She lectured on client development, associate retention, and office integration issues, all with equal panache. Within her practice group, Eva broached more technical topics, like how to select a perfectly partial jury (no one ever wants a truly impartial jury), how to deliver a winning opening statement, and how to cross-examine even the most hostile witnesses. No matter the subject, all eyes were riveted on Eva as she spoke with graceful eloquence, imparting knowledge that belied her years.

To her partners, Eva was the face of the firm. She represented everything Wilson Everson wanted to portray. She embodied the firm's ideal image to its clients, the media, and graduating law students. Oh, those law students. All the top firms in New York competed to wine and dine the best-of-the-best students from the best-of-the-best law schools by offering the best-of-the-best salaries and perks. And if these junior geniuses were blessed to receive an offer of permanent employment at the end of the summer, they would become full-time first-year associates with compensation packages that approached $200,000 a year. Eva was often called upon to lecture to those denizens of the recruiting office, usually when they were only summer associates. Like everyone else, the students were immensely captivated by everything Eva.

The "Summers," as they were called, worked for junior associates, under the supervision of senior associates who had to answer to the partners. These kids – few were ever over 25 – received more than $3,500 a week as the partners worked to convince them that Wilson Everson was the best firm in New York. These poor kids had to suffer through two-hour lunches at the finest restaurants in Manhattan, attend ice-cream hours in the afternoon, participate in the Lawyers' League softball games, and be treated to Broadway plays on Wednesdays evenings. Box seats for Yankees and Mets games were available every weekend, and no one was expected to take the subway or even Uber to the game – car service limos were made available, day or night.

Every once in a while, an associate would actually assign the Summers real work to be performed – perhaps research or writing – but not too often, for fear of offending the mollycoddled Summers. The assignments were never arduous – for fear rumors of slave labor would reverberate through the halls of their law schools when the Summers returned in the fall. Regardless of the quality of the work produced by these evolving adolescents, it was foisted on unsuspecting clients who were billed $335 an hour for their time. At least the firm recouped a portion of the millions they spent each year entertaining the pampered darlings.

Years later, some of these little sweethearts would become partners. At the most competitive firms like Wilson Everson, an entering class of seventy-five, newly-minted lawyers would be culled to no more than ten by the end of their fifth year at the firm. Those who chose to roll the dice and remain at the firm – or were lucky enough to escape the annual December winnowing of the associate ranks – would be further harvested by their tenth year, when they were eligible for partnership consideration. In some years, none of the original seventy-five would be elevated to partner but, more customarily, two or three lucky counselors would be knighted with the millionaires' mantle. First-year partners would collect well over a million dollars each, and the compensation curve after that was very generous.

Every June, Eva would identify a few Summers (usually young women) who caught her eye and mentor them through the three months of summer camp for young plutocrats. She eschewed the tradition of placing a few layers of associates between the Summers and the partners to protect the Summers from the partners who were screamers and throwers. The layers also protected the partners from the Summers who deserved to have things thrown at them.

Eva had a knack for identifying potential superstars. Her partners never figured out what inner sense Eva possessed allowing her to separate the prodigies from the pabulum, but she had the accuracy of Stephen Curry from outside the arc. She would invite one of the young women to her office, hold all calls, and spend an hour probing the student about her parents, hometown, hobbies, and life ambitions. The women would squirm nervously hoping the conversation would turn to a work assignment, but it rarely did. Eva genuinely wanted to get to know them, to know who they were and what made them tick. And no matter what, once she met them and spent even a modicum of time with them, Eva never forgot a name. Never. This served her well, not just with Summers, but also with everyone Eva encountered – colleagues, adversaries, clients and judges. Some thought it insecurity, most just appreciated it as part of her genius.

Sometimes she'd invite one of the young women to lunch at Aquavit or La Grenouille, two of her favorite chow haunts. That she deigned to spend hours, precious non-billable hours, chatting with them about travel or boating instead of tending to the needs of the world's CEOs communicated volumes of unspoken flattery. Eva's interest was always repaid, usually in orders of magnitude. When they joined the firm and advanced through the associate ranks, these women were beholden to Eva, and to her clients. She had created her own pseudo-sorority of the most successful women lawyers in the firm (ironic as, back in her college days, she detested sororities). She invited her favorite mentees to join her on client pitches, teaching them to make initial contact with potential clients and how to reel them in. As a result, her practice group of eighty-five lawyers was the most dynamic and profitable in the firm. Accordingly, Eva's was the most envied practice group in the firm. The older male curmudgeons resented Eva's celebrity status and stratospheric compensation, but even they had to respect the way she had created a superlative practice group.

A rock star.

# CHAPTER TWO

Directly across the park and north a few blocks, on 65th Street and Broadway, Gillian English and Janice Garramone were sipping cappuccino. Their daughters, Cara English and Roxanne Garramone, were seniors at the prestigious Convent of the Sacred Heart, a trio of ivy-covered mansions on Fifth Avenue and 91st Street housing an elite all girl's school, the alma mater of Gloria Vanderbilt, Paris Hilton, Lady Gaga, and other heiresses, celebrities, and trust funders. It was already mid-August and, once the Southampton Polo Festival concluded on Labor Day weekend, all attention had to be redoubled on the countdown to the SATs and ACTs.

Every summer, the mothers of juniors and seniors would probe their sources to find out which girls got accepted to the "best" colleges and who they used for SAT and ACT prep. Gillian and Janice were already making inquiries to get the "right" tutors lined up; not just any tutor would do.

"Sally Plimpton said her Fiona used a Yale graduate who's tutoring high-school seniors until she has enough money for law school. And the three kids she tutored last year? They all got into their top choices," Gillian told Janice. "That's good enough for me."

"I think we're going to use a boy who worked with some Spence girls last year," said Janice. "He worked for Kaplan and now he's started his own tutoring service. I've heard great things about him. Also he's not too bad on the eyes, so Roxanne won't mind putting in the time with him." Janice knew that *she* wouldn't mind having young Hank Blaser around either. The young man was smart and yes, not too bad on the eyes. Downright sexy in fact. Janice's husband, Mario, was more and more involved at his bank and Janice longed for a male who would listen to her and look at her – even if he was closer to her daughter's age, even if she had to pay for him to be there.

Gillian and Janice were unique among their peers. They really were friends, not just moms who smiled politely at each other at school events. They had been through a lot together and had emerged even closer and stronger.

Gillian was a young widow; her husband Mark killed on that clear blue Tuesday morning in September 2001 when a 757 crashed through his 101$^{st}$ floor office at Cantor Fitzgerald in the World Trade Center. His body was never found. Their daughter Cara was only a young girl when it happened.

Her entire world torn apart in an instant, Gillian was devastated. When it mattered most, Janice was there for her, day and night for the next year. When money became an issue, Janice and Mario lent Gillian money for Cara's $61,000-a-year Sacred Heart tuition, knowing full well they would never get it back. It didn't matter.

Mario had been scheduled to meet at the offices of one of his bank's clients in the first tower the afternoon of September 11th. Had the meeting gone forward as planned and had the attacks occurred later in the day, Mario would have perished, and it would have been Roxanne and her sister Jessica growing up fatherless. But Mario was not there, Mark was. Mario knew Mark would have done his best to help support his widow and their family so he vowed that, to the extent it was in his control, he would do the same – Gillian should not have to struggle financially to raise her daughter without Mark.

Gillian entered a downward spiral. Her dramatic weight gain and exhaustion were obvious to all. The black circles under her eyes never seemed to disappear. Her fiery red hair grew grey as Gillian gave up chasing her roots. Her sharp green eyes were dulled, along with her zest for life. Gillian turned all her focus on Cara and on her own aging mother, Audrey, living in Gillian's childhood home in Bethlehem, PA. If not for them, there would be no point to any of it. They would both be lost without her; she had no choice but to soldier on.

In a tragically ironic twist of fate, just a week before the attack, Gillian and Mark had met with Adam Costello of Northwestern Mutual Life to consider life-insurance options. The meeting had been positive, and Adam filled out the forms for Mark to secure a terrific tax-efficient investment vehicle – $5,000,000 of variable life insurance – prudent given his enormous Cantor Fitzgerald income. On Monday, September 10th, Mark received the documents from Adam and read through them. As he was preparing to sign them, he noticed a small typographical error. Adam had misspelled Cara's name in the beneficiary section substituting "Carol" for "Cara." Mark put the papers in the briefcase, reminding himself to call Adam the next day to fix the mistake. He never got to make that call. Gillian and Cara never got the $5,000,000.

# CHAPTER THREE

Janice Garramone had just turned fifty – eighteen years younger than her husband, Mario. Fifty required more time at the gym than forty did, Janice reasoned, and she logged in the hours necessary to keep herself in great shape. Her rigorous routine of free weights and Pilates complemented her Atkins-inspired diet, resulting in a fifty-year-old woman with the body of a 35-year-old athlete.

Janice and Mario enjoyed improving the lives of others. They made a sizable contribution to their daughter Roxanne's old summer camp in Hendersonville, North Carolina, saving the camp from bankruptcy. This was even more admirable as Roxanne had long since outgrown the camp – the Garramones wanted other children to have the same opportunity and fun Roxanne had enjoyed when she was a kid. They were also significant benefactors of Boston College, where they met. The dean knew he could always count on them whenever the school really needed help to round up the support of their financially well-heeled friends.

But no matter how good they were, and how much good they did for the world, life was not all crackers and cheese inside the Garramone home. The CEO of Mario's bank, New York Savings & Guaranty, was failing in health and the whispers were that Mario had the talent for the position. The only criticism of Mario was that he lacked international banking experience. In an effort to round out his resume, Mario began spending increasing time in London, Singapore and the Middle East to earn his international stripes. That meant significant time away from home, and Mario's absence would breed wandering eyes – and hands.

At 68, Mario appeared relatively fit, although most of that was due to genetics. He rarely engaged in any cardiovascular exercise more strenuous than weekend golf, other than the gratification of his distended libido. He also kept himself tanned – not just tanned, but George Hamilton tanned. But it looked good on him, not like the orange mien of Donald Trump. Mario was sartorially obsessed, compulsively buying the best clothes and out-dressing his peers. He was particularly proud of his ability to wear purple, lavender, and light blue. He abjured the traditional white shirts of the banking world, opting instead to always make a bold fashion statement wherever he went.

He always wore "braces," as he called them (suspenders to everyone else on the planet). If he wore a belt, he'd wear it off center, with the buckle to the right of the first belt loop on the right side of his pants, just to be different. This "off-center buckle" look actually became a trend with the junior bankers who worked for him. It was the only office on the planet where the junior staff wore their belts pulled to one side of their body. Clients would sometimes ask the bankers why they wore their belts off-center, but no one had the nerve to explain they were just following Mario's odd example. Some of the junior ones didn't even know why they did it – they just did it. The final trademark of Mario's ensemble was his colored socks. When Mario walked into a meeting with his purple suits, belt askew, and pink socks ... well, it made an impression. All in all, not what one would expect from a conservative senior officer of a major bank.

Mario wanted to stand out, he was addicted to attention. He craved it any way he could get it. The young women at the bank (and outside the bank for that matter) doted on him, providing the validation he so badly needed.

Mario's sister, Anna, was a psychiatrist in Buffalo. They chatted every few weeks on the phone. Once, in a moment of uncharacteristic self-reflection he asked what she thought about his insatiable need for attention.

"Oh Mario, you know my policy on this," she hesitated.

"Yes, yes, but come on, you're the only person who's known me my whole life," he cajoled. "You must have some insight ..."

"Mario. This never works," Anna interrupted. "We agreed – I won't analyze you, and you won't give me financial advice. It's only going to end up in us fighting," she pronounced.

"Anna, c'mon! I mean it! I really want to know what you think!"

She sighed. "You mean like the clothes, the super tight, purple slacks you wore to my house last Easter?"

"Yeah. Just this once – what's your professional opinion."

"Okay," Anna said finally. "But just this once."

"Okay, I promise," Mario said.

"I think, my professional opinion is, either you have really bad taste, or you think you're Prince."

It was the last time he asked his sister to analyze him.

Mario did go to therapy for a while. He saw Dr. Michelle Pearlstein weekly for about two years. He found her attractive even though, or maybe even because, she was the opposite of Janice. Dr. Pearlstein perfectly embodied Mario's perception of an upscale, Upper West Side liberal feminist. Her refusal to adorn her face with makeup, or her hair with dye (she let the gray show, she didn't care!) was ... refreshing. She had a sort of muted brilliance to her skin he found fascinating. Her eyes were myrtle green, but more captivating for their piercing nature, than simply for their color. When Dr. Pearlstein focused on him, Mario saw a clarity in her eyes that he was sure allowed her insight into his thoughts. When she crossed her legs and revealed her toned calves, he found himself wondering about her exercise regime, imagining her tight, muscular body in one of those form-fitting Lululemon tops he just loved seeing Janice parade around in at home. Dr. Pearlstein never wore anything form fitting, much to Mario's chagrin. He was left to wonder about the shape of her body – and wonder he did. Sometimes, during their sessions, Dr. Pearlstein would have to summon Mario's thoughts back to reality. Her legs could be quite distracting.

"Mario. We were talking about your constant fantasizing," Dr. Pearlstein said.

"Hmmm? Yes, we were."

"You seem distracted today," she continued.

Mario shifted uncomfortably on the couch. Intelligent Jewish women were so hot, he thought. Smart, in control. Her skirt seemed to inch up as their session progressed. Did she do this on purpose?

"I want to recommend something, I think it could be helpful. I have a group session. It's every Tuesday at 7, a group of five – two men, three women –"

I like those odds, thought Mario.

"– the sessions are structured around common issues the members of the group are coping with –"

Was she talking about sex? Was that the common issue, hyper-sexuality? What else could it be, Mario thought. What else was there?

"– anonymity is respected. In fact, no one in the group even knows each other's last names –"

Like a secret sex club, Mario thought. Like in that Kubrick film. What was it called? The one with Nicole Kidman...

"– everything that is discussed in group remains completely confidential." Dr. Pearlstein took her glasses off, placing them on the small table next to her.

Mario's head filled with images of Nicole Kidman, naked, wearing nothing but glasses. Nicole took her glasses off...

Nicole sat in group, naked, unembarrassed. Everyone else had clothes on. The session was ending, the others made their way out as Nicole approached Mario. "Mario," she said with a smile, "I really loved what you shared in the session today." She blushed. "It made me...kind of hot."

Mario smiled, and leaned in to whisper in Nicole's ear. "Well, maybe I can help you with that..." He embraced Nicole, slowly lowering his hand down her naked back, over her hip, down to her inner thigh.

"Oh! Mario," Nicole gasped.

Dr. Pearlstein sat in her leather armchair, watching.

"Mario," she said. "Where did you just go?"

Mario closed his eyes and smiled.

"Mario? We have to end the session now, but I want you to think about the group therapy idea."

Mario blinked. "Hmmm? Oh, yes, yes of course ..."

Although she came close, Dr. Pearlstein was never able to persuade Mario to join the group. He was deathly afraid someone would recognize him, and he would be "outed" to his bank. He started seeing her less and less frequently. Eventually, he began to cancel sessions, purportedly because of his international travel and their professional relationship grew to a gentle close.

About eight months after their last formal therapy session Mario called Dr. Pearlstein and asked if they could have dinner so he could bring her up to speed on things that were happening in his life. He valued her good counsel and was anxious to share some of his latest internal conflicts with her, especially since his own sister had refused to give him any psychotherapeutic assistance. Dr. Pearlstein rationalized that Mario was no longer a client; there was no reason they couldn't share a dinner together. Moreover, she missed hearing Mario share his challenges and exploits. She agreed.

They met at Bar Boulud, on Columbus Avenue and 64ᵗʰ Street for a workmanlike French dinner. Dinner was casual and they caught up, laughed and drank. And drank more. Dr. Pearlstein didn't even feel herself becoming ensnared as Mario convinced her to enjoy a drink at her apartment after dinner. Tall, handsome, tanned and well-built, Mario was extremely convincing when he set his mind to it.

Mario bedded Dr. Michelle Pearlstein that evening, and three more times over the next month. Then, having satisfied his craving to dominate this woman, as he had to dominate all the women in his life, Mario moved on. Dr. Pearlstein would never hear from Mario again. She realized she had been used but was not totally disappointed with the experience. She shared her reflections and feelings with her own therapist, and the entire incident served to rejuvenate her sexual awareness and relationship with her husband.

All the international travel was not easy on Mario, but he was deft at the minutiae of piecing together his itineraries. He always traveled with a younger banker whose primary job was to make the reservations, coordinate the ground effort, outline the agendas, line up the right people for meetings and accompany Mario throughout his journeys. The work wasn't difficult: all the travel was first class and Mario always stayed at Ritz-Carlton and Four Seasons hotels.

Not surprising to anyone who knew Mario, his travel companions were usually young female investment bankers. They were all tall with long blonde hair, blue eyes, long shapely legs, healthy California surfer-type looks. It was amazing how many of these seemingly identical, climbing young bankers Mario was able to cull from the ranks. It was also amazing that Janice didn't have a clue what Mario was up to. Mario was very adept at never introducing any of these women to Janice or mentioning their physical characteristics at home.

With Janice consumed by their daughter's SAT preparation, Mario took off for London and Athens to round up mezzanine financing for one of his largest clients, a European real-estate conglomerate, EuroHoldings, LLC. One week in May, Mario came home on a Friday afternoon flight into JFK. Thanks to an airport ground workers' strike in Greece, not an unusual occurrence by any means, his flight was delayed two hours at the gate in Athens. He didn't really mind as he and Melanie Hunter – the latest young banking beauty to be seduced by his promises of promotion, as well as his handsome smile, first class tastes and body that wasn't so bad for a man his age – drank mimosas while waiting to take off. They had just spent two amazing nights at the Ritz in London before bedding down together again at the Divani Apollon Palace and Spa on the Athenian Riviera for four nights.

The Greek meetings had been canceled while they were in London, but Mario's wife would never know that. The opportunity was perfect for them to spend four days cloistered together on the beach, at the pool and primarily, in Mario's sumptuous suite overlooking the picturesque Saronic Gulf. They spent the days on the beach, where the 5'10, blue-eyed, naturally blonde and well-built Melanie admired Mario's fitness.

On their first afternoon in Greece, after Mario explained

that the meetings had been "postponed" for a while, Melanie watched Mario emerge from a swim in the sea. For an older man, she thought, he's pretty damn fit. He plopped down next to her. "Hey! You crazy kid, you're going to fry up in this sun. Here," he reached for the tube of Bain de Soleil sun-block lotion, "let me fix you up."

She laughed. "You just did me an hour ago!"

"Well, this stuff wears off. You can't be too careful," remarked Mario. But the irony of Melanie's comment about *doing her* was not lost on him. His dick twitched forward a bit at that comment.

She laughed again and rolled over on her stomach. He slowly applied the lotion to her back.

"Mmmm...," she cooed. "So nice. Wait a sec."

She sat up, reached around, and untied her bikini top. "Everyone else is topless! And hey, this is Greece, after all. Besides, I don't want you to get lotion all over my suit. I just bought it last week especially for this trip." She held the pose for an extra second, Mario's eyes filling with her incredible young breasts.

She rolled over onto her stomach again, he spread the lotion lower. She slipped her thumb into her bikini bottom, rolling it down just enough to reveal the creamy white of her cheeks below the tan line. "Make sure you get under the waistband. People often burn there." She knew exactly what she was doing to him.

Mario spread the lotion on her leg, slowly circling his hand up, tantalizingly close to her soft, warm inner thigh. She shifted slightly, just enough to part her legs imperceptibly...

He knew exactly what he was doing to her.

Barely making an effort to conceal his erection, Mario regaled Melanie with his meteoric rise through New York S&G and his seemingly imminent coronation as CEO. "I'd need a close ally in the junior ranks to be my eyes and ears about what people are thinking and saying about the tone at the top," he murmured, applying more lotion to her shoulders. She was enthralled. Melanie, he promised, would report directly to him, with her immediate supervisor knowing of the business arrangement, but never suspecting the illicit nature of it all. As he reclined on his beach lounge to steal the fullest view possible of Melanie's entire body, Mario told her their "meetings" should not occur in New York where tongues would wag.

"It would be better, and a lot more fun for both of us, if we schedule our time together in other places – South Beach, Santa Monica, Vail – where no one knows us, and we can really enjoy each other's company." What he meant was: "I don't want anyone to know I'm having resort romps with you. But you just come along and service me while I make empty promises to you about your future."

After that first full day of teasing on the beach, their sexual energies were running so high they were both intoxicated with desire. For much of the day, Mario had engaged his conspiratorial mind in an effort to orchestrate his way into Melanie's tiny bikini bottom. Throughout the day, every time he glanced longingly at her breasts, she smiled approvingly. The way she sat up on occasion, turning to her side facing him, gave Mario all the assurance he needed.

It was Melanie who gave the initial opening to Mario. Subtly, he suggested that they meet around 6:30, "either in the lobby, or in my suite, it really doesn't matter much to me" before venturing out to the beachside tiki bar for a drink before their 7:30 dinner reservation at Mythos, the hotel restaurant. Melanie smiled slyly, "What about before dinner?"

"What do you mean," asked Mario.

"It's 4:00 now. What am I supposed to do until 6:30?" she asked innocently. "Can't we get together earlier?" she asked quietly.

Mario's state of arousal made it difficult for him to even think clearly – and it made it difficult for him to get out of his chair suavely.

"Fine idea," he replied, anxiously. "Shall we each shower, change and then . . ."

"I have an idea. My skin is always so dry, and you've been such a doll making sure I had enough sunscreen on today. Why don't we go to my room now, let me grab a quick shower, and you can make sure I have enough lotion on me to keep my skin moist après-sun?"

"Are you freaking kidding me?" Mario mused to himself. No way. It couldn't be this easy. He even wondered if it could be some kind of a trap. But then he concluded that he was an irresistibly attractive man and it was inevitable that young and nubile Melanie Hunter would desire him.

Not wanting the enthusiasm to wane even a scintilla, he agreed that Melanie's idea was terrific, suggested they leave the beach immediately. He watched with great interest, and a bit of temporary disappointment, as Melanie sat up, reached back, and fastened her bikini top once again. They walked back towards the Divani Apollon and Melanie pushed the button for the 12th floor. Melanie was in an executive room, a class two levels below Mario's deluxe suite. Her room was not palatial, but for their immediate interests it had all the requisite features: queen size bed, fully equipped minibar, and beautiful views of the Saronic Gulf.

"I'll just be a sec," Melanie piped cheerfully, walking briskly into the bathroom, leaving her white beach cover-up on the floor outside the closet.

Mario twisted the feeble red plastic tie on the top of the door of the mini bar, and helped himself, removing a can of Corona Light and triggering the automatic charging device – a gadget he begrudgingly admired, but found annoying. Listening to the shower run, he allowed himself an excited grin and stepped onto the balcony.

Like a schoolboy, he felt giddy waiting for Melanie to emerge. It wasn't Janice's fault that he hadn't felt like this about her for years – it was just the inevitable familiarity of marriage. For a moment he considered joining Melanie in the bathroom, images of them naked in the shower filled his mind, Melanie fondling his manhood while he soaped her body. But before his thoughts could reach their natural maturity, he heard the shower stop. Melanie emerged from the shower in a short, dark blue silk robe, the kind every traveling female executive keeps rolled in a corner of her suitcase. She slid open the door to the balcony, joining him. She tipped her head back and peered into his eyes, sliding her arms around his waist. They embraced for about five long minutes before Melanie took Mario's hand and led him into the room.

As advertised, she produced a small jar of Clinique Deep Comfort Body Butter and handed it to Mario. She took two steps back, released the sash of her robe, and let the robe slip to the floor. There she stood, totally naked, her perfectly athletic body still glistening with beads of water from the shower. Raw desire guiding his actions, Mario knew what to do and eagerly set about it. Dinner plans were cancelled, and they screwed mercilessly for hours. Melanie rode him like a porpoise at Sea World, enjoying her dominance over the senior vice president of her bank. Later, grilled octopus, stuffed squid, and a lamb dish with avocado mousse were delivered to the room, but the food was not the most memorable part of the evening. Her only disappointment came after Mario's second orgasm, which left him unable to raise his flagpole again – until around 6:00 the next morning.

The next morning, over breakfast on the terrace of the bright, contemporary lounge overlooking the Gulf, they planned their next out-of-office rendezvous, or at least Mario did. He wanted it to occur during the second week of September, when both his daughters would be back in school and he had taken care of the quarterly bank paperwork due Labor Day. Accordingly, the second week of September was really the only week he could get out of the office and frolic. Proffering a little white lie, he told Melanie that EuroHoldings was about to acquire a massive hotel just north of Miami, in Bal Harbour, and he wanted to be on site to handle the final negotiations himself. Of course, when the time for the trip came, they would get to Miami and he would tell her the deal had caved – not that big a stretch, deals cave all the time. Then, they would remain in Miami Beach for the four days. Mario had no misgivings about getting this amazing goddess alone again in a bathing suit – or out of one.

It was no wonder that the trip to London and Greece was the highlight of Melanie's budding career – so far. What could be better for a girl from Chapel Hill? It had been six days of first-class travel, limos, luxury hotels, meals served by elegant waiters in white gloves, room service carts of pastries, cheeses, fruits and always wine, always champagne. Her companion was the second most influential man in the bank and he had just promised her a wonderful opportunity – albeit as a glorified escort and snitch. He earned high marks as an attentive lover, to boot. After earning her MBA at Duke's Fuqua's School of Business, Melanie never thought that getting a job and climbing the corporate ladder (to the top of the corporate bunk bed) could be this easy.

As their plane entered the final glide path for landing at JFK that afternoon, Mario and Melanie gathered their belongings. The seating area on their American Airlines 777 First Class Flagship Suites consisted of six-foot, six-inch beds with drop-down armrests, privacy dividers, power ports, leather headrests, several large tray tables, a guest seat and countless pockets and bins in which to store things. There were a lot of things in a lot of places.

Mario shoved all his papers into his brown, well-heeled Tumi briefcase. Mixed in with his papers was a letter Melanie was writing to her college sorority sister, Stacy Ponder. It was an apology:

> *Dear Stace,*
>
> *I am SOOOOOO sorry!!! I can't believe I won't be at your wedding!!! I feel absolutely awful, but there's nothing I can do. My boss needs me on a very important trip to Miami that same weekend. It's a really big deal for the company, a closing for a EuroHoldings hotel, and I'm up to my eyebrows on this one.*
>
> *But it's more than that Stace, I hope you're sitting down! I'm in love, I mean really in love. It's my boss, Mario. I know, I know – but this is different! He wants to take such good care of me. It's first class all the way, and he is really opening doors for me with my career. And he's so handsome and –*

Stacy would surely understand. After all, large corporate deals and handsome sugar daddies were what they aspired to when they were Pi Phis at Duke.

# CHAPTER FOUR

Carly Burke was gorgeous – simply gorgeous. At 5'7, with light brown hair and the most striking emerald green eyes imaginable, she was also fun and feisty, making her way through New York with her midwestern accent. Born just outside Wichita, Kansas, she had attended KU for two years before getting pregnant by her high-school sweetheart, Tommy Sugar. It turned out Mr. Sugar was not that sweet: within five years of their all-American wedded bliss, he had impregnated two other women. So, divorced, with two young kids, and only twenty-two years old, Carly was on her own for the first time in her life. She got her paralegal certificate and then a job at Hinkle Morris, a thirty-five-lawyer firm in downtown Wichita where she hoped to find a real husband. Carly enjoyed her time at Hinkle Morris and grew attached to several lawyers there. They all told her that she should have gone to law school because she was smarter than most of the junior lawyers at the firm. And she was.

Hinkle Morris' biggest client was Boeing. Their Wichita facility had manufactured aircraft since 1929. During World War II, they employed over 40,000 workers, including President

Obama's grandmother. Since the war, Boeing churned out thousands of civilian and military aircraft, becoming the preeminent aircraft manufacturer in the world.

When she was 28, Carly was named lead paralegal on a major antitrust suit filed against Boeing by the federal government. The case dragged on for four years with Boeing retaining several law firms to coordinate its defense, as was often the case with massive litigation efforts. Among the firms engaged was Bergman Troutman, a Dallas-based firm with offices around the country. Hinkle Morris served as local Wichita counsel, with Bergman's New York office serving as the lead counsel. For Bergman, heading up the effort was powerhouse litigator Harris Hirschfeld.

Harris was an oaf. At 6'2, 260 pounds, he had let himself go years ago. He was sixty-four years old and it was a struggle just to get around the office. He promised himself that he would join the New York Health & Racquet Club and resume working out ... one of these days. But he knew he never would. He was clumsy, a poor dresser, and burdened with chronically bad breath and mustard-colored teeth. He was socially inept, especially around men. Around women, he used his power within the firm to impress them – or at least so he thought.

Despite this, Harris Hirschfeld knew a good billing opportunity when he saw one and, as a result of his massive financial hauls every year, he had ascended to the head of his practice group. There was no other litigator in all of New York who could bilk clients faster or more smoothly than Harris. He was a legal genius and genius has its rewards: he raked in a handsome $5.5 million every year, more than enough to keep his patient wife, Becky, happy. Her needs were modest and her own inheritance large, and she eschewed the fancy wardrobes most of her friends sought so dearly.

In addition to working with her Hinkle Morris cast of Kansan characters, Carly Burke assisted Harris and his firm in the coordination of discovery among all the law firms on the Boeing case. The discovery process in that case would last two years, involve 78 depositions, and require the exchange of 4.5 million pages of documents. Carly was ideally suited for the job: she was methodical, well-respected, and had a billing rate far less than a New York paralegal.

Shortly after she began to work with Bergman Troutman, and with Harris in particular, Carly sensed that Harris was interested in her. Harris, objectively unattractive yet an extremely intelligent man, had a fondness for young women. This had caused him no small headaches in the past.

Seven years earlier, a young associate got pregnant and named Harris as the father. It turned out that the father was really a waiter in an Upper West Side Turkish restaurant, a one-night stand, but the damage had been done. Although he was not the father, Harris had been the woman's lover for three years, not exactly a secret among his partners, associates, or even the support staff at Bergman Troutman.

The whole thing was messy. Harris didn't want his affair with the young woman to become public knowledge and, even though he wasn't the baby's father, he felt trapped into supporting the associate and her bastard kid. Harris being

Harris, he went so far as to throw around his ample weight to protect her job when she earned lackluster annual reviews from the other partners.

He was able to keep the affair from impacting his career, but he had to reveal to the partnership, and his wife, that he was being accused of fathering the baby – which meant he had to admit to them the existence of the affair with a young associate. Well, he might not have told his wife all the details, but it was enough to give her a sense of his philandering ways. It put him in the dog house for quite some time with Becky.

Becky Hirschfeld was 5'2, blonde, and still as cute as when she was voted Miss Sunshine at college in Jupiter, Florida. Not wanting to be judged by the cost of the clothes she wore, Becky was content in jeans and a ponytail, and she looked damn good in them. Fitness was Becky's obsession. It seemed the more weight Harris gained, the more Becky was determined to keep herself in top physical shape. She busied herself volunteering as a board member of the Metropolitan Opera and the Alzheimer's Association, and was very involved with her son's school, Riverdale Country Day – one of New York's most prestigious private schools. Despite beauty, social standing, finances, interests, and intelligence, she carried herself in a very ordinary manner. You would never know she had inherited a multi-million-dollar fortune, or that she was married to one of the premier lawyers in all of New York.

The confession and revelatory details of Harris' affair was the lowest point of the Hirschfelds' marriage. Becky flew off the handle, and cognac glasses flew across the room.

Alone while their daughters were at a movie, Harris and Becky came to terms (and almost to blows) about what had transpired. Feeling more alone than she ever had in her life, Becky probed Harris for more details. She was not sure why she wanted to know more, but she did – or thought she did. Whenever Becky thought about that awful confrontation, she sometimes wished she knew every single detail about her husband's sordid affair – and sometimes wished she knew nothing at all.

The whole mess made her more resolute than ever to maintain her good looks and erogenous body. Not for Harris – she had no sexual interest in him anymore; he was a disappointment and embarrassment to her. Perhaps she wanted to draw looks from other men, or perhaps she wanted Harris to see what he had tossed to the curb, but she wanted to look good.

Bergman Troutman lost two clients because of Harris's chaotic sex life. Another potential client, the country's largest textile manufacturer, pulled out of an interview because the company's female general counsel was offended that a middle-aged man was preying on women younger than her own daughters. Harris heard a lot about that from his partners. At Bergman, partners could lie, cheat, steal, or bang whomever they wanted, but if it affected the bottom-line, there was hell to pay. Harris's compensation was negatively impacted not just for that year, but for the two after that. He never told Becky about that. Becky didn't even know what Harris made per year. Harris liked it like that.

Carly didn't know about Harris's history. She just knew that at the end of every day, after the last team meeting, Harris always found a way for the two of them be the last ones at the table – or at the bar. While she was truly stunning and could have any man she wanted, she found Harris's innate intelligence intriguing. He seemed to know everything about everything. He was as fluent with the outlook of the Federal Reserve Board as he was about politics in Ukraine or the Yankees frustrating inability to land a decent fourth starting pitcher. And he was not somebody who just bluffed his way through a conversation, as most lawyers do. No, he really did know everything about everything. No matter the subject, Harris was an expert and that turned Carly on.

After spending time with Carly at several depositions, and becoming absolutely infatuated with her, Harris concocted a plan. The Boeing case was being litigated in New York and all the pre-trial work would be performed there. Carly had been working with Boeing for years through the Hinkle Morris firm. No one on the team knew Boeing's documents the way Carly did. It only made sense, Harris reasoned, that Carly should move to New York for a few months to get his team up to speed. After all, it was less expensive to move a single paralegal to New York than to relocate seven lawyers to Wichita. Harris telephoned his co-counsel at Hinkle Morris, Bill Stuart, and suggested the plan. It was left to Carly to decide. It was a big decision, and not an easy one; she had two young daughters. Lawyers signed up for long bouts of travel and inhumane hours; paralegals didn't necessarily bargain for that kind of disruption to their lives. But when Bill Stuart presented the opportunity to Carly, the eager paralegal jumped at it. The opportunity for a fully paid excursion to

Manhattan for several months was just too good to pass up.

Carly's parents lived only five blocks from her house, and they loved having their granddaughters around, so they were thrilled to babysit for a few months. Besides, they were both only fifty-two years old, so they were not exactly infirm. Bergman Troutman's relocation group would identify a few apartments for Carly to choose from. Boeing would pay for it. Harris could easily convince Boeing that the cost of the apartment was far less than the cost of the billable hours Carly would spend sitting on an airplane every week flying back-and-forth from Kansas to New York.

Carly was from the country, but she hadn't exactly fallen off the turnip truck. She knew that Harris was probably behind this little scheme and that suited her just fine. It was just one more clue that he was becoming more interested in her and she knew she would be able to work that to her advantage. She just didn't know how yet.

She waited. One Friday, during a particularly grueling deposition of Harris's witness, Bobby Stephens, Carly reasoned the time was right for her to explore the extent of Harris's infatuation. Partly because during Stephens' grilling, Harris seemed more fascinated by the side slit in Carly's red plaid Diane von Furstenberg skirt than the actual deposition. She enjoyed spending time with him, but she also enjoyed a good game, and that's what Harris could be to her. After all, he had been prancing and cooing before her for weeks now, playing his own game. As a beautiful young woman who had been divorced at such a young age, Carly had seen many men morph into peacocks before her eyes. She was keenly aware that the object of such games was to get her in bed. She held all the cards and she knew it. As far as teasing Harris, Carly had no end game in mind – at least not yet – but how exciting would it be for her to see how low this pillar of the New York Bar would kneel before her? Why not? She had been on the receiving end of so much gender-based exploitation, it seemed only right. Turnabout would be fair play.

Harris loved a good bone-in ribeye. And Smith & Wollensky's was his favorite beef joint in Manhattan. He was also fond of Peter Luger's, but he tired of the long cab ride to Brooklyn, the cash-only policy, and the abruptness of the burly German wait staff. So, when he was in the mood for a good piece of meat (other than those he ogled in the office), he called Hank, the manager at Smith & Wollensky's and asked to have his favorite table reserved. Hank was a tall, former busboy turned waiter turned manager, whose 6'3 frame, well-fitted suits, and slicked-back black hair made him a commanding figure. But Hank was just a receiver who had a few connections. For example, Steve Hammond, a regular at Smith & Wollensky's, was the manager of Joseph A. Bank, a moderately priced men's clothing store on Madison Avenue. For Christmas one year, Steve allowed Hank to be custom fitted for two suits. Hank lived in those suits. In exchange, Steve was always seated in the Oak Section on the right side of the restaurant, where celebrities and athletes dined nightly. In the dim lights of the bustling night spot, Hank looked terrific in his Armani-wannabe clothing. Then shortly after midnight, each evening would end with Hank sitting on the filthy orange plastic benches of the 7 train as it lumbered into the bowels of Queens where he shared a third-floor walk-up apartment with his mother. Even in the custom-made suits he was just another schlub on the subway.

Harris enjoyed the pomp and ceremony with which Hank always greeted him. It was a rather thick and sappy show Hank put on for his regulars. He would fawn all over them, tell them how good it was to see them, how well they looked, and anything else they wanted to hear in exchange for the $20 bills they would foist into his outstretched hand as he led them to their table. It was a dance of phonies – Hank pretending to give a shit about these people, and the guests feigning embarrassment, but thrilled that their dates and clients could see what big deals they were.

After the deposition and the post mortem with the witness in his office, Harris suggested that a steak dinner would be a good way to close out the week. He had his assistant, Myra Gladman, call Hank to reserve a table for four – Harris, Carly, the witness, and Boeing's assistant general counsel who had traveled with the witness to help prepare him for the deposition.

Myra was a Long Island divorcee who was not sliding into late middle age with particular grace. The natural greyness of her hair was unavoidably visible straight down the center part, despite her attempts to dye it an interesting shade of merlot. The skin on her face was thoroughly wrinkled, resembling more a turkey's wattle than a member of Manhattan's glitterati. Associates and clients were surprised that Harris had such an uninspired-looking woman minding his schedule and all his office activities. But Myra knew everything about Harris's office, and his personal life. Getting rid of her would have proven impossible or, at very least, very expensive to the firm. And that's why the partners never questioned why Myra was still there. She knew everything there was to know about Harris's three-year affair, as well as four or five others he had "forgotten" to mention to his wife. Myra dutifully dialed Hank and fell into an easy familiarity with him.

"Hank, Mr. H. says he needs a table for four at 7:00 tonight. But if I didn't know better, I would guess it'll end up being just two."

"You do know better, Myra," Hank chuckled. "You always know better. And let me guess – Mr. Hirschfeld's guest will not be a male, an attorney, or even over 30?"

Hank would never dream of talking this way about any of the other regulars. But with Myra, their delicious bond of shared cynicism and gossip had deepened over the long years of circling Harris's orbit. They both snickered. "Some things never change, do they?" Hank offered. His voice belied just a slight hint of admiration underlying the amusement. Myra was thinking the same thing.

At the same time Myra was calling Hank, Harris extended the dinner invitation to his clients. "Thank you so much, but we have a 6:30 flight out of LaGuardia tonight," said Bobby Stephens, the witness and, more accurately, the day's sacrificial lamb. The young assistant general counsel was under strict orders to accompany Bobby on the trip, so he, too, would be on that 6:30 flight. But Harris already knew that. The reservation for four was just a ruse to make Carly feel more comfortable. Harris knew the other two wouldn't be joining them. And he was right. Myra was right also. So was Hank.

"Oh, that's too bad. You really would have loved it," Harris offered with feigned disappointment. "Next time you're back up here, we'll have to plan this out in advance." Back up here, Bobby thought? Are you fucking kidding me? I'd rather have root canal without anesthesia."

"Of course, that would be great," assured Bobby, already busy gathering his overcoat and trying to erase Harris, and the entire day, from his memory. Harris politely turned to Carly. "You'll still join me, I hope?" Of course she would. Harris thought he was orchestrating a clever way to get Carly alone for a few hours to see what might come of it, but it was Carly and her red plaid skirt who was conducting the music that evening.

Dinner with Carly at Smith & Wollensky's went well, very well. The balance of erogenous power between them had shifted several times, from the appetizer through the entrée, as each attempted to attain domination and be in control of the dinner, the conversation, and whatever would come of it. Harris regaled Carly with stories of all the major clients he had serviced, and all the big cases he had tried to successful jury verdicts. Carly smiled warmly and pretended to be palpably impressed. Harris trotted out all his mojo, but Carly, as a flourishing puppeteer, pulled the strings. After eating only half her steak, she excused herself and went to the ladies' room. She, and everyone else in the restaurant, noticed Harris gawking at her legs as the generous pleat opened and closed welcomingly on her plaid skirt with every step. In front of the mirror, she reapplied her lipstick, sized herself up, and decided the game would be even more fun if she unbuttoned one additional button on her pink chiffon blouse.

With her subtle and deliberate wardrobe malfunction in place (not that she even needed it, she knew she already had Harris's undivided attention), Carly rejoined the table. Just as Carly expected, Harris could barely divert his glance from her cleavage as he finished the last bites of the creamed spinach he always ordered with his medium-rare ribeye. Although he had earlier made noises about needing to be back in Bronxville by 9:00 p.m., Harris managed to let his concept of time waft away as he suggested that Carly order dessert and ordered himself a glass of Taylor Fladgate 20-year-old tawny port. He had no interest at all in the dessert, and probably not in the port either. Harris just wanted the night to last a little longer, so he could get his fill of Carly. Mmmm, the thought of getting a fill of Carly titillated him.

Finally, after dinner, and after waving around his black American Express card just enough that Carly had difficulty suppressing an eye roll at his ostentatious behavior, it was time for them to leave. As they stood and pushed themselves away from the table, Carly noticed the obvious bulge in Harris's trousers. That, more than anything else she had heard or seen that night, made her smile. The big fish had taken the bait.

Outside the restaurant, under the green awning with its white lettering, Harris raised his hand to hail a taxi for Carly. He would have given anything to go back to the hotel with her, but he was certain that would come about another evening, just not tonight. Carly stood on her tiptoes in a schoolgirl-like manner, gave him a peck on the cheek and got into the taxi, careful to make certain that when she sat down, the slit on the right side of her skirt fell totally open so he would have one last glance to arouse his mind during the 47-minute train ride to Bronxville.

# CHAPTER FIVE

va Lampedusa rocked the world at Wilson Everson. Her reputation as the nation's best female trial lawyer was well earned. And unlike many women, she was satisfied with that title, not finding it sexist at all. "There are literally thousands of female litigators in the United States, many of whom are excellent. To be called the best among this esteemed group of over achievers is a high honor, and I'm not certain I deserve such recognition," Eva had said while accepting her lifetime achievement award from the Litigation Section of the American Bar Association a few years earlier.

Because of her legal prowess, combined with her acumen as the firm's largest rainmaker, Eva was the most highly compensated partner in the firm. She made millions of dollars a year, considerably more than her crosstown rival, Harris Hirschfeld. Although she never discussed it with anyone, Eva kept tabs on the earnings of all the top lawyers in the city, gathering information from media reports, headhunters, and disgruntled partners in other firms.

Eva was never afraid of a challenge. Her latest

representation involved the defense of the biggest of big pharma. The company had developed an ADHD drug that was alleged to have caused suicidal tendencies in children. Seventy-four families sued and were threatening to form an MDL, multi-district litigation. If the families were to prevail at trial, it could cost the company hundreds of millions, if not billions, of dollars. Her defense would be that those side effects were not unique but were consistently found in all drugs within that class of drugs. A "class defense" was a tough sell and it would take all her smarts and guile to convince a jury. The tougher the case and the more the odds were stacked against her, the more Eva rose to the occasion.

As a young lawyer, Eva had been tenacious and unrelenting. She maximized every possible opportunity, volunteering to do extra non-billable work on cases just so she could learn more about the law or the client. She'd ask partners if she could accompany them to hearings or sit in on depositions just so she could learn. Her thirst for knowledge was boundless. That tenacity, combined with her incalculable intelligence, made Eva a giant in this bastion of legal giants. Eva charged hard and never stopped short. Days turned into nights and weeks into weekends. Whether she was a junior lawyer or seasoned partner, Eva rarely took a vacation. Protracted personal gratification would just have to wait. But she was not, she reminded herself, going to follow in the footsteps of her octogenarian partners who would likely die at their desks. Their widows and children would inherit vast fortunes, but the people who had toiled to earn those handsome sums would be long gone. No, there was a big world out there and someday Eva was going to explore it.

Eva's most fervent passion was travel. She was born in Cartagena, Colombia, a city on the sea, and some of the most beloved memories of her childhood revolved around trips she and her dad, a self-defined accountant, would make in the twenty-six-foot Criss Craft closed-cabin boat he had picked up as payment from a client who didn't have the cash to pay him for keeping the man's books. Eva and her father had many wonderful times on that boat, the Suite Life. In the waters not far off Cartagena, they would fish for mahi mahi and grouper early on Sunday mornings. Sometimes, on the most wonderful days, dolphins would frolic off the bow of the boat, escorting them through the crystal blue waters. On occasion, when the seas were calm and the winds listless, they would sail to the San Blas Islands of Panama, or to Catalina Island in the Dominican Republic.

Eva was fascinated by other cultures. Even Panama and the Dominican Republic had cultural mores far different from those Eva experienced during her childhood in Colombia. When she was young, her parents took Eva to Brazil and Argentina, and to her mother's hometown of Copenhagen, and she relished her time in those places. Eva was especially enthralled with Buenos Aires, all the beautiful women and their magnificent clothes! She was determined to become a model, or a designer, or the owner of a clothing line. No dream was out of reach.

During many of her childhood years, Eva convinced her parents to bring her to Rio during Carnival week. There, she was spellbound by the garish costumes, outlandish street parades, and otherworldly carryings on of the locals during that magical season. She loved frolicking in the waves off Ipanema Beach and was oblivious to the temperatures that often reached one hundred degrees. She was also unmindful of the rampant debauchery and drunkenness that pervaded those weeks of frivolity. Once, her parents took her for an evening inside the Sambadrome. Eva felt privileged to be among the 180,000 people enjoying 84,000 dancers and entertainers, representing twelve "schools" – who were actually performers from the local favelas, or slums – performing dances and ear-splitting music for sixteen hours over two nights. Eva loved it all, her eyes widening at the exotic sights, her ears filled with the wonderful sounds – she wanted more, and she knew she was determined to discover and visit all the colorful places she imagined, and even those she didn't yet know about.

But it was always the time on the water with her father that Eva craved the most when she was a little girl, and not just because she wanted her father's attention. She had a magical relationship with the sea. Eva would stay connected to the water through sailing, fishing, and yachting her entire life. When she was a young associate at her firm, slaving for the 270 hours a month the firm demanded of her, she still found time to join the Manhattan Yacht Club, so she could make use of their well-maintained sailboats all year round. Most summer Sunday mornings, Eva would venture out onto the Hudson, enjoy a good sail, and tie up back at the Van Vorst Street pier before any of her colleagues were even out of bed. Her work and the sea were her passions, not men. She had no husband, no serious boyfriends.

It's not that she didn't enjoy sex – she did, very much. She would only date men she considered her equal, intellectually and physically. With those conditions, Eva's dating pool was quite shallow. After all, she was one of the most intelligent, worldly, and attractive women in the city, and one of the most accomplished. A girlfriend who got close enough to know told Eva her men divided neatly into two categories: "Men who just can't match your expectations so they're shot down before they even step foot in the arena, and men who pass the requirements but end up intimidated by your success, wealth, and beauty." Eva laughed at her friend's assessment – but she didn't disagree.

On those occasions when Eva found a man she liked, she didn't hesitate to give of herself, and give in every way. She would shower him with gifts and thoughtful mementos, not to impress him, but to assure him of her affection. And after dark, Eva was not at all shy about sharing herself. Passionately. Completely. Sex to Eva was as much athletic and physical as it was intimate. Once she made the decision to bed a man, she anticipated that each encounter would be a three- or four-hour episode. That's what she wanted, that's what she gave, and that's what she expected in return. Most of her lovers were thrilled, and sometimes overwhelmed, by Eva's direct, unabated approach to sex. She had her favorite fantasies and positions, but what thrilled her most was when her lover suggested something she had not yet tried. Then, if she liked it, she would insist they do it several different ways to explore the possibilities and engage in an encore performance in the early morning hours.

Intimacy, though, was also part of Eva's sexual motif. When she was most aroused, Eva would allow herself to engage in the ancient Eastern spiritual practice of tantric sex. Always intellectually curious and keen to explore the best ways to enjoy life and experience the most intense peaks, Eva had studied the art of tantra through a Buddhist speech coach she had employed a few years ago to help with her delivery to juries. The two became close spiritual friends, although never technically lovers, while working alongside for two months in 2017. Eva had become fascinated with the concept of merging her physical and sexual wellbeing by making use of ancient tantra techniques. She learned the skill of attaining greater pleasure through various sexual and emotionally satisfying practices that would help in the amalgamation of her soul with that of her lover. It was not merely bondage or exciting sex games; it was a holistic approach to combining the needs of the mind, body, and spirit that gave Eva her greatest pleasures, and orgasms.

Eva had female friends, too. Many of them were former clients, or fellow lawyers from her two decades of practicing law in New York. When one spent as much time working as Eva, it was hard to develop friends separate from work life. Eva would socialize with her girlfriends at power lunches, side-by-side pedicures, and wine tastings at the clubs and restaurants in the city. In addition to belonging to Equinox, Eva was a member of the New York Athletic Club, a 150-year-old New York institution that had remained off limits to women until the 1980s. Eva enjoyed being one of the first female members of the club, and the male members enjoyed having her around. If women were going to be admitted in the very conservative and highly respected club, it was better that they be intelligent, athletic, and beautiful, rather than the out-of-shape banal crusaders who sought membership to one of the last bastions of male exclusivity in the city merely as a badge of honor.

On occasion, Eva would travel with her girlfriends and, when they did, it was agreed that those trips were to be female-only affairs. Some of her closest girlfriends were married, but they were all too happy to abandon their husbands, children, work, and household responsibilities to spend four or five days away with Eva and the rest of the ladies. More often than not, Eva would pay for everyone's trip because she had the money and would rather spend it on her friends than on silly materialistic acquisitions like fancy cars or fur coats. She'd take the girls off to Scottsdale or Hilton Head for three days of golfing and tennis, or to Canyon Ranch or Miraval for serious spa time. Often, Eva would hire a yacht, or even a megayacht, over 200 feet in length, and take her friends to sail with her among the islands of the Caribbean, the Mediterranean, the Maldives, or anywhere else that might be fun. Of course, there was one overarching rule to which they all agreed to abide – what happens on the sea, stays on the sea.

# CHAPTER SIX

After Mario Garramone's black Skyline car-service limo ferried him from JFK to his apartment on Park Avenue and East 84th Street, he said a pleasant "Good afternoon" to Jose, the doorman, rushed into the elevator, and pushed "PH" for the penthouse. If he wanted to beat the traffic to the Hamptons on a Friday night, he would have to change quickly and be sure that Janice and their daughters were ready to leave within the hour. No doubt they would be ready before him because the girls looked forward to their weekends in the Hamptons more than anything. When the elevator door opened into the foyer of their apartment, the girls leapt to their feet. Roxanne had been texting her friends, planning the weekend's festivities, while her younger sister, Jessica, had been pleading with Janice for another set of riding lessons. Mario hugged and kissed the girls, then Janice, and proceeded to the bedroom, pitching his suitcase and briefcase onto the bed. There, Janice brought him up to speed on the household events of the past two weeks while he'd been in England and Greece.

"We really have to keep an eye on Rox this weekend,"

Janice said. "She's going to a party with that Van Morrow boy and he has a shitty reputation with girls."

"Oh, she'll be fine," Mario assured her. "That's just part of growing up. She knows how to handle herself. That's one of the things her wonderful mother has taught her." He winked at Janice and patted her shapely ass. While Mario grabbed a quick shower, Janice hurriedly unpacked his suitcase, tossing the dirty clothes into the hamper for Rosa to wash over the weekend while they were away. As Mario was drying himself in the bathroom, Janice tried to organize what she thought he might need for the weekend. As she grabbed the few papers in his briefcase, she noticed one that was not in his handwriting. It was a woman's handwriting, full, pretty, and cursive. On personalized stationary with the initials MFH on the top of the forest green page. It was Melanie's letter to her sorority sister begging off from the wedding invite because of her business trip with her new "boyfriend," the man about to become the CEO of New York Savings & Guaranty. The letter Mario had unintentionally grabbed and shoved into his briefcase as they got off the plane.

It didn't take Janice more than a few seconds to realize what had happened in Europe. As she did – as all those rumors and snide innuendos she had been hearing for months raced around in her mind – the color drained from her face. Her eyes filled with tears of shock, disbelief, and anger. At once, she knew it all to be true. Her Mario, her husband, had betrayed her. She read more of the letter. A weekend at the Greek Riviera on a topless beach with his associate? Promises of promotion? A *special position* in his staff? Next stop, Miami Beach?

EuroHoldings trips all around the country? Who was this Melanie and how long had this been going on? None of that really mattered to Janice right then. She was fixated on getting her family ready for their weekend in the Hamptons and not having anything disappoint those beautiful girls. But she didn't put the letter back in Mario's briefcase. Rather, she tucked it into a copy of *Jane Eyre* she kept in her bedside stand. Mario came back into the bedroom, having changed into khaki shorts and a light blue polo shirt. Janice managed a sham smile, and the girls were instructed to head downstairs to the car.

"Are you sure we have everything?" Mario mused.

"Yes. Positive."

And just like that, this lovely, healthy, wealthy, perfect American family was off to a weekend in the Hamptons. Only their whole world had just been shattered. They just didn't know it yet.

# CHAPTER SEVEN

Rolando, the Panamanian housekeeper employed by the Garramones for over a dozen years, greeted them when their car pulled into the driveway of their estate on the East End of Long Island. Janice had phoned him when their Mercedes M-450 exited the Long Island Expressway, about 30 minutes before they would reach the beach house. The house was impressive, the previous owners having taken great pains to preserve the architectural record of such a beautiful building. Conceived and constructed in 1906 by the architect Minard Lafever, it was one of the classic early mansions of Southampton. The house sat directly on the banks of Quantuck Bay in the Long Island Sound. Over the years, a series of additional structures were linked to the original wooden clapboard house through the use of ill-considered passageways designed by those far less proficient than Lafever. Nevertheless, the house was majestic and copious, qualities that appealed greatly to Mario's ego and appreciation of opulence. He was thrilled with its cavernous nature, so much room. Plenty of opportunities to be by himself.

This Friday, like every Friday, Rolando had dinner cooked

and warming. He presented Mario with his triple-olive vodka martini, and Janice with a glass of chilled Sonoma Cutrer Chardonnay as soon as they entered the front foyer and put down their bags. A platter of antipasto, including salami, capicola, mortadella, marinated artichoke hearts, and pepperoncini peppers sat invitingly on the dining room table. For the fitness-minded girls, there were carrots, celery stalks, broccoli spears, and hummus, as well as the homemade kale chips Rolando had just taken out of the oven half an hour ago.

No sooner had Janice completed her walk through of the kitchen to examine Rolando's dinner preparations, when her wine glass needed refilling. Rolando attended to that. It must have been a tough drive, he thought. He knew Janice usually enjoyed driving almost as much as Mario enjoyed sitting back and letting her take control of the car, the same as she took control of the family's affairs. But when Janice needed her fourth glass of wine less than 50 minutes after they had arrived, Rolando sensed that something was amiss.

The girls couldn't be bothered with dinner at home. Much as Mario enjoyed the Friday night formal family dinners when they all arrived in Southampton, he knew he could no longer compel the girls to sit at the table for hours while he enjoyed his traditional Italian Friday night fish feast. Roxanne was about to turn eighteen, and Jessica, sixteen. Jessica, however, was far more socially advanced and mature than her older sister. It was Jessica who received the greatest number of invitations for weekend fun in the Hamptons; she usually brought Roxanne along with her. As a result, the girls were never lacking for things to do when they arrived in the Hamptons on Friday nights. There are only two nights in any weekend, and there were plenty of boys to see, drinks to drink and joints to smoke.

"Where are you going tonight?" Mario asked them, trying his best to sound authoritative and paternal.

"The Friedmans are hosting a party for their friends from Australia," replied Roxanne.

"All right then, but keep an eye out for your sister and don't let her stray too far from you."

Little did Mario know that it was Jessica who was the cool, contained one in their little clique. She might have been among the youngest of the girls in the group that summer, but she had a maturity and womanly presence far beyond her years. Although she was the older sister, Roxanne was the one who had trouble holding her liquor or, even worse, holding back her feelings when she was attracted to a boy. Roxanne had a Taylor Swift-like penchant for falling head over heels in love with a boy after knowing him for barely a day or two, and then crashing back to earth with all the agility of a fourth grader's paper airplane. Subtlety was not a word that could be even remotely ascribed to Roxanne's approach to boys. The boys were usually quite enamored with Jessica, and Roxanne felt her fate was to corral and contain one of the leftovers – any boy she thought she could attract before he might fall prey to Jessica's long legs.

As soon as the girls were out the door, Janice went upstairs to the master suite. The events of the day had finally completely overtaken her and she felt like she was drowning. She had done an admirable job of collecting the girls and their bags and proceeding to drive the two and a half hours as if nothing had happened. And, to make matters worse, Mario had reclined in the car and fed her a relentless line of bullshit about how exhausting the trip had been, how many more lay ahead, but that it was all for the greater good because he was destined to be the next CEO of New York Savings & Guaranty. Any woman with less intestinal fortitude, or without her daughters in the back seat, might have sped up a bit and swerved the car into a steel post, killing her passenger, herself, or both. Nor had it been possible for her to change the subject. Throughout the unfortunate four hours of interminable traffic on the Long Island Expressway – and through the first four glasses of wine – she could think of nothing but Melanie's handwriting.

*"The great thing is that the timing is perfect,"* Melanie had written to Stacy Ponder. *"He has been preparing to leave his wife for years now and he told me I was the 'perfect incentive' for him to finally make the move."*

Whore, thought Janice. That fucking whore. As she contemplated how and when to confront Mario, the sedative effect of the Sonoma Cutrer took hold and Janice drifted off to sleep, fully clothed and fully deflated.

By the time Mario finished sitting with Rolando and telling him how he had conquered the international banking world the previous two weeks, it was already ten o'clock. One might wonder why Mario had the need to tell his house manager such things, but his insecurity was abundant. He might be a real player in the banking world, and a fairly handsome man, but insecurity had always been his Achilles heel and would be his ultimate undoing. With a gorgeous wife, two very together daughters, and an enviable and highly successful career, Mario had no objective need for validation. Yet he sought and, in fact, craved it at every opportunity.

For his part, Rolando was an attentive listener. He had a cushy job, managing the Garramones' property at a salary of $84,000 a year. The family came out to the house most weekends and Rolando prepared their favorite foods and provided general entertaining services, always with a smile. Whenever something went wrong at the house, Rolando was tasked with having it fixed. He didn't actually *do* any of the work himself. Rather, he called on his local cadre of Hamptons handymen, who would appear and take care of the problem. It was a small, sort of elitist fraternity of blue-collar, migrant workers who could command virtually any amount to service the spoiled Manhattanites who kept them busy throughout the year. Among this group, Rolando was near the top of the pecking order, because although he really didn't do much work himself, he was given a late model navy blue BMW and unfettered use of the house when the Garramones were not around. But most importantly, he was granted virtually limitless authority to hire his buddies to do anything the property may need: remove a tree, clean the chimneys, repair the appliances, service the cars, or anything else. It was that hiring authority that kept him in the highest regard among the mostly illegal immigrant worker community because scarcely a week went by when he did not need to retain someone's services.

Despite his generous salary, beautiful car, and use of the 9,600-square-foot home on the northern banks of the southern fork of the Long Island Sound, Rolando wanted more. Mario would have given him anything he wanted, partly in exchange for Rolando's turning a blind eye to the telltale signs of Mario's indiscretions over the years. But Rolando wanted more, so Rolando sold dope. When he visited his family in Panama in 2013, he carried a suitcase full of marijuana back to the states with him. Of course, he was very careful, packing bags of coffee around the dope to throw off the scent of any drug-sniffing dogs that might be checking the luggage of arriving passengers. He was surprised at how easy the entire process was, and thrilled when he parlayed his $15,000 investment into $80,000, courtesy of his cadre of Hamptons tradesmen turned distributors. Over the next few years, Rolando had several of his nephews from Panama visit him and required each to transport a suitcase full of dope as a condition of their visit.

One night, about a month earlier that same summer, when Mario and Janice were out at a Fourth of July party and he thought the girls were asleep in their room, Rolando had idled on the bamboo swing off the back porch and treated himself to a joint. It was after 1:00 a.m. and Jessica was thirsty, so she ambled down the stairs to pour herself a glass of sparkling water. She smelled the recognizable sweet scent of pot, which she was quite familiar with. On Friday summer afternoons, she and her good friends would go to the park and light up after school before going home and enduring their parents' bantering (and inevitable interrogation) during the endless car ride to the Hamptons. The dope helped make the trip more manageable.

Rolando was startled to see her, but there was no hiding

what he was doing. The joint was in his hand and the air reeked of the unmistakable smell of marijuana. The rest of what happened was somewhat blurry to Jessica. The next morning, she remembered Rolando sharing most of the joint with her. There was some passionate French kissing on the swing, and she had moderately rebuffed him when he attempted to put his hand up her shirt to explore her budding 16-year-old breasts. She didn't remember much more than that and she was not sure she wanted to.

# CHAPTER EIGHT

Unlike the wealthy and socially desirable Garramones who drove to the Hamptons every weekend, Cara's mother, Gillian English spent her weekends driving to the Poconos to look in on her elderly mother, Audrey. Gillian had been raised there, just outside Jim Thorpe, and attended nearby Lehigh University, where she majored in business administration. She began working in Bethlehem, Pennsylvania, as the Chief Financial Officer for a national telephone-research database, CallPro, in the early 1980s. The business took off and its success benefitted Gillian personally and professionally. As the company's profits soared, the owners wanted to take it public and they enlisted Goldman Sachs to draft the prospectus and bring the company through the various stages of SEC approval, culminating with what they hoped would be a successful IPO.

A debonair managing director, Mark Costello, was selected to be Goldman's principle liaison with CallPro. Mark had to work closely with Gillian to understand the financial structure of CallPro in order to best package and finance it. An avowed New Yorker, Mark initially found himself commuting the two hours back and forth to Manhattan every day thanks to Goldman's car service (one of the many perks of servitude at Goldman Sachs). But after a few weeks, a four-hour commute – even with Goldman Sachs's limos – gets to a man. Mark started spending a night or two each week at the Historic Bethlehem Hotel, known for its floor-to-ceiling palladium windows that provided glorious views of the city's historic shopping district. Bethlehem's best years had gone the way of the steel industry that once dominated this blue-collar town. The food at the hotel wasn't the most exciting for Mark, so he asked Gillian for some recommendations. At first, she suggested the Bethlehem Creperie, which Mark tried and found appalling. He politely shared his review with her. Gillian was embarrassed and chastised herself a bit for sending such a Wall Street hot shot to someplace he found so "minor league." She also smarted with a bit of local pride; she wanted Mark to see the best of her city.

The week after his initial epicurean experience in Bethlehem, Mark was eager to try something different. This time, not only was Gillian going to recommend something, she was going to accompany him to make sure he wasn't disappointed.

When Mark pulled up outside the house Gillian lived in with her mother, Gillian peeked out from behind the curtains and hurried outside, sparing Mark any awkward questioning from mom. After all, this was only a business dinner. Or was it? Gillian sauntered out into the sultry August night wearing a sky-blue skirt revealing, and accentuating, every golden inch of her legs. Her Calvin Klein blouse with era-appropriate 1980s-style shoulder pads, rested gracefully on her strong, balanced form, the buttons positioned so perfectly that Mark enjoyed a vision of Gillian he had never seen before. Her chestnut brown hair, always tied back in the office, was draped fully over her shoulders and brushed to perfection, highlighting its volume and sheen. And her makeup was unlike anything Mark had seen on Gillian in the conference rooms of CallPro. Gillian was gorgeous that night.

Dinner was a success. Mark loved the food (although later he wouldn't even remember what he ate that night). Soon Mark began spending more nights in Bethlehem. His colleagues at Goldman questioned why this project was taking so long, but he assured them that even though the company's books were in order, the accounting system was an irregular one that required his attention and expertise to bring it into conformity with the GAAP standards required for SEC filings. That seemed to satisfy them, and Mark continued to extend his time in Bethlehem.

By October, on some weekends when Mark returned to Manhattan, Gillian accompanied him. She was impressed and a bit intimidated by the city, but she never let on to Mark about that. At first, he took her to the fanciest and most impressive restaurants in Manhattan. But after a few weeks, he became more comfortable having his housekeeper prepare meals for them before she left on Friday nights. Alone in his apartment, on the 38th floor of the River Tower International at 72nd Street overlooking the East River, Mark and Gillian would eat whatever Lily had prepared, always accompanied by a lovely wine pairing. Saturday nights were usually their "grunge nights" when Mark and Gillian would order in pizza or Chinese, or they would go slumming at one of the city's hidden barbeque joints.

No one is quite sure which occurred first, Goldman's completion of its first round of financing for CallPro or Mark's marriage proposal to Gillian. Both happened shortly before Christmas 1989, making Mark's partners, and Gillian's mother Audrey, very happy.

Their marriage was filled with fun and excitement. Mark left Goldman for Cantor Fitzgerald in the summer of 1999 just as Cantor was on a major upswing. As a result, Mark was well compensated, and he and Gillian enjoyed regular trips to London, Berlin, and Tokyo. Gillian stopped working to start their family. When Cara came along later, Mark and Gillian made sure she had everything a little girl in Manhattan could ever want. Every Christmas and spring break from school they'd go on family trips to Disneyworld, Aspen, Bermuda or somewhere else that was simply magical. Often, they'd take Audrey along to babysit. While Mark and Gillian skied or snorkeled, Audrey adored her special time with her granddaughter, spoiling her as only a grandmother can with sweets and treats, and smothering her with hugs and kisses. Once these trips were over, Audrey was back in the Poconos to be seen on major holidays, but not much more than that.

After Mark's horrifying death in his Cantor Fitzgerald office on September 11, 2001, Gillian and her mother became close once again. Cantor Fitzgerald had no pension plan and the insurance policy Mark had sought to put in place had never been finalized due to that maddening typographical error. Gillian was suddenly left alone to bear alone the cost of their lifestyle: a

4,300-square-foot apartment on the Upper East Side, and all its attendant expenses. Before she knew it, Cara was starting at Sacred Heart and Gillian was overwhelmed by the cost of another full decade of private school tuition, and all that went with it – with no real source of income. Audrey dipped deeply into her life savings to help Gillian and Cara, but Audrey's savings were not very deep. Gillian would have to get a job, but she had been out of the workforce for over a decade and there were plenty of younger, more aggressive, more experienced, more educated former CFOs competing for the jobs Gillian coveted.

Gillian's single (mostly divorced) friends dated and cavorted about the city, but Gillian had not gotten over Mark's death and had no interest in diving back into the dating pool.

Janice and Mario had a genuine fondness for Gillian and they hated seeing her suffer the embarrassment of being the only mother of a Sacred Heart girl who struggled to pay the tuition, couldn't send Cara to camp, and was unable to be part of the Upper East Side host-and-be-hosted social scene. So they did what they could to help Gillian – and they could do a lot. But it all had to be done with a tender balance so as not to offend Gillian's understandable sensitivities. Because of the financial and emotional generosity of the Garramones, Janice and Gillian became even closer friends.

# CHAPTER NINE

In Southampton, Roxanne and Jessica went to the Friedman's, just as they had told their father, but they never went inside the main house. Instead, they made a beeline for the extravagant carriage house where 18-year-old Ben Friedman was living for the summer and hosting parties every weekend. Ben's parents trusted him not to engage in precisely the activities he engaged in every weekend. To show their confidence in his ability to make good choices, Mr. and Mrs. Friedman allowed Ben unfettered use of the carriage house, which only showed how out of touch they were with their charming son's nefarious antics.

The carriage house was built in 1947, two years after Ben's grandfather returned from World War II, and twenty years after the main house was finished. The carriage house, or "Ben's Den," as it was known to his friends, was widely known as a place with no rules, restrictions, or parental supervision. It was a large building with four small bedrooms, a kitchen, a dining area, and a spacious living room furnished with whatever couches and loveseats Mrs. Friedman and her upscale decorators had discarded from the main house during renovations. Three massive maroon and grey couches were arranged in a U-shape, with various fluid-stained, well-worn club chairs positioned at the back of the room around an antique mahogany card table. In front of the couches was a single five-foot-long French country coffee table, marred with burn marks and scratches, none of which had occurred during its forty-year tenure in the main house. Often, even when the Friedman's maid went into the carriage house to clean, the centerpiece of the coffee table was a twenty-four-inch high amber glass bong with a perc filtration system that passed the liquid through the base, and then through it once again. It was Ben's usual practice to substitute Southern Comfort for water, telling anyone who was sober enough to listen that the sweetness of the Southern Comfort would mute the acrid nature of the dope. An added bonus was that unwitting first-time users would find the draw from the bong to be sweet and palatable and, as a result, they smoked more and stayed dressed less.

As soon as they opened the door, Roxanne and Jessica were intoxicated by the smell of marijuana, the smooth sound of Prince and the sight of a half dozen bronzed and muscular teenage boys. This, they thought, would be fun.

Roxanne knew most of the boys in Ben Friedman's carriage house that evening, and she knew four of the girls already there. Of course she did – they all went to school together. Jessica recognized several of her sister's classmates from Sacred Heart, but she didn't know any of the boys there. After a few drinks, all that would change.

Ben and his friends were pouring screwdrivers and mimosas. They considered these "sophisticated drinks" and showed they were of a higher social ilk than the local Hamptons boys – the townies – who knocked back Budweiser at the local Hook House bar. Not wanting to seem uncool, the girls joined in sipping exotic cocktails, just as they'd observed their parents do on island holidays. And they did so with a high degree of pretention, though these spoiled socialite trust-fund brats had nothing to be pretentious about. Not one of them had a summer job; they all went shopping and lunching with limitless access to mommy and daddy's credit cards. None of the girls were familiar with the potency of mixed drinks; they were used to sipping Chardonnay and Pinot Grigio. Keenly aware of that "advantage," Ben made the drinks unfairly strong. After two drinks, or three at most, almost all the girls were usually making out with one of the boys.

Thoughts of unwanted advances, sexual harassment or any of the other gender-driven, socio-political concerns that had shaken the nation's consciousness during the #MeToo movement were the furthest things from the minds of these overly-stimulated teenage hormone factories. No, these sexually-fueled young women wouldn't mind the attention, or a few gentle advances, from some of Manhattan's most wealthy, handsome, and intelligent young men.

Although only sixteen, Jessica was not going to be left out of the fun. In fact, she was determined to have more fun than any of the older girls. It was Jessica who danced seductively with David Schneiderman, a senior at the prestigious Collegiate School for Boys in Manhattan, the nation's most exclusive boys prep school, founded in 1628. Its alumni included Cesar Romero, famous for playing the Joker in the original *Batman* television series; David Duchovny, famous for being a Golden-Globe winning actor in *The X-Files*; and John F. Kennedy, Jr., famous for being . . . well, John F. Kennedy, Jr. Like most boys who attended Collegiate, David Schneiderman was aware of its rich lineage and had the ego to prove it.

As they danced, Jessica hugged David so tightly it was almost as if he were wearing her as a second skin. David brought Jessica into one of Ben's bedrooms and handed her a joint. They got legless and, despite his turbocharged libido, David passed out on the bed before he was able to fulfill his testosterone-charged fantasies. She wasn't disappointed. She really didn't give a shit. She hadn't decided whether she wanted to be with him sexually or just tease him. Once David fell asleep, Jessica was done and wanted to leave. It made no difference to her that Roxanne was having a perfectly lovely conversation with Steven Seidman, one of David's teammates on Collegiate's varsity basketball team.

"Let's go. I wanna leave," Jessica insisted, emerging from the back bedroom.

"Why? What happened in there? Are you OK?" asked Roxanne.

"Yeah, I'm fine. I'm just like bored," replied Jessica. Roxanne's concern quickly turned to chagrin. "Look, I'm having fun and you can sit down and chill for a while. You were in there fucking David, or whatever you were doing for all that time. If you don't want me to tell mom and dad about any of this, just give me another half hour," demanded Roxanne.

With that, Roxanne turned her attention back to Steven.

Jessica turned her attention to deciding whether to flirt with another boy while biding her time. She knew her sister had the upper hand and, at least for this evening, she was willing to submit to that pecking order.

Roxanne and Steven kissed. He nibbled on her ear, whispering, "I'll take you home later, you can let your sister take the car and go home by herself now."

"I'd love that, but what would she say to our parents? I can't just send my kid sister home in a car while I'm sitting at a party drinking."

"Why not?" begged Steven, with growing excitement and a growing penis.

"First, my parents would kill me. And second, if she actually kept this secret, which is highly unlikely, she'd hold this over me and I'd have to pay for it forever," Roxanne explained. "Oh, and she's obviously high. That would be just great. I don't know what would be worse – if she got into an accident or if she stumbled into the house with those bloodshot eyes, stinking of pot. Neither option would end well for either of us."

"But it would be worth it," coaxed Steven, his steadily increasing erection doing all the thinking.

"Maybe for you, but not for me. Look, if you're serious about this and really want to get to know me better, we can hang out over the next several weekends. I'm not dating anybody and I'd like to spend time with you. Perhaps we can spend the whole summer together," Roxanne countered in a logical manner, with a poise beyond her years.

Roxanne may not have been as socially mature and

nimble as her younger sister, but she was very smart. If this boy really wanted anything to do with her, he would be around tomorrow. And if he wasn't, there would be dozens of others to take his place.

"Are you ready to go?" Roxanne asked Jessica.

"I've been ready for 20 minutes," Jessica retorted in her bitchiest voice. "If you're done sucking face, we can leave now."

It was 1:30 a.m. when the girls arrived home. They scurried upstairs and went to bed. Their mother was comatose after drinking all that wine in an attempt to obliterate what she had learned about her husband's Greek affair. Their father was sound asleep next to his wife with no clue that she knew anything about Melanie. Jessica was relieved that Rolando's blue BMW was not in the driveway, because she had been avoiding alone time with him for the past four weeks, since that foggy night they made out on the porch.

Jessica was trouble, but her family had no idea just how much trouble she would find over the next few years.

# CHAPTER TEN

Eva Lampedusa's corporate partner, Howard Rothman, asked her to accompany him to a meeting with Sheik Muhammad ibn Asneen Jabar, thirty-three years old and one of the sons of the Saudi king. The Sheik and his father had been longtime corporate clients of Howard's. Apparently, there was some sort of potential litigation in the offing now and Howard feared the Sheik was shopping it to other law firms.

The Sheik was in New York and staying at the Plaza, directly across the street from Wilson Everson. He kept an odd schedule, preferring not to deviate from Saudi time, so he insisted that all meetings be conducted in the middle of the night, New York time. The Sheik believed this gave him a competitive advantage during negotiations with sleepy business rivals and he was probably right. His nocturnal schedule also supported an active social life – the Sheik was a zealous partier. Alertness at night was a necessary attribute for navigating the New York dance clubs where he drank, snorted coke, and indulged in other sins prohibited in his own world.

On a Tuesday evening in early August, at 11:00 p.m.,

Howard and Eva were summoned to the Sheik's suite. When Howard and the king had first discussed the parameters for the meeting during a speakerphone call from Howard's office, the king sounded less than thrilled for his son to be potentially conducting business with a woman. In his most avuncular style, Howard convinced His Excellency that Eva was the finest litigator in New York and that taking a meeting with her was something neither the king nor the Sheik would regret. Besides, Howard added, Eva was a pleasure to look at. On the other side of the room, where she was seated leisurely on Howard's white leather couch, with the king unaware that Eva was listening to their entire speakerphone conversation, Eva rolled her eyes.

After the customary pleasantries at the Sheik's suite that subsequent evening, the royal ruler explained his dilemma. The Saudi government was having quality issues with Mitsubishi Electric Corporation's newly developed water treatment plant in Riyadh. They wanted to file a product liability suit against Mitsubishi, but the suit couldn't be initiated until the Sheik divested himself of a very large and highly visible asset – a super yacht he was buying from ... Mitsubishi.

It seems the insomniac Sheik had commissioned a $418 million ultra-luxurious super yacht a couple of years earlier. He had tendered a deposit – $100 million – and the massive vessel was almost ready for delivery. It was being constructed in a Greek shipyard by Mitsubishi Marine Industries. Mitsubishi Electric Corporation – which was about to be sued by the Sheik's father, the King – was a completely distinct corporate entity from Mitsubishi Marine that was building the Sheik's boat.

Still, it didn't look good.

The king was distressed about the entire situation and insisted that the Sheik extricate himself and the royal family from the mess, quickly and cleanly, regardless of the amount of the loss. The Sheik was content to realize an undersized recovery from his $100 million deposit if someone else would assume the contract. That is, for reasons of optics and to avoid a perceived conflict, he just needed to get out of the deal.

Eva listened and carefully absorbed the facts of the case. Super yachts are expensive, very expensive. In fact, eight of the ten most expensive luxury acquisitions in all of history have been super yachts. Even after making the initial purchase acquisition, the need for supplemental funds was a constantly demanding affair. Fuel prices, port fees, taxes and crew salaries all combined to make the total financial outlay massive. Consequently, it was often only members of the ruling families of oil-rich countries who could afford the super yacht life.

Eva wanted to promote herself to file and prosecute the litigation against Mitsubishi. But she immediately identified an insurmountable obstacle: she had consulted with Mitsubishi earlier in the year about a product liability concern they had brought to her for counsel – airbag malfunctions in the Mitsubishi Mirage vehicles. Because of that, she would be conflicted out of any litigation representation adverse to Mitsubishi. She needed to keep that information to herself right now. She knew that Howard would press her the next day about pitching to get the litigation. As the partner who introduced Eva to the conflict, Howard would be heavily compensated.

But what really intrigued Eva was not the litigation, it was something else – that brand-new ship. Almost everyone spoke their mind about options for the Sheik and they agreed to meet again on Thursday.

Eva kept her own idea to herself.

# CHAPTER ELEVEN

Eva went home and couldn't sleep. She started to envision the Sheik's problem as a once in a lifetime opportunity for her. If she could cobble together enough money to acquire the ship and structure it into a sort of floating vacation home/workspace for herself and some of her closest friends and investors – with a healthy portion of the ship being some sort of floating hotel – it could be the realization of her ultimate travel fantasy. It could also be the change she was seeking for her life. The details could all be worked out in time, and she realized she would have to cede some control to others who would be making huge financial commitments to make the project viable. But already she had a vision, a grand vision.

She knew the Sheik was not having traditional cruise ship cabins built; he was constructing spacious and ornate bedrooms. She could turn those bedrooms into individual abodes – or luxury suites, as she would call them – that would be sold to her investor friends who would be willing to take a gamble on her ambitious vision. Everyone would have to pay a massive application fee, of course, as well as hefty dues to whatever kind of condo association would be necessary to fund that portion of the enterprise that wasn't taken care of by the income from the hotel rooms.

Eva could totally eliminate a bunch of the cabins and replace them with even more common space for the ship's owners. She was on fire with ideas! A small fruit market could offer fresh fruits, vegetables, crackers, and such niceties as cheese and caviar so suite owners could enjoy snacks in their own luxury suites. A swanky wine and liquor shop would make available expensive spirits and unique wines from vineyards the ship would visit. She could install an opulent coffee bar, offering coffees from all over the world. A top-quality health and wellness center and gym would be absolute requirements for people who would be spending months at a time on board the ship. Perhaps she could even install a golf simulator/tennis practice center to attract business colleagues who would say they couldn't spend protracted periods of time on a ship and forsake their precious addiction to smacking little round white or yellow balls all over the Hamptons. The front wall of the tennis/golf "ball room" would be interchangeable, allowing people to smack either golf balls or tennis balls at it. And perhaps there would be a little self-serve mini bar and snack center in the back of the room. A small cinema was already part of the Sheik's original design, but Eva would enlarge it to accommodate more movie goers. The more she thought about it, the clearer she could see it – it would be magnificent.

If she could realize all the possibilities she envisioned, she could see herself spending much of her time on the ship, planning itineraries far in advance and making the ship her home when she was not actively trying cases for her pharmaceutical clients. These days, most pretrial preparation work that was done – including writing and responding to discovery requests, exchanging hostile letters with opposing counsel, and virtually everything other than arguing in court – was done remotely anyway. There was no reason why it couldn't be done from her comfortable confines aboard the world's first communally-owned megayacht.

Eva was single and forty-seven years old, with over $80 million in invested assets. She would absolutely relish sliding into semi-retirement while most of her colleagues were just hitting their stride. She could see herself traveling the world in the greatest style imaginable without any reservations or apologies. She just needed price concessions and investors. "Just?" she thought. But she could do it. She had achieved bigger conquests for her clients. Why couldn't she do this for herself? The Sheik, she was confident, would capitulate quickly with all the pressure from his father, the king; it was Mitsubishi that could gum up the works. Would they even entertain a transfer of the contract to her? But if they didn't, she reasoned, and with the Sheik walking away from the deal, Mitsubishi would be stuck with a huge white elephant and every day that went by once construction was completed would result in a diminution of the ship's value – just like a car. Ships, like cars, depreciate the day after they are built and even with Mitsubishi's vast financial resources, $418 million was a titanic financial outlay.

Eva spent the next two days huddled with her personal

financial advisor and a small corps of her closest friends. They all told her it was unworkable and a fool's errand. But the more Eva was confronted by naysayers, the more she was determined to make it work. She understood that not all great ideas bore fruit, but she was more successful than most in getting things done when she set her mind to them.

By Thursday afternoon, Eva knew her plan could work if some of the moving parts came together perfectly. First, she would have to convince the Sheik to take $50 million in exchange for his $100-million down payment on the vessel. That would enable him to get out of the deal quickly, avoiding extra costs attendant to the delivery of the ship and, more importantly, embarrassment. Eva also realized that fifty cents on the dollar wouldn't lose the Sheik, or his father, any sleep. Next, Eva would have to prevail upon Mitsubishi to reduce the purchase price from $418 million to $320 million. The Sheik had tendered $100 million; Eva would be responsible to raise the final $220 million. If she could get these concessions, from the Sheik and the ship builder, she would end up with a brand new $418 million vessel for $270 million.

The negotiations would be complex and multi-faceted, but Eva was indefatigable about her vision. The stars would have to align but if they did, this could be one of the most exciting ventures on the seas, and clearly the most exciting thing Eva had ever attempted in her already extraordinary life.

Thursday evening arrived, and Eva had dinner delivered to her office where she unveiled her grand plan to Howard. On several levels, Howard was surprised and upset by Eva's plan.

First, and most selfishly, he saw Eva's potential litigation representation of the Sheik and the king evaporate. No matter how many times Eva explained that she would be conflicted out of any product-liability litigation against Mitsubishi because she was already representing them in a separate matter, Howard refused to accept it. Howard also realized that if Eva was able to convince the Sheik to adopt her proposal, she would be spending appreciable time outside the office, resulting in a net decrease in her billable hours and revenue generated to the entire firm. This would affect not just Howard, but all the firm's partners. And the partners might just blame Howard for the decrease in their profits. Eva had been careful not to leak this information to Howard or any of her other partners prior to this time. With all this in mind, Eva had been cunning in her decision to have dinner delivered at 8:00 p.m., only an hour before the meeting with the Sheik, and after most of the partners had gone home for the day.

With his chubby jowls dropping downwards in a discernable pout, Howard trailed Eva as they marched across Fifth Avenue and up to the Sheik's hotel room. This night, unlike two nights earlier, Eva strode in confidently and it was Howard who lagged behind and was the junior varsity player on their team. Before they even entered the room, Howard had been rendered insignificant. This night was to be Eva's show.

As they began the introductions once again, the Sheik surprised Eva and Howard by announcing that his Excellency, the king, was on the speakerphone. This didn't phase Eva in the slightest. She was a poised and confident lawyer who addressed juries for a living and dealt out advice to captains of industry on a regular basis. Nevertheless, she respected the king and addressed him deferentially.

"Your Excellency, good evening. My name is Eva Lampedusa. I am here with my colleague, Howard Rothman, and it's my pleasure and honor to meet you."

The white plastic speaker box on the table in the middle of the room responded. "Good evening to you, Miss Lampedusa. My son has told me he met you earlier in the week. He and Abdul have said lovely things about you."

Eva wondered which of the Sheik's eight associates was named Abdul, as none had played much of a role in the discussions the other night. But it was no matter, as this was her night to dominate the discourse.

"Your Excellency, Sheik Asneen Jabar has explained to us the situation in your country regarding Mitsubishi and your concerns around the water treatment plant and the vessel. My partner and I . . ."

"Miss Lampedusa," interrupted the king. Eva was impressed that he pronounced her name correctly, as she had done with the Sheik. "Please forgive my directness, but I do not care about that silly boat. This was my son's folly and I cannot allow it to make me look like an ass when it comes to this company, Mitsubishi. I need to sue them because they have messed up my country's water-treatment plant. And the health of my people is much more important to me than my son's nautical recklessness. Do you understand me?"

"Yes, your Excellency," replied Eva, respectfully, while trying to hide her glee. The conversation was playing directly into her hands.

The king continued. "Have you and your partners come up with a way we can get out of this situation?"

Eva glanced at Howard who nodded. Eva responded, "Yes, your Excellency. We have considered a multitude of options we are prepared to present to you." Eva was bluffing. She had considered only one option.

"With all due respect . . ." said the king. Eva knew all too well from judges and opposing counsel that that phrase meant, "I don't care, just listen up."

"I don't want a lot of lawyer speak about 'a multitude of options,' as you call it. Have you all figured out a way that we can get out of this ship investment quickly and easily?"

"Yes, your Excellency." Eva knew to be direct and not to mince words when addressing a judge or in this case, a king.

"And what is that?"

"Your Excellency, I am prepared to make a contingent offer to you and Sheik Asneen Jabar of $50 million in respect of your $100 million deposit on the vessel."

"I see," said the raspy voice in the white speaker box. "And on behalf of which of your clients is this offer being made?"

"Your Excellency," Eva knew to begin every statement with the appropriate salutation, "I am making this offer personally."

Several members of the Sheik's entourage cleared their throats and looked at one another.

"I see," said the white box once again. "And what is that offer contingent upon?"

Eva explained that she needed a week to contact Mitsubishi and to discuss a discounted purchase price on the vessel. Nothing would be gained by sharing with the king the purchase price she sought to pay, or her vision for the intended purpose of the ship.

As if a scratched record, the voice once again began with, "I see." But the king followed immediately, "Miss Lampedusa, I regret not having made the trip to meet you. You sound like a fine lawyer. Most of the lawyers we deal with give us options and excuses. You have given us a direct answer. This is a very cogent proposition and it makes a lot of sense. We will give you two weeks to see what you can achieve with Mitsubishi. Won't you please keep us updated on your progress? And regardless, I suppose we shall be in touch again. I like your style and I would look forward to working with you at some point. Oh, and one last thing. This is not my boat, it is my son's. I would never have done such a foolish thing and I would like to think he won't ever do anything like it again." The king had just publicly rebuked his son in front of others, a most unusual occurrence.

After everyone stood up, shook hands, and bowed appropriately, Howard and Eva walked back across Fifth Avenue to their offices. Howard mumbled that if Eva were ever to deal with the king or Sheik in the future, Howard must be given credit as the originating attorney, since he had introduced them. Eva's mind was racing with all the things she had to get accomplished – and how Howard's self-interested and asinine comment epitomized the reason she wanted to go live on a ship.

What Eva needed at this point were two things: price concessions from Mitsubishi, and fellow investors who would share her vision of such a unique and exciting concept. One was in her power and, as for the other, she awaited word from Japan.

The next morning, Eva telephoned Mitsubishi Marine and began the dialogue.

# CHAPTER TWELVE

Harris Hirschfeld took 7:42 a.m. train into Grand Central Terminal, grabbed a buttered bagel and orange juice at Fred's Deli in the lobby, and ascended the escalator to the MetLife building. A few minutes later, he was in his office at Bergman Troutman on the 28th floor, directly above the Terminal.

Grand Central was a New York landmark, and Harris thought of himself as somewhat of an historian about this hallowed institution. He shuddered when people referred to it as Grand Central *Station* – it was a *Terminal*, after all, a place where trains *terminated*.

He had spent hours over the years studying the celestial ceiling mural poised high above the stampeding commuters, a beautiful work of art often taken for granted by the more than 750,000 travelers who scurried through its tunnels and alleys every day.

Harris also knew that 93 percent of those commuters were college graduates, something he had always found fascinating. Were 93 percent of the commuters pouring in on the Metro North trains arriving from Westchester and Connecticut, and only a non-collegiate 7 percent on the subways from the working-class neighborhoods of Queens and Brooklyn?

He knew about the Whispering Gallery on the north side of the terminal where you could stand at either end of the Oyster Bar ramp and whisper into the tiled walls and your voice would instantly travel up the curving archway, across the ceiling, and down another to be heard on the other side of the gallery.

As he did with most things in his life, Harris had studied Grand Central Terminal on his own time and in his own way. And as he did with most things in his life, Harris used that information to impress all who would listen to him.

Seated at his desk, he checked his computer to see which partners and associates had swiped their identification cards into the elevators that morning. That way, he could keep tabs on what time they came and went from the office, intel that would come in handy for the management committee's compensation deliberations in December. Today, he was looking for one name in particular – Carly Burke.

Once he saw her name illuminated on his screen, he felt an immediate jolt of satisfaction. She was coming to work early – a pretty good indication she had spent the weekend in New York, rather than returning to Wichita where she might have a hometown boyfriend. It made him happy.

Almost immediately, the happiness faded. Okay, she stayed in New York over the weekend – so maybe she had a guy in New York? What did she do this weekend? Who was she with? What did she wear? Damn it, did she get laid – that's what he really wanted to know. He needed to know the details – just like he knew exactly how many out-of-town tourists clogged up Grand Central every year (21.6 million). He was a possessive and jealous type, precisely the traits that had gotten him in so much trouble seven years ago.

"Good morning, Carly," Harris whispered gently into the phone. Speaking in a subdued voice was one of Harris's little tricks. It was a public speaking tactic, known to any experienced nightclub entertainer: if the crowd is chatty, don't try to top them. Go low, and they will come to you. It worked well in meetings, in front of juries, and with his clients, but some of his partners resented his arrogance and insecurity.

"Hi, Harris" responded Carly. "Did you have a nice weekend?"

"I did, I was at my son's baseball game. It was a great honor. He struck out six Horace Mann boys in only three innings." Even when answering a simple question about his weekend and time with his family, he needed to brag. It elevated his stature, at least in his own mind. Who referred to watching his kid's game as "a great honor?" Good to see his superciliousness hasn't dissipated over the weekend, thought Carly.

"That's great," responded Carly politely, rolling her expressive blue eyes and wondering why he was calling her so early. Although she already knew.

"Thanks again so much for dinner on Friday night," Carly offered.

"Great steaks there, weren't they?" Harris said it so proudly, as if he owned the damn restaurant.

"Yes, they were. It was also fascinating listening to you tell me about your career and all the amazing things you have accomplished," said Carly, almost gagging on the words as she spoke them.

"Carly, we have a very sensitive project coming up over the next few months and I need someone I can trust to run it. Not only do I think you're doing an excellent job here in New York, but it's ideal that you're from Hinkle Morris and not from our own firm. That really makes you the perfect candidate for this project."

Carly was intrigued. Had Harris designed a project specifically so Carly would have to work closely with him? Not entirely, Carly thought. She knew that her pathway to whatever she intended to acquire from Harris would mean she'd have work closely with him at some point.

"It sounds fascinating, Harris. What's it about?" Carly asked.

"I would be much more comfortable discussing it in person. Do you have any free time this morning to stop by my office?" Harris knew that Carly had nothing but time for him. He was a senior partner running a massive litigation department in one of the largest firms in the country and she was an imported paralegal, bright eyed and bushytailed in the big city. She was expected to be there whenever summoned, and she would be.

"I can come up now, if that would work for you," Carly offered, dutifully.

"Terrific," Harris muttered softly, again trying to command Carly's total attention. Ten minutes later, Carly was seated in a great big black leather chair across the desk from Harris. "You know, there's a history behind those chairs," Harris dropped it a little too casually, as if he hadn't rehearsed the anecdote he was about to tell. "Do you remember Senator Sam Rayburn?"

Carly had no idea who Sam Rayburn was. "Sam Rayburn? Yes, of course," she answered.

"Well, when I was in my second year at Georgetown Law, I did a summer clerkship on the Hill. Of course, I was always very adventurous and curious while I was there." Carly could hardly hide her disdain for Harris's unbridled arrogance – but she did.

"One day, I found my way to a storage room in the basement of the Capitol. I stumbled upon all kinds of furnishings and other paraphernalia – incredible historical items embodying the entire history of the Capitol building. In fact, it was like taking a tour of U.S. history. Those two chairs right there belonged to Senator Rayburn. Rayburn who, as you may remember from your studies of history, served in the United States Congress from 1913 to 1961. He served as Speaker of the House for 17 years, longer than any other man in the history of this fine Union."

Carly stared at Harris, trying hard to maintain a look of attentiveness and fascination while not wincing at his pomposity. It wasn't easy, though, when Harris said things like "this fine Union."

"At that time, all senators were given two new red chairs when they were sworn into office. A mark of a senator's seniority was the color of his guest chairs as the years passed. The longer he was in office, the more constituents and colleagues would sit in his guest chairs, and their leather would grow darker with wear. So, that chair you are sitting on was bright red back in 1913, when it was initially bestowed upon Senator Rayburn."

"That's really interesting," Carly said. She surprised herself; she was being sincere – it was kind of interesting.

"Now when I first came upon those chairs, they were almost falling apart. They were covered in more dust then we would find in the attic of my grandpa's stable. The wood was all cracked and nailed together, testifying to the enormous weight of the history that had been borne by those chairs. The horsehair that filled those cushions under you right now was sticking out, like needles through a cheesecloth. I had an old antiques dealer in Foggy Bottom look at the chairs and he teared up. Because of the storied importance of the chairs, he offered to do the restoration for half price. But don't think I got off cheap – it still cost me over $4,000 to get two chairs restored."

Carly remained impressed, not at Harris's bragging about how much he had paid for the restoration. Rather, she was struck that fifty years of lawmakers' fat fannies sat in these chairs, probably groveling, lying, begging, and bragging – the same as happens in that chamber today.

"Well, as much as talking about those chairs fascinates me, I called you up here for a more challenging purpose. It appears that the government has some of our most confidential strategic litigation documents from our US v. Boeing case."

"Come again? Litigation documents?" Carly asked.

"Yes. Not Boeing's documents, but ours – your firm's and

our firm's. Confidential documents related to trial strategy and our theories for defending the case."

Although she was not a lawyer, Carly was one of the best document-discovery people Harris had ever met. Her skills far surpassed those of the junior lawyers at Bergman Troutman. These tasks usually fell to junior lawyers or paralegals because junior lawyers were almost always too busy climbing the ladder to partnership. As a result, paralegals jumped into these more mundane tasks and spent months, sometimes years, searching through documents, in storage warehouses and online. They didn't mind the work because it was time intensive and, unlike the young associates who had to slave for hundreds of hours a month while earning a regular monthly paycheck, paralegals received overtime pay.

The importance of Harris saying the documents were "litigation documents" wasn't lost on Carly. During the discovery phase of a case, the parties were required to exchange documents from their clients' files, even if marked top-secret or confidential. Usually, those documents were covered by a confidentiality agreement, signed by a judge, detailing who could actually read the documents, and under what circumstances. Violation of that agreement was a very serious offense, with heavy sanctions imposed by the court.

But "litigation documents" were an entirely different story. A lawyer's work – including his thoughts, mental impressions, or strategy – was absolutely protected from disclosure. In fact, on those rare occasions where such litigation documents were inadvertently turned over to the other side, the receiving party was obligated to identify the documents immediately, notify the other side of their receipt, and return them quickly. Any copies that might have been made had to be destroyed.

"How do we know this?" asked Carly, genuinely fascinated by what Harris was saying.

"We were at a dinner about a fortnight ago honoring Judge Burke upon the occasion of his retirement."

Again, Carly thought, so fucking arrogant. Who uses "fortnight" in a conversation?

"Anyway, I joined Steve Krotz and another guest at the bar." Steve Krotz was the Assistant United States Attorney who was serving as the government's lead trial counsel in the US v. Boeing case. "Steve said to me – 'Harris, what do you think about the EuroHoldings situation?' I was caught off guard but, naturally, didn't let him know it."

Naturally, thought Carly. He's too cool to allow that to happen. But Carly knew what he was talking about. The government had recently initiated a separate antitrust investigation into EuroHoldings and was utilizing the same investigatory strategy it was employing in the Boeing case. Harris and his team were following the EuroHoldings case very closely and had just completed a major presentation for their client comparing the government's strategy in the two cases.

"'It's an interesting matter, that Boeing case,' I said to Krotz, 'but I don't really see any similarities.' But the look on Krotz's face told me clearly that he knew that we were closely mapping the EuroHoldings strategy. And if that weren't enough, he actually came out and asked why we would ever be comparing the Boeing case to the EuroHoldings case. I was gobsmacked."

Carly was following it all intently. "How would those documents ever get to the government? How could they know that we're comparing the two cases internally?"

"I don't know, but that's precisely what I need you to focus on – how were the documents turned over, whether the disclosure was inadvertent and, if not, who did it and why. And Carly, uncomfortable as this may be for you, I need to know whether they were turned over by a lawyer in your firm or in my firm."

"I totally understand. I'll begin on Wednesday, right after I finish cataloguing the exhibits from Mr. Stephens' deposition last Friday."

"Give that to someone else," Harris snapped, a little too impatiently. "This is a high-priority project, and I need you to begin work on it immediately. And don't accept assignments from anyone else unless you have cleared them with me. I don't want to lose your attention on this project at all."

"Got it. I'll get started on it straight away." As she got up and turned to walk out of Harris's office, Carly was extremely aware of Harris's fixed gaze on her ass. The form fitting maroon Donna Karen skirt she had chosen that morning had achieved the desired effect and Carly knew it. Still, Harris's laser-like stare annoyed her.

But this assignment intrigued her. At that moment, she was less interested in playing Harris than in discovering just how and why confidential litigation documents had been revealed to the other side. Harris and his fixation on her were not going away anytime soon. He would be available to her wherever, however, and whenever she wanted. That made her smirk.

# CHAPTER THIRTEEN

Saturday morning at the Garramones' Hamptons house had been uneventful. Mario awoke early and went for his three-mile walk through town, anxious to be seen in his new Adidas Stan Smiths, the tennis shoes that had been popular in the 1970s and were enjoying a revival. Mario prided himself on catching the trend at the right moment of popularity – just at that moment before everyone would be wearing them, when it was still noticeably daring.

Although Janice was awake when Mario left, she feigned slumber and remained in bed until she heard the front door chime, indicating that he was gone. She hadn't decided yet what to do about his apparently flaming affair with Melanie Hunter. All Janice knew for sure was that she was not going to let it throw her off her daily routine, something she held dear to her heart. Saturday mornings at 8:00 a.m. in the Hamptons meant Soul Cycle. Janice was one of the more fit and engaged women in the class. She was not there to meet men or have people stare at her great body. Soul Cycle, golf, yoga, tennis – it all kept her balanced, and balance was what Janice needed most right now.

The girls slept until after 11, but there was nothing unusual about that. The screwdrivers and dope probably added a couple of cycles of deep REM sleep, but Mario and Janice would have been shocked to see the girls downstairs much before noon on any Saturday morning. Roxanne was first downstairs that morning, sporting a green Dartmouth T-shirt over a pair of white cut-off jean shorts. Of the several colleges she had visited this past spring, Dartmouth was near the top of her list. She made it a point to buy a T-shirt from each of the colleges she toured.

She slithered into a seat at the butcher-block table in the kitchen and Rolando whipped up her favorite Saturday breakfast – an egg-white omelet with broccoli, mushrooms, red peppers, onions, and flax seed. Although Roxanne was not at all heavy, she shared with most 18-year-old American girls an unhealthy obsession about her weight. Her parents were not overly concerned. While the girls claimed to be skipping meals and eating sparingly, Janice frequently found Shake Shack wrappers and crushed pizza boxes in the garbage can – which made her happy. It reassured her that there were no demonstrable concerns of anorexia with her daughters.

Jessica did not emerge until closer to noon. She ambled downstairs wearing a pink bikini top and white gym shorts with the waistband rolled over itself, making the shorts even shorter. Even though she was the younger sister, Jessica was more developed than Roxanne. The shape of her breasts, almost peeking out of the top of her bikini, certainly did not escape Rolando's attention. He prepared her favorite Saturday morning breakfast – eggs benedict, with fresh salmon instead of ham.

While Rolando may have had many faults – and he did – cooking was not one of them. It was beyond reproach. His hollandaise sauce, made with all the freshest ingredients just that morning, could win awards at the finest culinary schools on the East Coast.

Finishing her breakfast, Jessica sashayed through the French doors and headed out to the pool, armed with her headphones, a bottle of Black Hemp bronzer lotion, and three back issues of US magazine.

"Is there anything I can bring you?" asked Rolando dutifully.

"Do we still have any of that rosehip iced tea you made yesterday?"

"Yes, shall I bring it out to you?"

"That'd be awesome," Jessica said over her shoulder, sliding open the bronze door latches of the majestic French doors as she stepped out to greet the gentle breeze of the Long Island Sound.

She shimmied out of her white shorts, exposing pink bikini bottoms, and reclined on the lounger to soak up the sun. She didn't feel at all self-conscious, no strangers could see over tall, old hedges that enclosed the property. Rolando came out with a pitcher of the chilly red brew and a polycarbonate cut crystal glass, which he placed gently on a table next to Jessica. The Garramones had a sacrosanct rule that no actual glass was to be used on the pool deck, ever since a tipsy guest dropped her glass while flirting with Judge Beagan at their Preakness-watching party nine years ago, resulting in Mario spending the rest of the night at Southampton Hospital having little pieces of glass removed from his foot.

Pouring the tea, Rolando couldn't help but steal a glance at Jessica applying her lotion. She wasn't trying to be seductive. She wasn't even aware that Rolando was watching her. Had she known, it would have creeped her out. For his part, Rolando was keenly aware that he shouldn't be staring at teenage girls. He was in his 50s; he knew it wasn't right. That night weeks ago, when he was making out with Jessica, could have been the end of his career – and of his liberty – had Mario found out about it. That simply could never happen again, he promised himself. Yet as the girls grew more mature and physically developed, Rolando felt himself staring. He just couldn't help it.

Alone in his own room, he tried not to fantasize about Jessica. He'd start thinking about other women, age-appropriate women ... but it was no use. He would inevitably succumb to thoughts of Jessica, almost always resulting in a violent masturbation session. He'd tell himself that his self-gratifying fantasies were a relief valve; it would prevent him from acting upon his obsession.

It didn't work. Here he was, filling his eyes with her young body. "This must stop!" he repeatedly reminded himself, or there would be irreparable repercussions. His mind drifted to his childhood, when his Uncle Hector spent a summer away from the family. At the time, Rolando was told that Hector was exploring employment opportunities in Peru. It was only years later that he learned that Hector had spent that summer in treatment for sex addiction, ordered by the court after repeated "incidents" with underage girls. But that was *Hector's* problem, Rolando told himself; it's not like it ran in the family or anything.

Once her Soul Cycle class ended, Janice purchased a hemp-and-chia seed smoothie from the nutrition counter at the gym. She was in no hurry to go home.

"Hey Janice. That was one of our most intense sessions in a while," wheezed Mindy Davis, one of Janice's closest Hamptons friends. Mindy was a little shaky on her feet and totally drenched in perspiration after 50 minutes of torture on the spin bike.

"Yeah, it sure was. But I needed that," replied Janice.

"Why? Something wrong?"

Mindy had always been there for Janice. An extremely accomplished litigator at a major New York firm – Janice could never remember which one – Mindy had been a great mentor and confidant as Janice dealt with the challenges of raising two over-privileged girls in the Upper East Side private-school world. Mindy's two daughters had successfully navigated those choppy waters years earlier; and one was graduating from Yale in the spring, the other was in her sophomore year at Oberlin.

"Just some shit at home, nothing serious," Janice lied.

"If it's not serious now, don't let it grow into something that could become serious," counseled Mindy. "Most large problems start as small ones that go unnoticed."

Janice seethed. She should only know. Mario's week-long fuck fest in London and Greece with some young hottie was serious enough already. This was no small problem, and it sure as hell wasn't going unnoticed.

Janice didn't know if she was ready to talk to anyone about it, even Mindy. On the other hand, of all people, Mindy would understand. Mindy's husband, Frank, had cheated on her with their nanny years ago – and it wasn't just a fling. It went on for eighteen months before Mindy found out about it. Then, everyone in Southampton knew about it. Nothing could ever be kept a secret in the Hamptons.

When it all happened, Janice was the only one Mindy confided in. Janice never forgot how candid Mindy had been when dealing with her most personal and darkest crisis. Mindy wouldn't let it destroy her; she maintained her strong and outgoing personality throughout the ordeal. Mindy told Janice she'd thought seriously about divorcing Frank but stayed in the marriage for their daughters. It hadn't been easy. There was virtually incontrovertible evidence that Ellie, the Swedish nanny, had slept with Frank in Mindy's marital bed when Mindy was away.

Mindy's girls had been at sleepaway camp in Maine that summer; Mindy was working diligently at her law firm in the city. Frank had been laid off from Citicorp and was working as a consultant out of their Hamptons home during the splendid summer months. Mindy would join him every Friday afternoon, remaining through Sunday evening, when she'd head back into the city. During those weekends, Ellie would retreat to her own room while Frank and Mindy went out as the quintessential Hamptons couple, attending all the social events and parties in town. At night they'd sleep in the same bed, without ever touching each other.

One day, Mindy's sister Jenna called her at the office, telling Mindy all about a blue dress she just had shortened and that she was planning to wear on a date that night. She asked Mindy if she could borrow her diamond earrings. "They're in the jewelry box next to my bed. They'll look great with that dress," Mindy told her. Jenna phoned the house to let her brother-in-law know she was coming over, but there was no answer. She had her own set of keys, she'd let herself in.

When she arrived, Frank was splayed across a wicker lounge on the back porch, eating a bagel and reading the *Times*. Jenna went up to the master bedroom and heard the shower running. Perhaps Mindy had come home for the day? Jenna peeked into the bathroom and saw Ellie's silhouette through the shower curtain. Ellie had her own bedroom and bathroom down the hall, so it was odd that Ellie was using Mindy's shower. Perhaps Ellie's shower wasn't working? She thought about it for a few minutes but didn't know what to make of it.

As Jenna went downstairs, Frank heard her footsteps and the screen door open behind him he said, without looking around, "Babe, would you mind bringing me another cup of coffee?" The intimacy in his voice was unmistakable. Instantly Jenna knew what was going on. And if that were not enough, the look on Frank's face was unforgettable once he turned around and saw Jenna, not Ellie, standing before him.

"I'm sorry, I thought ..."

Frank's voice trailed off. There really was no way he could finish that sentence. Saying anything else would only bury him deeper in the hole they both knew he was in. Jenna felt sick – literally sick to her stomach. This handsome, successful, charismatic man she and her sister had known for over thirty years and both dated – but her sister had won in marriage – was banging the nanny in Mindy's marital bed. Jenna felt a tightness in her chest and could sense bile rising up towards the back of her throat. She just had to get out of the house, which she did without a word to Frank, or to that slut nanny who was probably drying herself at that very moment in Mindy's monogrammed Wamsuttas.

In her car, Jenna's hands shook as she squeezed the steering wheel more ferociously than a 22 handicap strangles his club when attempting to hit a lob wedge over a stream. She was infuriated. Should she tell Mindy immediately, or wait until they were together in person? It couldn't wait, she decided. She dialed Mindy's number. Mindy picked up. "Did you get the earrings? I just know they'll look fantastic with –"

It was awful. Mindy was so cheery. Jenna interrupted her and told her everything that had happened at the house.

That was Ellie's last day in Mindy's bed, or Mindy's house, or even in the Hamptons. Mindy drove out to the house that night, walked in, and summarily fired Ellie, warning her to "stay the hell away from the Hamptons, the island of Manhattan, or anywhere else I might ever see you for the rest of my life." Ellie didn't want to know what vindictive act awaited her if she defied Mindy's explicit admonition. Ellie packed her suitcases, called a taxi, and was never heard from again.

Jenna never told anyone else what transpired that day, and presumably neither Frank nor Ellie shared the sordid details either. Mindy engaged in two hours of fact finding from Frank, which quickly and predictably deteriorated into a screaming match. Mindy learned that Ellie had been the instigator, seducing Frank in her bathing suit, apparently worn topless after the girls left for camp – or at least that's what Frank wanted Mindy to believe. Mindy shared some of the details with Janice, but mostly talked to Janice about her feelings of betrayal and guilt.

Now, with a smoothie in her hand, Janice stared at her sincere friend who had shared so much of her own marital travails. Well, Mindy had asked about her well-being, so Janice decided to test the waters.

"How did you come to terms with yourself and your marriage once you heard about Frank and that tramp?"

"What? Did Mario . . .? Oh, dear Janice, what's happened?"

Janice hadn't been ready to tell anyone what she had discovered, especially since she hadn't even confronted Mario yet. But there it was, an open question that Janice couldn't resist answering as she looked into the warm, comforting eyes of a true friend.

"I found a note," Janice began.

"What kind of note? To whom?" Mindy now sounded more like a litigator. "What did it say? Are you certain you read it properly? You know Janice, you can be prone to the dramatic. You could be upset about something that doesn't really exist."

"Trust me Mindy, I read it properly. One of Mario's young *colleagues*," Janice said, employing sarcastic air quotes, "was writing to a friend, telling her all about a trip she and Frank were enjoying together in London and Greece."

"Okay... Was it a business trip? Maybe she was just

telling her friend how fun it was to be on a business trip in Europe with a senior bank officer." Mindy, not wanting to jump to conclusions, but already knowing what was happening, was playing Devil's advocate. "That's pretty heady stuff for a young banker, you know."

"It started as a business trip but apparently the deal fell apart shortly after they got to London. But that didn't stop them from staying there for a few days. And then they flew to the Greek Islands together. He told me he was engaging in *'due diligence'* in Greece. *'Due diligence!'*" More air quotes. "On a deal that had already been cancelled, or whatever they call it. Mario promised to make her his 'special assistant'." The air quotes were really flying now. "And would be taking her on more trips so they could discuss sensitive things without anyone from the office overhearing them." Janice's fury grew as the whole story poured out of her, her lips pursed and her hands clenched.

"Alright, take it easy though. What did Mario say?"

"I haven't confronted him yet. I'm going to do that this afternoon." The tensions welled within her.

"What are you going to say?" asked Mindy, concerned.

Janice stammered. "I ... I don't know yet."

"Well, let's plan out your approach before you just stumble your way through it," said Mindy, now sounding definitive, like the aggressive litigator she was. "If you're right, we'll want to make sure we find out all the facts, and don't leave him any openings. He may change his story if things get ugly and you end up in a contested divorce proceeding. What you learn now will govern our approach."

"Our approach?" queried Janice. "I didn't have any approach in mind. I just want to find out what happened or scream at him – I'm not sure which one yet. Maybe both. Or maybe I'll just kill him. I wish I could open my eyes, and this would all have been a bad dream, and it would just go away."

"I know, but that's not an option," Mindy said in her most comforting tone. "Look, maybe he'll say he regrets it, it was just that one time, and that he won't do it again. Oh, and he must fire that woman. Immediately. Even taking her off his team is not enough. If she's still at the bank, she is toxic. But let's see what you learn."

# CHAPTER FOURTEEN

Eva was at her desk, deep into pharmaceutical studies on ADHD, preparing for her upcoming trial. Even though the trial was nine months away, Eva was already working on her opening statement and trial exhibits. She was known for being uber prepared, to the point of being obsessive-compulsive about every detail. She had a reputation for being a ruthless litigator who left nothing to chance.

"Ms. Lampedusa, there's a Mr. Kuroki on the phone for you," Eva's secretary interrupted. "But he's not on your schedule."

"I'll take it," replied Eva, anxiously.

"Hello, this is Eva Lampedusa."

"Greetings Ms. Lampedusa," Mr. Kuroki began. "I am calling on behalf of Mitsubishi Machine Industries and the Hellenic Shipyard of Greece." His speech was very stilted, it was obvious English was not his first language.

"Thank you," replied Eva. "I've been expecting your call."

"We've also been in touch with Sheik Muhammad ibn Asneen Jabar over the past several days. Your proposal to buy the Sheik's boat has been reviewed at the highest level of the

Shipyard and Mitsubishi Marine. I will spare you all the details of the negotiations among the Sheik, Hellenic, and Mitsubishi, but these are the terms that are being offered to you. You have proposed that Mitsubishi sell you the vessel for $220 million. After much deliberation, Mitsubishi is prepared to offer you the vessel at $220 million if you tender the money in cash within 60 days. We must have your wire on or before October 16. Alternatively, if you are proposing a mortgage, or any third-party-payment terms, Mitsubishi will sell you the vessel at $240 million. And the Sheik has agreed to your proposal that he walk away from the boat in exchange for your payment to him of $50 million."

Eva absorbed it all. She was more excited than a homecoming queen on prom night. Mitsubishi Marine was really going to sell this boat to her – and they were going to do it at the price she wanted! She thought to herself, $240 million with financing and $220 million without? Why would I want to give them an extra $20 million? There is so much I could do aboard the ship with that money. She recapped the transaction in her mind, like she had done about six times a day for the past few weeks. Mitsubishi was reducing the cost from $418 million to $320 million and the Sheik had already paid $100 million for which she would remunerate him $50 million.

"Let me make sure I understand this properly," recapped Eva. "If I tender $220 million to Mitsubishi and $50 million to the Sheik by October 16, the ship is mine free and clear?"

"Yes, but if you need additional financing, or additional time, the purchase price will be $240 million," reminded Mr.

Kuroki.

"I understand. Thank you for your consideration. Please relay my thanks and appreciation to Hellenic Shipyards and the Sheik."

Holy shit thought Eva, pushing the disconnect button and exhaling deeply. This could really happen! I could really get this boat and transform it into the community and adventure I've always wanted. She paused for a moment, her eyes resting on the law books that lined her oak-paneled walls. She stared at the people strutting down Fifth Avenue. She reflected on the fact she could soon trade these views for one of the South Pacific islands through a glass balustrade on the balcony of her new home on the ocean. Eva was not daunted by the fact she had to raise so much money in such a short period of time. She had already scribbled a list of potential investors and kept it on a handwritten ledger in the top right-hand drawer of her desk at the office. Hanging up the phone, she opened her drawer and reviewed the list.

Lorraine Williams was the first name she saw. When she was twenty years old, Lorraine had inherited a fair amount of money from her father, the owner of a Canadian paperboard company. In the span of thirty years, Lorraine had parlayed that $20-million inheritance into over $970 million. She was divorced, and reclusive. One of the richest women in all of Canada, she was constantly sought for interviews, press quotes, speaking engagements, donations, and the like. Lorraine was very charitable, and just last year had donated $125 million to the Toronto General Hospital to found a breast cancer research-and-treatment wing.

Eva's investment banker, Mario Garramone, and her law-school colleague, Harris Hirschfeld, were also on the list of potential investors. Eva knew they had money, lots of it. She didn't know how embroiled each of them was in his own personal affairs – and they had no clue that an inimitable offer was about to further complicate their lives.

Eva smiled as she went over the list of investors. Some would be larger investors than others, because some had greater financial resources, and some had greater egos. And those greater egos would require them to purchase the largest shares of ownership available; Eva was counting on that. To the extent those categories overlapped, Eva would be very happy as the wealthy members of her little club would purchase the largest shares. Less money for Eva herself to have to come up with.

Some of the people on her list might not want to join her venture at all. They might not have enough time to travel, or just be cash strapped. Others might have friends Eva didn't know who would be willing to give it a go. She wondered how she would decide who would be allowed to buy into her idea. What criteria would she use to determine who would fit into the community she would create?

As for governing the ship, Eva knew she'd need to form a board, consisting of an odd number of members – five? seven? nine? – directors who would set a strategic vision for the ship and oversee its management and finances. Of course, she would be the first chair of the board, as the entire enterprise was her baby. But after that, she would be comfortable turning over the reins to one of the other large investors. After all, they were all going to be handpicked and they were mostly going to be Eva's friends.

Even once she had raised the funds to pay the Sheik and Mitsubishi, the complexity of the plan would just begin. Eva's grand vision meant that every investor was a part owner of the ship. They'd each get their own luxury suite and the right to determine where the ship would go, what it would do, and a voice in all the ship rules. After that, they would be obligated to make semi-annual condo-association payments in support of the operation of the vessel. When Eva was done having it outfitted the way she imagined, the ship would have 45 luxury suites of varying dimensions and sizes. Four of the cabins, located on two floors of the stern corners, both port and starboard, would be the largest, each exceeding 2,800 square feet. Those were the prime real estate on the ship and Eva would sell them for the highest price. If she could land two financial whales, she would even be willing to forego one of those luxury suites herself.

Another brilliant idea Eva had conceived one night was the notion that she would develop at least half the ship as hotel rooms. "Visitor flats," she would call them; that was far more preferable to calling them hotel rooms. The ship would have luxury suites for Eva and all her wealthy friends, but others would be able to sail as visitors. If some of the visitors liked the ship – and at least eighty-five percent of the owners voted that they liked the visitors – the visitor could be invited to buy their visitor flats, or any unpurchased luxury suites. But first, they had to pony up a $25,000 application fee just to be considered. That, Eva reasoned, would limit the vetting and voting process to only serious potential buyers.

Costs for the running of the ship would not be insignificant. Eva set about calculating them, roughly. Annual dockage fees would cost around $450,000 and insurance would be in the $290,000 range. A reserve had to be established for maintenance and repairs – that'd run millions per year. A captain's salary would be around $260,000 per year and a crew of 120 would also command salaries totaling in the millions. Fuel costs alone could exceed $800,000 per year ... and the expenses went on and on. But on this day, at this moment, all Eva cared about was that she needed $270 million to pay to Mitsubishi Marine and the Sheik on October 16.

She knew she'd get it.

# CHAPTER FIFTEEN

As Janice drove home from Soul Cycle, she was an amalgam of anger, rage, and fear. She knew Mario would be home and she was steeled to confront him about Melanie Hunter and to find out how long he had been cheating and lying to her. Her red Saab 900S convertible made the turn onto Brentwood Lane. She immediately noticed that the family Mercedes was not in the driveway.

"Hello?" she yelled, walking through the door.

"Oh hi, Janice," yelled Rolando from the kitchen where he was preparing dinner for the family.

"Is Mario here?"

"No, he took an early walk and then Mr. Monahan called and invited him to fill out a foursome at the club."

"Oh, okay. What time did he leave? Did he say when he's coming back?"

"I think they have an 11:20 tee time," Rolando said.

Janice did some quick math in her head. They'd finish on the course by 3:15, have a beer or two in the clubhouse, and he'd be home no later than 4:30.

"Okay, great," replied Janice. She was relieved. She could put off the confrontation.

She trudged upstairs and peeled off her sweaty exercise clothes. Walking naked past the full-length mirror in her bedroom, she glanced at herself. She didn't look so bad, she thought. Her breasts were still firm, her legs long, and her skin tight. She never lacked for attention at the club, the gym, or virtually anywhere she went. She wondered what Melanie looked like. Melanie, the whore, she thought. She couldn't even bear to think that name, let alone utter it.

After showering, Janice donned her favorite bikini, a yellow Catalina suit with blue piping. Most 50-year-old women wouldn't dare to wear a bikini in the first place. Not only did Janice wear it, she rocked it. She strolled out to the pool where both girls were asleep on lounge chairs, each wearing headphones. Janice read for a few minutes and soon she was warm and sweating all over again. She walked to the pool shed, removed a few rafts, and threw them into the water.

"C'mon, let's swim," she said to her daughters.

She had to repeat herself three times before Roxanne woke up.

"Mom, can you *please* leave us alone? We're tired," pleaded Jessica.

"All you girls do is sleep," complained Janice.

"We're tired," they whined in unison.

Janice knew they had been out late the night before, and though she didn't know that they smoked dope or got drunk – or made out with boys they barely knew – she knew her girls were popular, and no angels either.

Janice walked over to the Bose poolside music system in the outdoor kitchen, turned on her Ariana Grande track on Spotify, and descended the three steps leading into the pool. And she didn't just turn it on; she turned it up so loud the girls couldn't ignore it.

"Alright, alright, I'm coming in," Roxanne acquiesced. "C'mon Jess, you have to go in, too. Where's dad, anyway?" She didn't really care where her father was, but if he were there, her parents would eventually take a walk or spend time together, leaving the two girls alone. She could only hope for that but, for now, she was stuck.

"Playing golf," Janice answered abruptly, but not so abruptly that either girl noticed. With that, she pushed off the bottom step, reached in front of her, and dove under the water, breast stroking the length of the pool. The girls grabbed the Styrofoam pool rafts, dragged them to the shallow end begrudgingly. They climbed onto the rafts as gingerly as possible, trying not to get wet. Inevitably, when they pushed away from the pool wall with their feet, their midsections sank into the water and they were almost entirely submerged.

"Who wants to take a trip to Stockholm before school starts?" Janice asked suddenly.

"Wait. What?" replied Roxanne. "What are you talking about?"

"Two of my mother's cousins still live right outside Stockholm, and I've always wanted to visit them and see Sweden. I just thought it might be a nice opportunity for the three of us to get away for a week before school starts."

"Wow, that'd be great," replied Roxanne, almost rolling off her raft as she turned to face her mother.

"But we have so much to do to get ready for classes," offered Jessica, thinking more of missed crazy end-of-summer Hamptons parties – and missed boys. Roxanne smacked Jessica in the arm. "Are you nuts? Didn't you hear mom? Sweden. How fucking cool would that be?"

"Roxanne. Language," scolded Janice.

"Would dad come, too?" asked Jessica.

"I don't know. It seems like he's been too busy for us lately. I thought it would be a fun opportunity for the three of us."

Jessica's sixth sense was quite keenly developed. "Too busy for us? What does that mean?"

"You know that he's been traveling so much the last year and he has so many pressures on him at the bank."

"Who cares," Roxanne chimed in. "I think it would be more fun if it were just like the three of us anyway. Whenever we go away with dad, he's like on the phone and the stupid computer all the time. This could be so much cooler."

"I don't want to go. You guys go. There are a lot of end of the summer events I need to be at," pleaded Jessica.

"You don't *need* to be at anything," her mother snapped.

"And these so-called *events* are just parties with boys you want to, like, meet or hook up with anyway," Roxanne said, siding with their mother.

"Hook up? Like sex?" Janice bristled, not at all hiding the tone of concern in her voice.

Jessica didn't like the direction this was going in. "No, Mom, it means just, like, meeting them and hanging out."

Roxanne made a huffing sound and rolled her eyes.

Janice turned away, hiding her smile from the girls. A week in Sweden, along with her daughters, to tell them all that was going on between her and their father, could be just the ticket. By then the confrontation would be over and she and Mario would be engaged in a preliminary dialogue about how to divide their assets amicably and move on with their lives. Since talking with Mindy and taking stock of her own self – her mindset and her body – Janice had preliminarily concluded that she didn't want to stay with Mario. He was a cheater and she deserved better. She was still young and pretty enough to move on. She had her own money and, when she was done with Mario, she would have even more. She didn't want to be that woman at the club that the other wives snickered at behind her back because her husband was known to be screwing around.

Thinking about quality time alone with the girls made Janice feel warm. Her parents were from Sweden and she really had always wanted to go there, having heard so much about it during her childhood. But maybe this was too much, too soon. She and Mario had never taken separate vacations. Time really was running up to the end of the summer, with so much to do to prepare the girls for back-to-school, including securing an SAT-prep program and tutor for Roxanne. Christmas vacation might be better. Sweden would look regal covered with snow and they would have time to really prepare for the trip.

Yes, Christmas. She and Mario would be public in their

divorce by then, so a trip without him wouldn't raise eyebrows. Appearances still mattered, at least for Janice and the girls. Apparently, Mario no longer cared about that – it was probably obvious to everyone in his office that he was screwing around again.

After her swim, and once the girls crawled back onto their lounges and put their headsets back on, Janice went to her bedroom and searched for the telephone number of Hank Blaser, the prodigy SAT tutor she had heard about from the Spence moms in the spring. She called his cell phone. "You've reached Hank. You know what to do." She left a message.

# CHAPTER SIXTEEN

J ust outside Westport, Connecticut, Marc Romanello was hitting golf balls off the perfectly manicured turf of the Southport Country Club. He wore canary yellow Vineyard Vines Bermuda shorts, an azure blue golf shirt, and a sweat stained New York Yankees baseball cap that almost never left his head anywhere he went. Marc was a passionate Yankees fan, and everyone who knew Marc knew that. In his home, one of the six bedrooms in the center of the house was a virtual museum of baseball paraphernalia dedicated to the Bronx Bombers. The room was packed floor to ceiling with treasured Yankees memorabilia, such as an autographed black-and-white photograph of Yogi Berra and Phil Rizzuto taken at the Yankees spring training facility in Fort Lauderdale the spring right after The Scooter had been voted the top defensive player in the '51 World Series. Marc was particularly fond of Berra and Rizzuto, his fellow Italian-Americans.

His most treasured relic though was an autographed jersey of the greatest Italian-American Yankee of all, Joe DiMaggio. It hung in the most prominent spot on the center wall of the room, behind UV-protective glass in a custom-made polished bronze case, illuminated by its own separate track-lighting system – like the Mona Lisa.

Other autographs in the collection included mortgage checks signed by Babe Ruth and Lou Gehrig, baseballs signed by Chris Chambliss, Roger Clemens, Mel Stottlemyre, and Joe Torre, and random papers signed by at least twenty-five other former or current Yankee players.

Marc knew almost everything about the Yankees. In October 1977, Marc was home from college and his father took him to the World Series at Yankee Stadium for his birthday. It was a particularly idyllic, warm night. Marc, his father, and 56,405 other fans were part of history as Mr. October, Reggie Jackson, smashed three home runs en route to the Yankees 8-4 defeat of the Dodgers. It was one of the best nights of Marc's life … up to that point.

Marc raised his son, Alexander, to be a Yankees fan as well. Although Alex was only a young boy during the Yankees' 1995 to 2009 dynasty, Marc indoctrinated him with stories of Yankees lore and took Alex on frequent trips to the stadium to see the "Core Four" of Andy Pettitte, Jorge Posada, Derek Jeter, and Mariano Rivera play outstanding baseball night after night, capturing the heart of the City. But it was to no avail. By the time Alex turned twelve, he had become a Mets fan. To his credit, he weathered the decades of squandered potential from those blue-and-orange squads that were always predicted to contend for a division championship, yet usually finished with barely more wins than they had losses. All that losing had a silver lining though. Alex learned the importance of being true to a cause he believed in. While his father beamed at the thought of another Yankees playoff or World Series, Alex was content to root for next year . . . and the year after that, while his schoolmates made fun of him.

Like Becky Hirschfeld, Marc also sat on the Board of Directors of the Alzheimer's Association. The father of Yankees manager Joe Girardi had suffered from the dreaded disease for almost fifteen years before succumbing to it and Joe was an ardent supporter of the organization. So Marc and a few other board members got invited into the Yankees dugout and clubhouse for pre-game activities on several occasions. Even Marc's son Alex, the consummate Mets fan, was over the moon meeting the many Yankee greats during those visits.

Marc had many Yankees hats, but some he favored more than others. These days, his go-to hat was a New Era navy blue hat, made in Bangladesh and approved and officially licensed by Major League Baseball (as if there was such a thing as being unofficially licensed). On the front of the cap was the classic white interlocking "NY", introduced by Babe Ruth's Yankees in 1922. Marc prided himself on knowing that the famous logo predated the Yankees – it was first designed by Tiffany & Co. as part of a Medal of Valor for John McDowell, a New York City Police Officer who had been shot, in 1877, in the Hell's Kitchen section of Manhattan, chasing down burglars who had stolen $120 worth of cigars from Cortney's Liquor Store.

The logo on the outside of all Yankee caps was identical, but it was the colors and the inside that made each unique. The white band inside the brim of Marc's cap was brown and irretrievably soiled with well-earned sweat stains from various softball games and too many rounds of golf to count. Written indelibly with a Sharpie on the right side of the formerly white band were the first few letters of his last name; the rest had been obscured by months of perspiration. On the opposite facing side of the inside of the cap were the numbers 203-263, the first few letters of his Connecticut phone number, written into the band so that, if Marc had been foolish enough to leave it somewhere, the finder of the disgusting head gear would call to return it. The rest of the phone number, like most of his name, had been worn away with use. But he never left that damn cap anywhere. Much to the chagrin of his wife, Karen, Marc wore the cap everywhere he went.

Although he had been a member of the crusty country club for 20 years, Marc had only taken full advantage of the facility recently, as he wound down his investment banking practice. Citibank had been very good to him, but Marc had lived through so many corporate restructures and changes in management, that it was not the same bank he first joined after graduating from University of Rochester.

Marc graduated from college in 1980 but was not quite ready to join the world of grown-ups, so he attended law school at Columbia University, made law review, and graduated fifteenth in his class, before renouncing the legal profession and going to work at Citibank. He was well respected, revered, and appreciated by all who worked with him; but Marc was ready for a new challenge, and golf seemed to present that opportunity.

When his first wife, Lauren, died at only 42, Marc raised two children by himself until he met Karen. They married within eight months of their first date.

After Lauren's death, their friends were very supportive of Marc. They waited respectfully and, when the time seemed right, they encouraged him to dive back into the dating pool. They started fixing him up on dates with women lucky enough to be deemed suitable candidates. At first Marc was uneasy, it had been twenty-five years since he'd "dated." But soon he began to appreciate all the opportunities his newfound status presented. Besides being intelligent and wealthy, Marc was forty-seven years old, tall, objectively handsome, and possessed those two most elusive-but-sought-after characteristics: charm and confidence. Marc was the unrivaled center of attention at any cocktail party or club dinner. Now that a sufficient amount of time had passed, the community was anxious to see which fortunate female would end up being Marc's life companion.

There were many new restaurants in Westport, and since Marc fashioned himself a foodie, he was keen to try them all. Money was no object; he was more interested in finding an appropriate companion to enjoy these experiences with him. Some of the women he dated were intellectually compatible and they would last for a few weeks. Others might not be so worthy, but they were very attractive and nubile. They used him for his social status and fine dinners, he used them for sex. Most of these encounters would not last beyond a couple of dates, and he sometimes wondered if they knew he was just using them. But most didn't care, as they were on the arm of a gorgeous, charismatic, generous, and genuinely kind man. Sex with Marc wasn't so bad either, he was as generous in the bedroom as he was in public.

His late wife's close friend, Amy Bradenton, introduced Marc to quite a few women. Amy thought he was a very hot catch – she would have loved him for herself, had she not been so deeply in love with her husband. But she felt she was doing a service to both Marc and the deceased Lauren by trying to find a good stepmother for the children.

Karen Lundquist had worked with Amy years earlier when they were both executives at Estee Lauder in New York; Karen had been General Counsel while Amy was Director of International Sales. Though Karen was four years older than Marc, Amy thought they were a good match: they were two of the most refined, intelligent, well-traveled people she had ever met. By now, four years after Lauren's death, Marc was not at all uncomfortable meeting women who were suggested to him by what he deemed to be reliable sources.

Amy sent an email to Marc and Karen, setting them up virtually. Marc followed up that same afternoon, inviting Karen to join him for dinner at Isle of Capri, an upscale Italian restaurant on the upper East Side of Manhattan the following Friday evening. Marc's expectations weren't too high: Amy had fixed him up with some terrific women, most were nice enough and reasonably intelligent, but none had that certain panache Marc required. Marc arrived early, as he almost always did for appointments, and got the best table in the house. In the back of the restaurant, facing the door, he would be able to spy Karen the moment she walked in – buying him a little time before he greeted her. He wasn't going to run away if she proved to be hideous, but he wanted to see what was in store for him.

She texted him from a block away, so he knew she would be walking through the door within moments. He also knew, or at least she had said, she was 5'10 and blonde with blue eyes. When the door opened and the most beautiful woman he had even seen walked over to his table, he was smitten. Uncharacteristically, he hugged her and gave her a kiss as soon as she was close enough. Immediately, he knew this would not be their last date. And soon after, he knew she would be the last person he would ever date. Eight months later, to the day, they were married.

As Marc was hitting balls on the range, his iPhone rang in his golf bag. He ran over to answer: cell phones were not permitted on club grounds, he had forgotten to turn off the ringer.

"What the hell are you up to, good looking?" He smiled, hearing Eva's voice. Eva and Lauren had been friends since childhood, and they had all shared many nights, and even vacations, full of fun and incredible memories. After Lauren's death, Eva and Marc became quite close, but they made a conscious decision not to get involved in a romantic relationship. It would destroy their friendship. At that time, they were both hard-charging professional climbers who were as relentless in their romantic pursuits as they were in their business endeavors. There had been one weekend, though, about five years earlier, when Eva sensed that Marc was down, as his son was away at soccer camp and his daughter at riding camp. Eva booked a spa weekend for them at Canyon Ranch in the Catskills, promising Marc relaxation, time on the tennis court, massages, full pampering – her treat.

The setting was glorious and subdued, and the first bottle of Caymus Cabernet Sauvignon was a smooth follow up to their pre-dinner extra-dirty Beluga vodka martinis. Less than 30 minutes after dinner, they were in Eva's room, naked, and the promised tennis and massages for the weekend gave way to forty-eight hours of unabashed sex, inestimable orgasms, and garish quantities of eating and drinking. But as they drove back to Manhattan on Sunday evening, they vowed that would be the last time they did that for fear of ruining a very important friendship, and they never repeated that intimacy.

"I'm hitting golf balls. In the sun. By the water. Having fun. And you? Saving capitalism from the threats of a socialist revolution?" teased Marc.

"I'm busy planning your future," retorted Eva.

"Again? Every time you come up with a great plan, it explodes all over both of us. Besides, unless my future includes a membership at Augusta National, I'm not sure you can get my attention right now."

"Would a brand new 455-foot megayacht do it for you, smarty pants?" queried Eva.

"Yeah, and so would a Gulfstream G-650 or a new Bentley, and they're just as likely to come my way as your SS Fantasy. What the hell are you talking about?"

Eva told Marc the story, and that all she needed to do was raise $270 million in the next two months.

"*All* you need to do?" Marc quipped. "That's it, just come up with $270 million?" He laughed hysterically, drawing stares from two older club members on the driving range. "You might as well say you need to commandeer a 787 or get appointed Secretary of State. Are you fucking nuts?" bellowed Marc. The older members' stares turned into dirty looks.

"I have a plan," responded Eva coolly. Marc was one of her closest friends and she wanted to try her approach on him and Karen. She also badly wanted for them to join her yachting adventure. But even if they didn't, they were all so close that Marc and Karen would provide solid advice – as friends, as well as successful business people in the finance world – about her pitch and the likelihood of making her fantasy become a reality.

"When can you and Karen have dinner?"

Walking away from the range now so his conversation would not be heard by others, he responded: "We're going to see some of Karen's friends in Florida next weekend. Maybe when we get back?"

"Screw that. You always brag that you are scaling back, spending less time at the bank, enjoying your life. I'm about to give you the most enjoyable future you could ever imagine, and you tell me to wait two weeks? Tonight – or tomorrow at the latest. I insist."

Marc laughed. "Alright. I'm glad to see you haven't lost your touch. I'll pick up some salmon on the way home. Come over to the house tonight around 7 o'clock."

"You're the best. I knew I loved you for a reason," replied Eva, thrilled, and a bit nervous to make a presentation that very evening.

"I'm irresistible.  We both know that," exhorted Marc.

# CHAPTER SEVENTEEN

L orraine Williams was reclusive, but not antisocial. As the richest woman in Canada, she had to protect her privacy. Her daughters, Lacey and Linda, were 36 and 34 years of age, respectively. Lacey had been close to her father. He had groomed her to take over the family business. But when her parents got divorced and her mother obtained control of the family's pulp-and-paperboard business, Lorraine pushed Lacey aside just as she did her husband.

Linda, the younger sister, harbored a tremendous amount of enmity toward her mother. They had never been close, and Linda resented the fact that Lacey had been the favorite. As a teen, she'd rebelled in every way possible – drugs, alcohol, and casual hook-ups with strangers. After her parents' divorce, Linda decided it was time to strike out against her mother. She filed a series of very public lawsuits against her, claiming breach of fiduciary duty and charging her mother with overrunning the family trusts. Even more offensive to Lorraine was the fact that Linda provided interviews to the press, violating her mother's privacy and confidence. The lawyers could take care of the lawsuits – and they did – but Lorraine was infuriated and devastated by the public disclosure of the most private aspects of her life.

Linda gave one particular interview to the *Toronto Star* hinting that the young women Lorraine retained as personal assistants were her lesbian lovers. It was a lie, and one – not least because of her strict Catholic upbringing – that Lorraine found most hurtful and unforgivable. Linda also suggested that her mother entered into countless contracts, agreements, and partnerships with the express intent of defrauding her business partners. Linda knew how to undermine her mother – allegations like that would have a real impact on Lorraine's ability to do business on a multibillion-dollar level.

At fifty-eight, with nearly a billion dollars in personal assets and not much bloom left on her rose, Lorraine couldn't afford to be pilloried and exploited by the Canadian gossip pages. She had loved her husband very much through thirty-one years of marriage. But his affair with the editor of a Montreal newspaper was blown up and fully laid bare by the rival tabloids in Toronto. Much as Lorraine wanted to stay married, she couldn't pretend to ignore a five-year affair and all the humiliation it brought to her personally and professionally. It was not total reclusion she sought, but she'd welcomed withdrawal from the social and business communities of Canada.

During the preliminary stages of a forestry-rights lawsuit filed in Portland, Oregon, many years ago, Lorraine's in-house counsel had recommended Eva Lampedusa as the ideal trial lawyer to handle the case. It took two years of litigating, but Eva got the case dismissed through a motion for summary judgment, saving Lorraine over $90 million. More importantly, Eva and Lorraine struck a deep and personal friendship that had persevered for the next decade. When Lorraine saw Eva's name on an incoming call toward the end of August, she was only too glad to answer on the headset she wore in her office.

"Eva! How are you doing this summer? Escaping the heat and spending all your time in the Hamptons?" asked Lorraine.

"I wish. Union Carbide has been haranguing me for the past three weeks to become engaged in a massive gas-leak incident in the Philippines. I'm afraid it could become another Bhopal and I just don't feel like spending the next six years of my life flying back and forth to Manila and dealing with bottom-feeding plaintiff lawyers."

"So just say no," offered Lorraine, fully cognizant of the case, and having a fair estimate of the fees it could generate for Eva and Wilson Everson.

"That's easy for you to say. You have enough money to buy ... India. It's my partners who aren't making this easy. The Trump White House is pretty lax on regulatory enforcement. There's just not a lot of massive environmental litigations being filed in the U.S. these days. This India thing is massive and could keep them busy for years. So, the guys downstairs are sucking off my business teats and they want me to keep on pumping."

"But I thought you wanted to focus on pharmaceuticals and get rid of the mining cases because you got sick of dealing with people like me," Lorraine offered with a not-too-subtle giggle.

"You know you were my favorite client, Lorraine, but it's not that simple. My partners are virtually underwater in their billings the past few years. They're clamoring for me to bring in this case and hand it off to them," explained Eva.

"Well, that doesn't sound too difficult. Especially for you."

"Yeah – but I can't do that. And I won't do that. If a client wants to hire me because of my skill and reputation, I won't just go out and participate in a beauty pageant, get the retention, and hand it off. Once I did that, my reputation would be shot and I'd never get another case again," explained Eva.

"Untrue. You're the best there is. Anyone would be foolish not to hire you. But I get it. It's your integrity and reputation that make you such a formidable litigator. Anyway, I know you didn't call to have me talk you out of a case. What may I do for you, my dear?"

"Remember when you called me a few weeks ago and said you wanted to disappear from the face of the earth?" Eva asked her old friend.

"All too well. Why, does your friend Richard Branson have a spaceship slot to sell me?" quipped Lorraine.

"No, even better. A yacht – a huge yacht. And not to sell you – to have you come in as a part owner."

"I already have two. You know that. We keep the 'Paper Perch' in the Med and the 'Paper Pompano' in the Caribbean. What makes you think I would want another one, silly girl?"

"Because this is a unique boating and exploration community I'm building," Eva said.

"What the hell does that mean? Sounds like a sales pitch,

if I've ever heard one – and I've heard a lot. If you want to keep my attention for even a minute on the subject, you'll have to do better than that."

Eva launched into a detailed explanation of her dream. In exquisite detail, she told Lorraine all about her vision of putting together a consortium of good friends with extensive travel experience and high net worth to purchase and run the 455-foot megayacht. The ship would circumnavigate the globe, stopping wherever its owners had predetermined. Eva and the captain, and maybe a few other owners, would set the itinerary twelve to eighteen months in advance. Those with an ownership share would be free to come and go whenever and wherever they chose. Unlike a time-sharing arrangement, though, owners would be purchasing shares of the all-inclusive enterprise, like a condominium concept, and would have their own luxury suites. Luxury suites would vary in size depending on the amount of the investment. Homeowners' association fees would be steep, but fair. The goal would be to establish an evergreen fund to pay for fuel, salaries, docking fees, insurance, port-agent-interaction costs – everything needed to make life onboard as comfortable and luxurious as possible. By paying the steep association or management fees – anywhere from $30,000 a month to $100,000 a month – owners wouldn't be constantly nickel and dimed about additional expenses.

With growing enthusiasm, Eva explained that a certain number of smaller cabins would be kept separate from the ownership's luxury suites and could be rented out to visitors for a week or two at a time. With a ship this unique and luxurious, rental rates could fetch as much as $3,000 a night and would supplement the funds attended by the luxury suite owners.

Lorraine was impressed. "Sounds like you've really thought this thing through," she said, with admiration. She sat back in her chair, put her elbows on her desk and folded her fingers under her chin. "Tell me more. It sounds like quite a complex environment. Who's going to run this thing?"

Surprised at how excited she was herself, Eva continued. "We're going to require quite a staff, perhaps as many as 100. At the front of the house, we'll need the equivalent of a hotel management team. This is not just to manage the hotel rooms, but to pamper us and take care of us in the most luxurious style you can imagine. I envision hiring a general manager who oversees the whole operation. And the infrastructure under him would be the same as a luxury hotel – housekeeping manager, head chef, yoga instructors, nutritionists, concierges, and sommeliers from the finest hotels – probably Ritz-Carlton and Four Seasons. People who have dealt with folks like you and me. They need to understand, and be able to cater to, our demands and predilections, no matter what. And maintain strict confidentiality."

"Will we have Julie from the *Love Boat* telling us when it's time for shuffleboard and karaoke?" snickered Lorraine.

"Absolutely not." Eva's tone was firm. "This is not a cruise line. No casino, no disco, no shuffleboard, no karaoke, and no hundreds of chairs around the pool. I envision a refined, mostly older, clientele. Dignified. Lectures. Seminars. And with a ship that size, 100 people will seem almost empty. Cruise ships that same size haul over 1,000 people back and forth between two ports, like a subway at sea."

"And who would give the lectures? Us? I wouldn't want to have to work when I'm on vacation," asserted Lorraine.

"We'll have an Entertainment Team who'll identify and book experts – scholars, great artists, influential political figures – to sail with us for a few days and deliver a lecture or two a day in exchange for their passage. We'll hire end-of-the-road entertainers from our younger years who may not be relevant to the mainstream music industry, but people we'd love to have play for a few nights. People like Tony Orlando, Cat Stevens, Boz Scaggs. They could get away from it all for a few nights, be pampered and adored like they were in the 70s, and just play a few sets."

"Shit girl, you've really got my attention now. Keep going."

As Eva continued, she sat back, closed her eyes, and envisioned her dream coming to life. "The great thing is the ship is almost completed. We have a few months to raise the capital and with it, configure the interior however we like. I imagine we'll want to have four or five separate dining rooms, so we don't get bored with the same surroundings every meal."

"That's a lot of kitchen staff for not a lot of people" Lorraine said.

"True, but we wouldn't have all the restaurants open for all the meals. We can rotate them. We could have an Indian restaurant, a steak restaurant, an Italian restaurant, and a pub. We could do Chinese, Turkish, seafood or whatever the hell we like. We could feature different cultural influences in the restaurants, depending where in the world we would be at the time."

"And exactly where would *we* be going?" Eva's repeated use of the word "we" had not gone unnoticed by Lorraine.

"Everywhere! With the itineraries set over a year in advance, we'd have plenty of time to make port reservations, coordinate fuel stops, transfer personnel on and off the ship and allow us to make our airplane accommodations."

"Honey, you know that I don't need years to make flight plans," Lorraine said. "Roger and Charles are always ready. They keep the plane fueled and can register a flight plan in less than an hour, anywhere I need to go."

"Oh Lorraine. I don't think I really need to remind you that not everyone's as privileged as you are. Now, back to the ship! Because all the luxury suite owners will be people who've traveled to all the world's major port cities on business – New York, London, Venice, Sydney, Hong Kong, Shanghai – we would not have to re-create all that on the ship. And of course, when we do go into these ports, I would envision us spending five or six days there."

"Five or six days?" inquired Lorraine. "Cruise ships usually just dock for a night, maybe two at the most."

"That's why you always retained me – because you needed a good lawyer. You don't listen," scolded Eva in a friendly and teasing manner. "This is not a cruise ship. Think of it more as your floating home."

"So, we do go into those ports, or we don't?" asked

Lorraine, a bit confused now.

"We do, but when we arrive, it's not just a 'hit it and quit it' visit like the business trips we've all taken. In advance of our arrival, we'll have refined local experts, maybe even retired mayors or chamber of commerce people on board for a few days, explaining what we need to do and see in those cities. They can also help us make reservations and gain access to places even you couldn't get into on your own."

"Darling, there is nothing I can't get into, and you know that," Lorraine said.

"Except the pants of that UBS guy you were chasing all over Aspen last year. You were like a schoolgirl driveling over her first crush. You didn't get into his life, his hotel room, or his Calvin's," Eva reminded Lorraine. Eva enjoyed being able to rib Lorraine about that fiasco. The list of Lorraine's failures was a short one.

Lorraine smiled. "Never you mind about that. But as long as we're on the subject, will there be men on board for us?"

"I'm not trying to raise all this money just to create a floating Chippendale's. You can bring on board whomever you like. And I'm sure there will be single men sailing in the visitor flats. Just keep your paws off anyone I bring aboard!"

"Oh, is there someone I should know about?"

"Never *you* mind about that. Now let me get back to the itinerary. So, you see, besides going to the major cities, we would be able to scout out and explore some of the lesser visited port cities."

"Keep going," Lorraine sighed, fully aware that Eva had

just shut down any further inquiry about her love life.

"For example, on the West Coast, we would vote every year to decide if we wanted to visit San Diego, Los Angeles, Santa Barbara, San Francisco, Seattle, Portland, or Vancouver. We might pick two one year and three the next. And – this is the best part – we can explore remote places most people never get to visit in a lifetime."

"I'm still listening," responded Lorraine, now anxiously intrigued.

"Way beyond just Los Angeles or New York – or even India or South Africa – think Borneo, Bali, Easter Island, Christmas Island, Tonga, Fiji, those kinds of places."

"How do we select luxury suites?" Lorraine asked, bypassing a few steps and putting the cart before the horse.

"Well first, I have to gauge interest and raise the money over the next eight weeks. And it's not just the capital but making sure I can cobble together the right mix of people to make the community interesting, relatable and fun."

"Screw that. I'm in. How much did you say you need – $370 million?" asked Lorraine, abruptly.

"No, $270 million," Eva corrected.

"If you can get $170 million from other friends – which I have no problem believing you will do if you speak to them as determinedly as you just spoke to me – and, *if* I get the biggest luxury suite on this little concept ship of yours, I'm in for $100 million."

"Are you shitting me?" blurted out Eva, shocked.

"No, but my lawyers are going to want to read over, or

even help draft, all the papers. I do pay those buffoons a great deal of money to represent my interests and protect me from scammers. You're not a scammer are you, my dear Eva?" joked Lorraine.

"For $100 million, I'll be whatever you want me to be," responded Eva.

"Good. So, you got my money already. Now get off the phone and call some of your cute guy friends and get them to pony up some money and join this little adventure of ours. Oh, and the next time we speak, you are going to tell me about who you're flirting with, or dating, or fucking these days. I got the little brush off you just gave me. We'll revisit that when we next chat, sweetie."

"Lorraine, you're the best," exclaimed Eva, almost squealing with delight. "I love you to pieces."

Lorraine laughed. "Well, go find a captain, or some other investors, who'll love me in a different way, darling!"

# CHAPTER EIGHTEEN

On the handwritten list of potential investors Eva kept inside the pearl-handled drawer of her mahogany desk, Dr. Liam Perlmutter was next. Dr. Perlmutter, a cardiologist, was a former client from Jupiter, Florida. But he didn't make his money in cardiology; rather, he was an enterprising inventor. He had invented a variation of the pacemaker and had made hundreds of millions of dollars selling it to hospitals, cardiologists and, most importantly, insurance companies around the world. Eva first got to know Dr. Perlmutter when he was involved in a patent litigation against Medtronic, one of the world's foremost manufacturers of medical devices, and one of Eva's best clients. Eva and Dr. Perlmutter had become good friends and Dr. Perlmutter had hosted Eva on his 160-foot yacht on several occasions. But now that he was getting up there in age – he had just celebrated his 70th birthday – he wanted less to do with all the responsibilities and headaches of fuel costs, selecting ports, hiring crew, and everything else that goes with running one's private yacht.

Although Liam was astute enough to recognize the

limitations that come with aging, such as not being able to do all the things he used to do, he nevertheless envisioned himself as a hip young spirit. He wore his white, wavy hair in a pony tail, something that was not at all common for someone his age. He frequently wore designer jeans that came with rips across the thighs, as well as the latest version of whatever Jordan or Lebron basketball sneaker line was being peddled by Nike. But as much as all those were items Liam wore often, he was almost never seen without a brown leather or suede vest; those had become his trademark. In a phone call, Eva had shared her dream with Dr. Perlmutter and he seemed very onboard to be a major player.

Shortly after their call, Eva made sure to just happen to be visiting an old college roommate on Jupiter Island. It seemed only natural, that while there, she pay Liam a visit.

Liam happily welcomed his old friend. Of course, that was partly because he always enjoyed ogling Eva, harboring the same fantasies as most men had of her. Eva had known Liam for eight years; he could be a real curmudgeon at times. She knew he could also be misogynistically aggressive with women, despite his forty-plus years of marriage to his charming wife, Danielle. He'd often regale women at cocktail parties with stories of how he was such a generous husband, portraying himself as a caring person – before moving in for the kill. He had had numerous affairs. Eva cringed at the thought of him naked.

Liam was thrilled to see Eva. He was even more delighted by the sight of her lavender linen blouse clinging tightly to her chest. The lace of her camisole was peeking out and, when the wind blew just right, Liam saw the outlines of Eva's nipples.

So he was very primed to hear more talk of Eva's one-ship navy.

"But how are you going to decide who the owners will be?" inquired Liam.

"They will all be people I know and trust. But even more importantly, they will be people I like and like spending time with," said Eva. "People like you." Liam was delighted with the compliment. Eva fought back vomit as she allowed those words to flow forth through her lips.

"And what about money? Aren't you concerned that they have enough money?"

"Of course, Liam, that's an absolute prerequisite, silly. The initial core group I'm looking to put together will each have to put up at least $20 million. Now, for the smaller luxury suites we can take investors in the $6-million to $20-million range. I envision about five or six luxury suites at the higher price and around 40 luxury suites at the lower level. After that, we'll have dozens of hotel rooms that'll provide weekly income to keep our expenses down." explained Eva.

Liam listened attentively "Why do you want hotel rooms anyway? Won't that just water down our community with transients who have no connection to us, who aren't in our financial league?"

"Not exactly," replied Eva. She didn't miss the fact Liam had used "our" and "us."

"Because the ship will be comprised of luxury suites, rather than the normal, boring state rooms you'd find on a cruise ship, these luxury suites will be sought after by friends like yours and mine – millionaires and billionaires. The visitor flats – that's the term we're using for the hotel rooms – will be renting for around $2,500 to 4,000 per night. And Liam, you need to understand that those hotel rooms are critical to our income stream. Plus, it will be fun to welcome dozens of new people aboard every week. Otherwise, we'll all get bored seeing only each other's faces day after day."

Eva continued, "People in our circle don't travel on those massive cruise ships that are like floating cities. For God's sake, their swimming pools are DNA cesspools. It's disgusting the way their passengers line up by the thousands to go to a mess hall three or four times a day and help themselves to whatever calorically rich slop is being dished out to them, at assigned tables. That will not be the way we live at all. *Not at all,"* she added for emphasis. "On our ship, there will be four or five dining rooms, modeled after our favorite international restaurants."

"But if we're not going to have thousands of people on board, how are we going to fill all of these restaurants?"

"We're not. It's that simple. Every night we'll open two or maybe three of the restaurants. And I expect we'll only have a total of 20 to 30 covers per night at each restaurant. We're not running a fraternity house where people strap on the feed bag and eat as if they've never seen food before. These restaurants are going to be gourmet quality. The food will all be made to order and the menu options diverse."

"What happens to our luxury suites when we're not on the ship?" inquired Liam.

"They're empty. Or you can allow your family or friends to

use them."

"Can we rent them out?" asked Liam, sensing a money-making opportunity here. He didn't make $880 million by performing cardiac surgery. Liam was a creative inventor and investor, taking seemingly simple ideas, infusing them with a bit of capital, and parlaying them into huge financial successes.

"That's an interesting question," pondered Eva. "I guess I'd be concerned that doing so might cannibalize our rental pool, adversely affecting the occupancy level of the visitor flats. And those, as I just explained, will comprise an important part of our revenue."

"But you said these'll be our own luxury suites, like our homes on land, right? We are free to decorate them and do anything we like with them. Right? So, if that's the case, why can't I rent mine out? I do that with our farm in Wellington and a two-week rental can pay for six months of upkeep for the horses and stable hands."

Liam was pushy, and Eva knew it. For a moment, she questioned whether his personality and financial temperament were ideally suited for the ship. After all, this was her baby and she didn't want someone to hijack the entire concept to turn it into his own money-printing enterprise.

Eva laughed (although she really didn't find it funny). "Liam, you're really something. I really hadn't thought about people renting their luxury suites out. But that's something we can certainly discuss when we all get together and figure out the structure of the management and governance of this venture. So, how shall I gauge your interest – strong, moderate, or not interested?" asked Eva, anxious to bring the conversation to a close.

"Put me down as a 9," said Liam, always eager to define the terms in his own parlance, rather than accepting someone else's.

Eva realized that this might not be quite as simple as she had thought. But raising $270 million in just two months, she knew she was going to have to endure some obstacles. Liam was very wealthy and that's exactly what Eva was looking for right now. Besides, he had an insecure streak and when surrounded by smart people, he became sheepish, a little less direct and offensive. Or, at least that's what Eva hoped.

"A 9 it is," responded Eva, resignedly. "I'm not sure what that even means, but as luxury suites start to sell, I'll call you. Then, it's either a yes or a no. Fair?"

"Sure," Liam agreed. He was already hooked on the concept. He just wanted more time with Eva and she knew it.

# CHAPTER NINETEEN

When Harris Hirschfeld's phone rang, and his assistant told him that Eva Lampedusa was on the line, he smiled and hoisted the receiver quickly. Eva had that effect on most people, men or women. Besides being stunningly beautiful, which got the attention of most men, she was also a good friend to anyone who had spent a period of time with her. Harris fell only into the former category. He wasn't particularly interested in her friendship. Like many men, he was enamored by her sexual elegance. He also saw her as a rival in the world of top New York litigators, and that competition spurred him to take her on, in any way he could.

"Hello, Harris here," Harris said matter-of-factly into the phone. He couldn't help himself. Harris was utterly self-important and bombastic and there was nothing he could do to suppress those traits.

"How are things down there in the expensive part of town?" Eva ribbed, teasing Harris. His firm had just signed a twenty-year lease at the highest commercial real estate rate in the city and the firm was being ridiculed in the real estate rags for vastly overpaying.

"Terrific. Back from the stresses of the Hamptons, I'm sitting tall in the saddle and raring for the fall trial term to begin." The courts slowed down immeasurably during July and August, when judges and lawyers took their vacations. Now, September was here, and Harris had a full calendar of cases on the court's trial docket. The way he said it, though, bristled with haughtiness. Here we go again, Eva mused, fresh off her conversation with Liam, another arrogant male.

Eva spent the next 40 minutes explaining to Harris her idea. Harris listened, asking intelligent, probing questions. A seasoned trial lawyer, he knew more was to be gained from listening than speaking. At one point, Harris's assistant knocked politely and stuck her head through the door to announce that one of the members of the firm's IT team was standing outside the office, waiting to work on his computer. Harris waved her away as he continued to listen to Eva's presentation.

"Eva, you've outdone yourself this time. I have a tough enough time keeping up with your press clippings and trying to steal your clients," Harris joked, in his patented whisper. "And now this – your own U.S.S. Lampedusa? It sounds absolutely divine, but I still have to work for a living." Harris wondered how Eva would be able to take so much time away from her practice, while simultaneously contemplating which of her clients he could poach while she was away.

"It's not retirement, Harris," Eva went on. "It's like having a vacation house that's available to you all year round.

When you have time to spend on it – over the summer, or during your kids' Christmas or spring vacations, or even for a long weekend – you would just fly to the ship and stay as long as you like. You can leave your clothes there and fly in and out when you like. Unlike retirement, by having this amazing retreat you could recharge your energy between cases and could come back even bigger, better, and stronger." She knew just how to appeal to Harris's oversized ego. "And, during the summer, Becky could stay on it with the girls. They like to travel, don't they?" She asked, already knowing the answer.

"Who else will be on this little floating wonderland of yours?" Harris asked, with more than just a modicum of sarcasm.

"Well that's the thing," Eva said, tantalizing. "My friends, people who are cool and fun like us," she almost gagged as she said it. "The richest people in the world."

Suddenly, Harris sat up tall in his chair. He envisioned Warren Buffett, Bill Gates, Mark Zuckerberg as his next-door neighbors on this yacht of Eva's. He knew Eva was friendly with Lorraine Williams – maybe she'd already called her? There were two ways to appeal to Harris, and Eva knew both. The first was rank seduction, the other was to dangle potential business opportunities in front of him.

Both played to his insecurity. He may have been amazingly successful, but he was very insecure. Most of Harris' fortune had been inherited from Becky's father who died just four years after they were married. Until then, Harris had been faithful to Becky and had a genuine friendship with her father. Becky's dad considered Harris to be almost like a son to him. In fact, when Becky's brother Glenn destroyed his own investment banking career, and almost destroyed the family with his coke addiction, it was Harris who stepped in and talked him into rehab. Harris personally addressed the criminal charges against Glenn and spent countless days with the district attorney fashioning a plea agreement to save Glenn's brokerage and trading licenses. As a result, Becky's dad left 80 percent of his entire fortune to Becky and Harris, with the remaining 20 percent in a trust for Becky's brother, with Harris as trustee.

After Becky's father passed away, Harris began to screw anything in a skirt. It wasn't that Becky had let herself go – she had kept in great physical condition. At 38, she looked barely older than when she was a 19-year-old L'Oreal model. Wherever they went, she drew the attention of every man in the room. The only thing more flawless than her tight, athletic body was her wrinkle-free face and the way her bronze skin framed her stunning blue eyes.

Harris was still attracted to her, but he had an insatiable desire to bed other women, beautiful or not. It was his way of asserting his dominance and conquering his insecurities. Becky's sexual interest in Harris had waned completely. She found it disgusting and incomprehensible that he'd carry on affairs with women half his age. His pudgy body and breath like rotten eggs didn't help either.

Harris had money, Becky's money, and Eva knew that. She wasn't hunting after his compensation from his work as a litigator; she knew he had more money than that, and it was those deep pockets Eva needed.

"Well, it sounds like an interesting idea. But I think I'll wait a year or two to make sure it gets off the ground ... or out of port." Harris laughed at his own joke, he had pleased himself with that line. "Then we'll see how things are and I shall entertain the possibility of buying a luxury suite on your ship," he said, pompous as ever.

Eva fought the impulse to hang up at this point. Like a waterfall in Yellowstone, all her reasons for finding Harris noxious cascaded through her brain. He was arrogant, supercilious, condescending and patronizing. She really couldn't stand him. But she could sure use his money to get this venture moving. He wouldn't spend much time on the ship, she reckoned. For him, it would be a trophy. She could already envision him bragging about it to all his friends, if anyone was truly his friend and not simply a hanger on. But if and when he did come on the ship, Eva was convinced that her more comfortable and confident friends could put Harris in his place and keep him there. That would be kind of fun to see; she let herself daydream about that for a few seconds. He would not be able to dominate on the ship, the way he did in his law firm and among his circle of socialites.

Also, there was Becky. Eva had met her on a few occasions and found her to be a very pleasant person. Eva enjoyed her company. Maybe while Harris was busy saving the world for corporate America, Becky and Eva would have a chance to get to know each other better. Regardless, Eva knew not everyone on the ship would be her best friend, so she kept her eye on the big picture: raising enough money to hit that magical $220 million mark by October 16. And Harris was her fat cash cow. Eva had to close Harris and she knew it.

"That sounds like a reasonable and prudent approach Harris. If I don't see you over the next few months, I'm sure I'll see you at Law Day." Eva was referring to the New York Bar Association's Law Day annual dinner at the Waldorf, held the Wednesday before Thanksgiving, which all top New York litigators and judges attended.

"That's right, and next year we'll be in touch and I'll buy one of those large luxury suites on your ship," responded Harris, playing right into Eva's hand.

"Not large at that point, Harris," answered Eva. "I need to get the large ones sold over the next two months. But by next year, some of the smaller units should still be available and we'll be thrilled to have you onboard." The bait was set. Harris would bite. Eva had no doubt about that and she smiled at the simplicity of her tactic. She only wished she had been sitting across from Harris, perhaps wearing a low-cut blouse, to really make the kill. But then again – no, she always felt like a piece of Arthur Avenue prime rib the way he'd stare at her, even in the most serious of business settings. She would do this over the phone and get even more satisfaction that way.

"Wait, what do you mean? If I am going to do this, I don't want some paltry little cabin on the bow of the ship where I'm going to get banged up and down with every large wave, listening all day to the drone of the anchor chain being lowered and hoisted back up," Harris asserted, surprising Eva with his nautical knowledge. "I will want a right proper sized luxury suite," declared Harris, once again exercising a manner of speaking that no one else used since the turn of the last century.

"Sweetheart, I don't know what to tell you. I would love to have you aboard, and I'd love to get you in one of the larger luxury suites, but I need to get those sold now. So, unless you're going to buy one this week, or give me a winning lottery ticket so I don't have to hock my friends for this money, I need to keep banging the bushes. Of course, if any of those luxury suites are available next year when you want to join us, you'll be at the top of the list."

"How many of those large luxury suites do you still have left?" A small, but noticeable, hint of desperation had crept into Harris's voice. He knew he needed to be included in an opportunity he didn't even know existed only an hour ago. Eva was good, and she knew it.

"Three," she lied.

"And how much are they going for?"

"$30 million each." She lied again. She was really targeting $20 million, as she was going to collect that amount from Marc Romanello and Liam Perlmutter, but if she could squeeze an extra $10 million out of Harris, that would be $10 million less that she would have to beg someone else for. It would feel good to beat this fat bastard for the extra $10 million. Sure, he would have to get a bigger luxury suite than anyone else, but that would be fine. It still wouldn't be the biggest luxury suite on the ship. That would be Eva's. And Lorraine's, of course.

"And how much will the upkeep or condo association fees be on an annual basis?" Harris asked, almost sheepishly.

"Harris, that sounds like the old adage about the guy who

wants to buy a Rolls-Royce and asks the salesman about its gas mileage. It's going to be expensive. You'll have to deal with that. We have to fund the payroll for the entire crew, cover fuel and port costs, maintain a capital reserve, procure insurance, and underwrite the dining services and other onboard enrichments. If that's too much for you, I completely understand," stated Eva flatly.

"Okay, I'm going to have to chat with Becky about this," Harris replied, with an uncharacteristic degree of humility, acknowledging that he was not the sole decision maker over the family finances.

Eva was done with the conversation and done with Harris. She had baited the trap and Harris had swallowed every last ounce of what Eva was serving. She knew Harris was too egotistical to allow this opportunity to pass him by – and he could afford it. Becky's father had left them around $400 million. As an insightful lawyer who always did her homework, Eva had investigated the Surrogate Court's file on Becky's father's estate and had discovered the exact amount he had left for Becky, Harris, and Glenn. Yes, there was $400 million to play with, and Eva was confident she had just snagged $30 million of it.

# CHAPTER TWENTY

It was 7:00 p.m. when an excited Eva Lampedusa rang the bell at Marc and Karen Romanello's home in Southport. Framed by massive Corinthian pillars, it was a large white neo-classical house, 9,400 square feet that spanned three structures. Out back, a 55 by 25-foot salt-water swimming pool was surrounded by sixty-five rose bushes and a bevy of wildly colorful annuals that bloomed in the summer. The estate boasted over four and a half acres of some of the most expensive real estate in Connecticut, with a tennis court at the far end of the property and a golf driving net off to the side, right beside the perfectly-manicured putting green. And it featured a gazebo where Marc and Karen had exchanged their vows a year ago. The entrance to the house led directly into a regal center hall, highlighted by an expansive, stunningly detailed stained-glass wall that spanned across the separate wings of the house.

Eva toted a bottle of 1995 Clos Pegase Cabernet Sauvignon Hommage Artist Series Reserve. She knew it was Marc's favorite. Marc answered the door, his sun-kissed face smiling beneath his beloved Yankees cap, and greeted Eva with a warm bear hug and kiss.

"You look great, my old friend," he said, giving Eva the once over. "But you always do."

"You should know," Eva whispered, in case Karen was within earshot. Marc smiled approvingly at the label and disappeared into the dining room to select just the right Riedel decanter for such an extraordinary wine.

Eva and Karen had met numerous times and they had become good friends. Marc had never disclosed that he and Eva had slept together during that Canyon Ranch weekend. In fact, he hadn't told her about that weekend at all. It had happened well before Marc met Karen, so why even bring it up? When Karen first met Marc, he spoke of Eva regularly and consulted her frequently when he was making business and personal decisions. Karen suspected the two of them had been an item at one time, but it was clear that their friendship was sincere and respectful, and Karen admired that.

"Is that Eva?" Karen yelled from the kitchen, where she was overseeing the salad preparation.

"Hi, Karen. Yup, its me." Eva's Louboutin heels clicked loudly against the black and white marble floor of the great room as she made her way towards the kitchen.

The women hugged and kissed, and Karen left the dinner preparations to Maggie, their cook/house manager. "We can enjoy this with dinner," Karen said as she accepted Eva's bottle admiringly, "but I just opened a great chardonnay to have with our crudités. Would you like a glass?"

"I wouldn't just *like* one, I *need* one," laughed Eva.

They retreated into the estate's magnificent library, where Karen spent much of her days reading. She reclined in her grandfather's rocking chair. The chair was special to Karen. She had mentioned it to Marc when they were dating, and he bought it from Karen's aunt in Minneapolis and surprised her with it on their wedding day. Eva sat across from Karen on a beige Eames lounge chair.

"I hear you've got a new venture on the horizon," Karen began.

Marc, who had just prepared himself a Purity vodka martini – two olives, two cubes – joined them. He brought glasses of chardonnay for both women. Sitting on the piano bench, under a spectacular twelve-armed crystal chandelier, resplendent with polished brass and three dozen crystals with 24 cuts each, he chimed in. "Yes, please tell us more. I've filled Karen in about our conversation, but we both have tons of questions for you."

Easing back in the Eames chair, Eva took a long sip of her drink and began her soliloquy. She described the circumstances that led to the opportunity to purchase the ship. She told of her dream to create a unique sailing experience, aboard an ultra-luxury yacht, surrounded by "like-minded" people. She also relayed to them her recent conversations with Lorraine Williams, Liam Perlmutter, and Harris Hirschfeld. Having outlined her concept for several people now, she felt more comfortable with her pitch. It also made it easy that Marc and Karen were like family to her. Eva did not feel judged. The three of them had batted around various business propositions over the years, with varying degrees of acceptance or success. They were all highly successful people who were not reliant on any one dream to make their fortunes.

The conversation continued for about an hour. Then Marc excused himself to turn on the gas grill at the outdoor kitchen by the pool. Well before Eva had arrived, Marc had soaked two cedar planks in a bottle of red Vina Unzaga, a cheap Spanish wine popular with college kids. Rather than soaking cedar planks in water before cooking, Marc preferred to use wine, so the full flavor of the cedar would be enhanced by the flavor of the grapes and blend into the fish. Unlike most chefs – who used white wine – Marc preferred to use red table wine. He found that the inexpensive wines had a more robust flavor, inappropriate for refined drinking, but wonderful for cooking salmon.

Karen posed a few questions to Eva that hadn't been raised by any of the other potential owners. "I understand that each individual owner will be able to decorate and furnish her luxury suite however she sees fit, but who will be responsible for decorating and appointing the common areas of the ship?"

Eva hadn't really considered this. "Gee, that's a great question. There are many designers who fashion the interiors of cruise ships and private yachts. I suppose we would engage one of those companies."

"I don't know if you remember but when I was studying architecture at the University of Michigan, I minored in interior design," Karen said.

"And . . .?"

"Well, I'd be happy to take a crack at it. This could be kind of a hobby for me. I wouldn't want to be paid; it would just be something fun."

Eva was intrigued. "That sounds great. You'd be willing to do this even if you don't end up buying a luxury suite on the ship?"

"Oh, we're buying, alright. You may have to help me convince Marc, but we'll be part of it, that's for sure." The ladies smiled, clinked their lead crystal glasses and Karen proposed a toast: "To a ship run by women."

"To a ship run by women," Eva parroted. Just like that, Eva had secured another investor.

# CHAPTER TWENTY-ONE

B ack in her cubicle, Carly Burke tried to figure out how the government could have obtained confidential litigation documents in the Boeing case. She really did care about this assignment, and not just because Harris gave it to her. She enjoyed probing, and part of a litigation-paralegal's responsibilities was diligent sleuthing. Powering up her laptop, Carly clicked on the PowerPoint presentation comparing the Boeing case to the EuroHoldings case.

Most of the names were familiar to her – people who worked on the trial team. Some were from her firm, Hinkle Morris back in Wichita, but most were from Bergman Troutman, Harris's New York firm. How could she possibly be able to trace who may have shared confidential information with the US Attorney's office? As a paralegal – and a visiting paralegal at that – Carly didn't have unfettered access to the firm's email records that would confirm who shared what with whom.

So, always looking for an excuse to log onto social media in the office, Carly decided to research Facebook, Instagram, and Twitter, to see if any of the Hinkle Morris or Bergman Troutman lawyers shared any common friends with the attorneys at the US Attorney's office.

At first, Carly was bored stalking the Facebook pages of her co-workers. But as she drilled deeper, it became kind of entertaining. For example, she found out one of the junior associates, Max Clurman, was a standup comic on weekends. She typed his name into YouTube and saw the man she knew as a buttoned up, straight-laced litigator doing a thirty-minute obscenity-filled routine that would make Kevin Hart blush.

Marcia Coleman, a thirty-four-year-old demure senior associate in the office, was a major player in the club scene in Manhattan. She frequented One Oak, the Pyramid Club, and some of the most trendy, expensive downtown clubs in New York. Carly was shocked, but smiled approvingly, when she saw Marcia's club outfits: blouses barely concealed her nipples, skirts barely larger than a handkerchief. "Damn," thought Carly, "that girl really brings her A-game outside the office. I never would have guessed that one." On her Facebook page, Marcia had an entire photo album of parties she hosted with her roommate, Melanie Hunter, a rising young banker at New York Savings & Guaranty. Carly was especially intrigued by selfies Melanie had posted from her recent trip to Greece with her boss, Mario Garramone. An intriguing business relationship thought Carly.

It seemed like no time at all had passed, but Carly had spent the better part of the last five hours in social-media investigation. She wondered whether she was barking up the wrong tree. Maybe she should have begun with a visit to the IT department to gain forensic access to the office email system. But, she reasoned, these were relatively intelligent people – it was unlikely they would be transmitting confidential litigation documents via email, to the US Attorney's office. So, she continued her research – at least that's what she was calling it.

Around 4:30 p.m. the same Marcia Coleman stopped by Carly's cubicle to ask her how she was doing digesting the Stephens deposition from last Friday. Carly was a bit flustered and stumped. She couldn't tell Marcia that Harris had removed her from the deposition project for this clandestine assignment. At the same time, Carly had to suppress a grin as Marcia – queen of the late-night sex trousseau –- was wearing a pink and green Lilly Pulitzer blouse, with a light green sweater tied around her shoulders. A far cry from the see-through House of Harlot dress Marcia had worn to a New York Giants players' party at the Boom Boom Room in the Standard Hotel last Saturday night. That dress must have gotten her laid, thought Carly.

Carly adroitly steered the conversation to the email that circulated earlier in the day concerning the firm's acquisition of a small boutique entertainment law practice.

"How will this affect you?" Carly asked Marcia, aware of Marcia's interest in litigating entertainment law.

"I don't really know yet. I looked at the roster of associates coming over and there's no one in my class year. That's always a good thing when it comes time for partnership consideration."

"Oh, you shouldn't have any problem making partner," Carly flattered, avoiding the subject of the Stephens deposition digest that Carly had forgotten to assign to someone else, so she could work on Harris's project. "You're so smart and your writing's excellent," Carly went on. If the firm knew about Marcia's slutty nocturnal persona, she wondered, would it help or hinder her chances at partnership? Certainly, Harris would be a fan.

"Say, I have a girlfriend coming in from Wichita to spend the weekend with me and I promised to take her to some of the more interesting New York clubs," said Carly. "I don't know which are hot these days. I don't even know how to get her into these places. I've heard you have to be on a list and even on a list, it can cost $50 at the door. True?"

Marcia perked up at the topic, never suspecting that Carly knew anything about her nightclubbing expertise. "Yeah, that's true for people who don't know their way around the system. Where do you want to go?"

"Well, that's the thing – I don't know where to go," confessed Carly.

"What are you looking for – a foodie place, great music, or rich, single men?" asked Marcia with a directness Carly had never seen from her.

"Are they mutually exclusive? All three sound great. Harris took me to Smith & Wollensky last week and I really liked that. I think I'll take my friend there for dinner, but I'm sure she wouldn't say no to meeting rich single men afterwards," admitted Carly, a bit embarrassed. After all, she was a nice Midwestern girl. At least, that was her play in New York.

"I'm sure you wouldn't either. I know, I always enjoy it." Marcia raised an eyebrow and grinned conspiratorially. "I know some really good party promoters in town. They always let me and my friends in for free."

"Free sounds good," responded Carly. "But why?"

"Because the conventional wisdom is that when attractive, available women are in a club, men follow in droves and those men will pay the steep cover charges and buy the women drinks all night long hoping their *investment* will pay off. The men meet the women, the men buy drinks for everyone, sex is available for anyone who wants it, the bar makes money. Everyone is happy. Get it? Now, is there any particular part of town you'd like to party in?"

"Anything you could do for us at all would be terrific," said Carly, feeling a little guilty for having spied on Marcia's private life. "We really don't care where we go."

"Let me see what I can do for you. And just between us girls, Harris loves his food and wine, but his taste for indulgences doesn't stop there, if you know what I mean," offered Marcia. "You are beautiful and kind. I'd hate to see you get hurt."

Carly was getting caught up in the moment. She felt obliged to confide in Marcia. "Yes, I know exactly what you mean. I've met plenty of guys like that since my divorce. Between us girls, as you said, I totally see what he is, and I know how to manage the situation."

"Good," responded Marcia. The look on her face suggested she had a knowing sense of what was going on and may have been on the receiving end of Harris's advances in the past.

# CHAPTER TWENTY-TWO

It was the Monday of Labor Day weekend, the night before the unofficial end of summer, and the Hamptons were in full swing. Roxanne and Jessica Garramone were at a party at Billy Doplinger's house. He was another boy from Collegiate School, that alone made him very attractive. Roxanne had known him for about five years. Mario and Janice had no reason to be concerned about their daughters because the Doplingers were good family friends. They all shared the same values and approach towards raising teenagers in elite, private Manhattan schools.

Billy was on the tennis team and he played almost every day during that summer, preparing for his senior year. He had been an acne-scarred awkward kid when he started at Collegiate but nature, sunshine, the weight room, and years of tennis had transformed him. A combination of his deep tan, blonde hair, and recently formed muscular upper body made all the girls take notice.

He and Roxanne were quite close, and Roxanne was not about to do anything to jeopardize that friendship. Jessica, on the other hand, was an entirely different story. She had run into Billy several times in Waldbaum's over the summer and had noted the obvious improvement in his physique. Not only had she noted it, she'd actively fantasized about Billy while she was making out with other boys. She had seen him shirtless and was taken by how well defined his shoulders and chest had become – she wanted to know how the rest of him looked. So as soon as she learned that Roxanne had been invited to Billy's party, Jessica campaigned to get herself included in the invitation even though she was two years younger than Billy and Roxanne.

Billy expected to have at least forty kids over, so having another one or two more was no big deal, so Billy told Roxanne she was welcome to bring her younger sister. Billy had seen Jessica around that summer, he knew she was tall and voluptuous – more than her sister. He didn't know she was sixteen. Not that it mattered. For Billy and his friends, if the girl was attractive and willing, the boys wouldn't hesitate. Jessica was both.

Mario and Janice Garramone attended the end of summer bash at the Parkview Club, an exclusive enclave of the rich and famous. Gentlemen had to wear jackets in the dining room at all times, ties were strongly recommended. For women, pants were frowned upon and shorts prohibited. Although Mario was clueless, Janice knew this would be their last Labor Day party at the club together. Janice had not yet built up the reserve, or strategy, to confront Mario, but it was as inevitable as the annual closing of the club pool next week. They had been on the waiting list for three years to get into this iconic institution, and had been members for fifteen years, but that was all about to end as abruptly as their marriage.

Mario wandered the large, oak-paneled room, where cigar smoking was once de rigeur but had now been prohibited by the newer, more health-conscious members of the club, much to the chagrin of the octogenarian members. Clad in his bright red country club slacks adorned with an entire pod of little green whales and topped off with a green jacket (as if he had just won the freaking Masters), Mario strutted around the room like a peacock in full plumage. After all, he was now the Chairman of the Membership Committee, one of the most influential positions in the club. And, if all worked out well, he was about to become the CEO of New York Savings & Guaranty. He had life by the balls, he thought. But his own balls had wandered one too many times and were about to get squeezed in a matrimonial vice.

"How'd you hit 'em today?" Mario asked Blue Worthington, a banker they called Blue because he had only worn blue shirts to work for the past 30 years.

"'Bout the same. "Blue sighed. "It's tough to get better when you're getting older."

"I shot an 80," Mario bragged. Everyone in the Parkview Club knew that whatever score Mario reported was due to be at least six strokes lighter than his actual gross score. He was known for not carding penalty shots, dropping a ball where he had lost one, and hitting two or three times out of a sand trap but claiming he had just struck the ball once.

Mario towered over Blue by about six inches, making it easier to look past Blue as they chatted, constantly swiveling his head around to check out the female talent. Doc Deehl had a new young squeeze, Mario noted with admiration. And Steve Keneally's daughter, fresh off a divorce, had been working out. Mario stared at her ass. Was she even thirty yet?

"So how have you been, my long-lost friend?" piped up Mindy Davis, the only woman in the room who knew about Mario's dalliances with Melanie Hunter. She shocked Mario out of his fixation on the young Keneally's behind. Mindy didn't really care what Mario said in reply. She was just engaging her litigator's innate sense of veracity-checking, taking Mario's temperature to see how forthcoming he would be with her, Janice's closest friend at the club.

"It's been a great summer, but it flew by so fast," responded Mario. It was the most banal of the classic end-of-summer statements.

"Yes, that always seems to be the case, doesn't it," replied Mindy, keen to probe deeper, but not wanting to overplay her hand. "Have you been traveling much?" She was baiting him.

"Yeah, and that's a grind," complained Mario. "Seems like it never ends. I'm always living on an airplane."

"Well, with that fancy bank of yours, you're traveling first class and being pampered, right? Secretaries, associates..."

Mario laughed. "I certainly don't fly steerage, but it's grueling nonetheless," avoiding Mindy's inquiry about traveling companions.

"So, what does the fall hold in store for you?"

"More travel, I'm afraid. It looks like I am going to have to spend a lot of time in California over the next four months. The flights there are direct, so that's not so bad. But what I really hate, though, is the traffic in LA."

"Where do you stay out there?"

"Usually on the beach – Santa Monica. My faves are Shutters and the Lowes. I mean, if I'm going to go all the way out there, I like to wake up and take a walk along the ocean. With that three-hour time difference, I can take a good jog at 5:00 a.m. and no one back here is looking for me yet."

*Faves?* What heterosexual male over 16 says "faves"? This guy is way too full of himself, she thought. And jogging on the beach? C'mon, Mario hadn't jogged a step in twenty years. Besides, Mindy was very familiar with those hotels. In fact, during a fling with a Disney executive six years ago, she spent four fabulous days, and especially nights, at Shutters. It was the most romantic hotel she'd ever stayed at. No businessman would stay in Shutters by himself.

"Great hotels. Isn't it a little bit of a downer to be in Shutters alone when all those lovebirds all around you are enjoying their morning coffee on their verandas overlooking the ocean?"

"Not really, I just enjoy the quiet of it all," lied Mario.

"Is your work out by the ocean," asked Mindy.

"No, it's downtown, I'm afraid. Wilshire Boulevard. That's why I hate the traffic. Driving from Santa Monica to downtown LA in the morning on the 10 is only thirteen miles, but it can take an hour and a half."

He's such a bullshitter, thought Mindy. No reasonable person would endure that long drive unless there was a damn good reason to be staying in such a romantic hotel on the beach. The Peninsula, Beverly Wilshire and Four Seasons were all right there by his office. Those were all outstanding hotels. Why would anyone endure 90 minutes of extra traffic each way? Janice was right – he has a little traveling concubine, or some local slut, he's banging at the beach. Who knows if he even has any business out there?

As these thoughts were going through Mindy's head, Mario caught a glimpse of Lynda Vandermeer and her newly acquired, and inappropriately outsized, breasts. She knew her pink Roberto Cavalli dress was more than a little unbuttoned, doing nothing to hide the sides of those bronzed headline grabbers, and she relished it. Mario continued speaking to Mindy, but his eyes focused completely on Lynda's tits. Mindy saw what was happening and wanted no more of this. She silently vowed to help her friend Janice screw this guy over. He had it coming. He was traveling the world with a young mistress, staying in sexy beachside hotels, and now trying to size up, (and screw if he could get the chance) half the women of the Parkview Club. Mindy reached up, gave Mario a peck on the cheek and, with all the fake sympathy she could muster, whispered, "Poor darling, don't let all that travel get the best of you. I must be heading out now. I have a conference call with Tokyo and they don't have a lot of sympathy about my celebrating Labor Day weekend at a cocktail party when they're facing inquiry by the SEC." Making her way under the ornately adorned archway separating the front exit from the main parlor, she was aware that Mario was checking out her ass. This was attention she did not covet, and he would pay dearly for it.

On the other side of the room, Janice seemed to be immersed in conversation with her girlfriends but was really immersed in multiple glasses of chardonnay. She wasn't a golfer or a tennis player, so she had nothing to add as the women extolled each other with stories of their birdies or set-point breaks from the summer's last week of tournaments.

The conversation turned to Federer and Nadal, and their prospects in the upcoming US Open. I bet they don't cheat on their women, Janice thought to herself.

# CHAPTER TWENTY-THREE

It had been almost a month since Gillian English and Janice
Garramone had met at Starbuck's by Lincoln Center and
first discussed potential SAT tutors for their daughters.
Janice had the money to hire whomever she and Mario wanted for
Roxanne. A mom at Spence had recommended that bright kid,
Hank Blaser. Twice over the summer, she had called him, but he
never returned the calls. Janice checked with the Spence mom
again and found out Blaser spent most of his summer in Ko
Samui, a sleepy beach town in Thailand.

That sounded wonderful, Janice thought. She allowed
herself to daydream about fantastically irresponsible days and
nights on the beach with no parental obligations. Wonderful: a
little reefer, cold beer, and no-strings-attached sex anytime and
anywhere. Just fun, no responsibilities. Like after her senior year
of college when she travelled through Amsterdam, or after she got
her MBA from New York University and she blew off steam in the
Maldives. If this kid was really such a great SAT tutor, Janice
had to get him for Roxanne. She pulled her white iPhone from her
purse and lazily punched in the number one more time, ready to

leave yet another message for Hank, perhaps sounding a bit more miffed this time.

"Hank Blaser," came the booming voice after only one ring. She wasn't expecting Hank to answer, and certainly not to sound as powerful as he did.

"Oh hi," she stammered, "My name is Janice Garramone and I got your name from Sally McPherson, whose daughter, Ellen..."

"Oh yes, you left a few messages for me last month. Sorry, I was away for a bit," Hank said, offering no suggestion that he'd been completely off the grid for most of the summer. "Your daughter is going to be a senior at Sacred Heart this fall, isn't that right?"

"Yes, that's correct," replied Janice, impressed that this young man had listened to her messages, and even more impressed that he'd retained that information.

"Tell me a little bit about her. I like to know some background about students before I commit to working with them. This is an intensive process and it only works if both of us are committed to achieving the same goal."

Janice liked what she was hearing, the kid sounded mature and logical. And whoa, he hit it hard and direct right out of the box. Janice liked that. It didn't hurt that in the back of her mind, Janice couldn't help but think of Sally McPherson's description of Hank as "a combination of Matthew McConaughey and Zac Efron."

"Well, Roxanne is an ambitious young woman who's a very diligent student." Janice said, finding herself saying what

171

she thought Hank wanted to hear. "She loves math, but also excels at creative writing."

Hank was intrigued – most of the high school students he dealt with were either great at math and science, or they were accomplished in the humanities. A student who excels in both? That usually translates into exceptionally high SAT scores. "Did she take the PSATs?" The preliminary SATs were often a pretty good barometer of how a student would do on the SATs.

"Yes, she did."

"And?"

"720 on the math. In writing I think she got a 750."

Hank smiled. Roxanne would be a more than capable student.

Hank was no slouch himself. After graduating from Dartmouth, he was recruited by J.P. Morgan as a junior analyst in New York. Not long into his apprenticeship he knew corporate life was not his calling. He dropped out of the mainstream career path and took up SAT tutoring with the Stanley Kaplan Testing Center.

No one got rich working at Stanley Kaplan, so he decided to cut out the middle man and go into business for himself. The parents of his students were paying over $60,000 a year for private school tuition in Manhattan, more than Hank had paid to attend Dartmouth, an Ivy League university. Some Manhattan parents would write a proverbial blank check to get their kids into great colleges, and he wanted to tap into some of that cash. His decision was a splendid one. In his first year as a private tutor, Hank grossed over $200,000, not bad for a twenty-eight-year-old. The fact that much of it was in cash (and most of it unreported on his tax return), made him smile even wider.

Hank Blaser knew all he needed to know about the Garramones' ability to pay for his services. Being no fool, Hank had Googled them. Everything he read indicated that the Garramones would have no difficulty paying his rate of $900 per hour. Hank's girlfriend, Stephanie Gallagher, charged $1,000 per hour to tutor high school kids and had more than a few clients who didn't blink at that rate. But Hank didn't want to hit four figures. It could draw the wrong kind of attention: IRS, or the gossip-mongering *New York Daily News* always on the lookout for an item about those crazy Upper East Siders overpaying to indulge their rich kids. No, $900 an hour was more than sufficient to afford Hank quite a decent life in the city. No need to be greedy.

"Well, from what you've told me so far, Roxanne sounds like a highly accomplished student, and I would look forward to meeting her."

"So, you do have time to work with her?" inquired Janice, excited.

"I have the time, or we wouldn't be having this conversation," Hank sounded a bit condescending, but didn't really mean to. "I would have to meet her first, though. You see, since we'll be working together for several months, I want to make sure that our personalities, and approach to studying, are simpatico, if you know what I mean."

"When should we start?" Janice said.

"The tests are given in October, November, and

December. I suggest we forgo the October test to allow us enough time to begin the work. Plan on Roxanne taking the November test, then if there's any problem, she'll have another shot in December."

Janice was savvy enough to understand that things could go wrong on any particular test date. If Roxanne had a cold, or a fight with her boyfriend, or even her period, her test performance could be affected. Hank had made a good point and again, Janice was impressed.

"So, I'm happy to meet her, and have our initial session this week," Hank said. "What's Roxanne's schedule look like?"

"This week sounds great," Janice responded. "Would we be doing this at our apartment, or somewhere else?"

"It depends. I'm tutoring several students this semester, all over the city. If I've got someone else near you, I can certainly drop by and tutor Roxanne at your home. If not, I usually tutor students at my place."

"Whatever works for you works for us," responded Janice.

Hank sounded so responsible and adult. Janice was thrilled that she had lined up her first choice to tutor her oldest daughter.

# CHAPTER TWENTY-FOUR

Janice's friend, Gillian English, also needed an SAT tutor for her daughter, Cara. But there was no way she could pay thousands of dollars for a tutor, and Cara was just not a good enough student to do well on the SATs without a tutor.

It was all so frustrating. There were many nights Gillian found herself crying in her bedroom, alone with a bottle of wine, wondering how she was going to make it after Mark's death. Raising Cara, and taking care of her mother, Audrey, back in the Poconos – all by herself. It was a lot.

Gillian had tried one job after another. Once an up-and-comer as a CFO at CallPro in Pennsylvania, Gillian was now a 47-year-old widow who had been out of a steady job for over 20 years. Oh, sure, she got hired once in a while, but whenever layoffs came Gillian was always among the first to go, because she was among the last hired.

Sacred Heart School helped with Cara's tuition – providing scholarships and financial aid. Cara might not have been the brightest student in the school, but she was the friendliest, adored by her teachers and classmates alike. Her red hair and freckles testified to her late father's Irish heritage. It made Cara proud that she looked like her father. She'd only had a few years with him before 9/11, but her memories of him were strong and wonderful.

Gillian and Janice met for drinks and caught each other up on their summers, and what lay ahead for the fall. Gillian's concern about Cara's SATs had only grown more intense since the last time they'd seen each other in the spring. Janice filled Gillian in on the Garramone family summer, leaving out the most important part – Janice discovering Mario's affair.

Janice was careful not to play up her summer of parties in the Hamptons, it would only make Gillian feel even more inadequate. Gillian filled Janice in on Cara's experience as a junior counselor at Camp Summit, a highly regarded Christian-based camp in Hendersonville, North Carolina. Cara oversaw a cabin full of eight-year-old girls and was the assistant riding instructor. She had always loved horses, but riding was a very expensive sport and Gillian knew there was no way she could afford for Cara to pursue it in New York. Some of the girls from Sacred Heart rode on Saturdays at the New York City Riding Academy on Wards Island, just a few minutes away from Manhattan by car – but light years away from the experience of any public-school kid. Dressage and jumping were the "in" disciplines, and families jockeyed to identify and purchase horses with the best lineage in those domains. The only girls who rode horses were from ridiculously wealthy families, and Gillian and Cara no longer fit into that group.

Janice broached the subject directly. "Gillian, I had a

lovely conversation with that SAT tutor who was recommended to us, Hank Blaser. He seems like a great guy and he's got time available." Gillian's attitude veered between anger and jealousy. Janice knew Gillian couldn't afford a tutor, much less one as highly coveted as Hank Blaser. Gillian wished Janice wouldn't even go there – the entire subject was simultaneously stressful and distressing to Gillian. Janice barreled on, aware that Gillian couldn't afford the same opportunity for Cara. "I thought because the girls are so close, it might make sense for him to tutor both of them at the same time. They may also focus better if they are doing it together. And a little healthy competition between them every week might also motivate them. Of course, Mario and I would pay for all of it."

Gillian's eyes welled up, her emotions getting the best of her. Janice and Mario had been so generous to Gillian and Cara since Mark's death, it was overwhelming. Gillian could never imagine there was even more to come.

"That would be amazing, wonderful. But I can't ask you guys to do that."

"You didn't. I offered it. And please don't mention the finances of it again. Let's just figure out the scheduling and get it going," insisted Janice.

"But those tutors are a fortune."

"I just told you, let's not mention the finances of it again," Janice said, firmly. The money really didn't matter to Janice at all. She was more than happy to spend Mario's money. She was going to divorce Mario. There was absolutely no way he would contest the payment necessary to tutor their daughter. Janice was only adding Cara to the process. And, she thought to herself, I can just imagine what people would think of Mario cutting off funds already promised to tutor his daughter's closest friend whose father had been killed on September 11th. Mario would be portrayed as a heartless bastard – perhaps (hopefully) it would make the papers. His reputation was vitally important to him.

Janice considered mentioning the arrangement to Hank, but no need – Hank, like every young man who had met her, would be charmed by Roxanne. There's no way he'd want to lose her as a client, even if Cara was added to the equation.

This would only be the tip of the iceberg. She intended to initiate many financial commitments that Mario would never suspect as being out of the ordinary. Then, when she served him with the divorce papers, he would have to take affirmative actions to close those payments, most of which would involve their daughters and their futures. He'd be stuck. Either be portrayed as a jerk when he could least afford negative publicity – with his lifetime dream promotion to CEO of the bank only a few months away – or pay up.

"That would be so wonderful," Gillian gushed. "I can't begin to thank you enough. I didn't know how I was going to ..."

"Stop that," pleaded Janice. "The girls grew up together, celebrated every birthday together, and have been in how many plays and musicals together?"

Gillian smiled at the memories of Cara and Roxanne dressed in their costumes from *Peter Pan, Grease,* and *HMS Pinafore.* "You're an angel, an absolute angel. There's a place in heaven for you and Mario," prattled Gillian.

If you only knew, thought Janice. That bastard won't be getting anywhere near heaven.

It was done. "Terrific. You get me Cara's schedule, I'll track down that elusive daughter of mine and get hers, and I'll set up the first meeting. They'll have the first session at our apartment, so I can tell Hank about our arrangement," explained Janice. "Oh, he'll want to know Cara's scores on the PSATs, so get me those." Cara had scored inside the top 20 percent – not bad, but nowhere near as good as Roxanne.

"I can't thank you enough," Gillian gushed one more time.

"Stop it now, it's our pleasure. And that is absolutely the last time I'll hear about it. Now, I've got a 10:00 a.m. appointment at Michelle's to get my nails done and I don't want to take a cab." Michelle's was the hottest boutique salon on the Upper West Side – Janice regretted mentioning it the second she'd said it. It was tricky with Gillian. "The way I've been eating lately, I can sure use the exercise, but I need to hoof it now."

Gillian now felt even more self-conscious. Not only was Janice picking up the tutoring tab, which could run up to ten grand, but now she was complaining about staying in shape – and she was a size four. Gillian had gained thirty pounds since Mark died. She was eating virtually everything in the snack aisle at Food Emporium, ballooning from 136 pounds to nearly 170. Plus, she was drinking, sometimes a bottle of wine a night. She knew she looked awful. With every pound she gained, her self-esteem plummeted. As the weight increased, she stopped bothering with applying make-up and dying her grey roots.

Her wardrobe was also limited – the trendy and flattering

clothes all the other Upper East Side moms wore were out of her financial reach. She ambled around the city wearing unflattering black Lululemon stretch pants and large blousy tops that resembled muumuus.

Gillian was keenly aware that there was no end in sight to her desperate financial straits and that she was destined to be alone once Cara left for college. She hated herself for all of it, but she couldn't think her way out of it.

She had convinced herself there was nothing she could do.

# CHAPTER TWENTY-FIVE

Although Dr. Liam Perlmutter was not in regular contact with Eva, he was extremely excited about his investment on the ship. It hadn't taken Eva long to convince him that he needed to get out of Florida, and away from his old cronies, to enjoy the final decades of his life. She told him Danielle deserved better than to be parked in Palm Beach, "God's waiting room," for the rest of her life. Eva appealed to Liam's need to be included in the finer things in life. From Eva's first call to him, Liam did not have a single dinner with friends when he didn't discuss the ship. He was obsessed with it.

Liam may have been a multi-millionaire, but his friends all considered him to be cheap. If there was a way to stick someone else with the tab, Liam knew it. If there was a way to get something cheaper than fair market value, Liam knew it. And if there was a way to make money out of nothing, Liam knew that, too.

There was only one detail of the ship finances that worried Liam – the condo association fees. He knew they had to be steep to manage the ship as a first-class operation. If some of the other owners backed out – or if the hotel revenue fell – those fees could go through the roof. So, Liam took it upon himself to help Eva drum up as many paid-suite owners as possible. At first this concerned Eva – she didn't know any of the people Liam was contacting. But Eva's mentor, Lorraine, convinced her that this was a good thing – she had to let go of the reins to some extent. Eva finally agreed to Liam's suggestion that he scare up a few of his Palm Beach colleagues.

Carmine Scantello was not what Eva had in mind. The sixty-five-year-old retiree had owned a construction company in Brooklyn. He was a big, rough guy. No one would confuse him with Zac Efron. But Carmine was more than a construction company goombah. He had graduated from St. John's Law School, courtesy of the US government after serving with the Green Berets during two tours in Vietnam. He built his construction company not by performing work on existing buildings, but by purchasing property and actually erecting the buildings.

He started small, with a medium-sized lot in Bensonhurst. No other contractor in all of Brooklyn wanted to touch this property – it was entangled in a hornet's nest of zoning regulations. But Carmine knew what he was doing. With his law-school background, he knew how to navigate the system and, after only a few months, he got all the needed variances to put up a catering hall. He ran it himself for a year, then sold it to the son of the don of the neighborhood crime family at a very nice profit.

He used that windfall to make his first foray into Manhattan real estate, buying four walk-up tenement buildings on Second Avenue between 48th and 49th Streets. Each had street-level retail space, with small, dark apartments upstairs that had been allowed to drift into a sorry state of decrepitude. Carmine had to buy the property, and then buy out the retail leases and a few holdout tenants upstairs who thought they could hold him up for a killing. But Carmine was not a man you wanted to play those kinds of games with. He prevailed quite rapidly.

Time was money and money was the goal. He tore down the tenements and erected a nineteen-story apartment building. Wisely, Carmine decided he did not want to be in the landlord business, so he sold the apartments as condominiums, fetching anywhere from $600,000 to $2 million per unit. From there, Carmine's business was off to the races. Within ten years, he had developed a real estate empire valued at $200 million. Smaller construction companies retained Carmine for his legal expertise, and he developed a profitable, and intellectually stimulating, side business advising on permitting, zoning, variances, and all the other legal maneuvers that meant the difference between success and bankruptcy.

After amassing a small fortune, Carmine bought a winter condominium in Palm Beach, following the well-trod footsteps of so many other New York Italians and Jews. He intended on living a quiet life of retirement, relaxing in the sun with his beloved wife. But right after Carmine bought the condo, his wife passed away from a massive heart attack.

Carmine had met Liam Perlmutter standing in line for bagels at The Original Brooklyn Bagel Company on Military Trail in Palm Beach. He overheard Liam explaining to his wife, Danielle, that these were the best bagels in Florida because "they boil them, the same way they make them at the Carnegie Deli." That got Carmine's attention.

Liam was born and raised in Brooklyn, practically next door to Carmine's old stomping grounds in Bensonhurst, so the two men chatted about their school days playing stickball in the streets with pink Spaldeens. This began their friendship. Later, Carmine provided critical construction advice to Liam when Liam was building his new home along the Intercoastal waterway.

Liam was keenly aware of Carmine's social insecurity. Although he had vaulted to the pinnacle of financial success amongst his *paisans*, Carmine had never really broken into the world of the rich and famous. He was handicapped by his thick Brooklyn accent. Nevertheless, one night Liam decided to run the notion of Eva's boat by Carmine. Carmine was so overwhelmed by the idea, it made Liam uneasy. Carmine's eyes welled up with appreciation. He understood that Liam was doing something special for him, inviting him to dive headlong into the deepest end of the pool of patricians. Carmine was intrigued by the deal: a Japanese company building a 455-foot tube of fiberglass and steel in Greece, originally for a Saudi Sheik, then acquired by a hot woman lawyer from New York, that would ferry hundreds of American sophisticates to the most remote regions of the globe. After a call with Liam and Eva, Carmine committed to buy one of the smallest units sold, a $6-million luxury suite.

Cindy Miller was like a niece to Liam. He'd dated her mother for a few years and, even after they broke up and Liam married Danielle, they had all remained close. Cindy always called him "Uncle Liam." When she was just thirteen, Cindy's mom died, and Liam and Danielle helped Cindy's father raise Cindy; they all shared the pride when she went off to college at Washington State University. Her freshman year, she met Dave Sunnyday, who was majoring in Indian Studies. Cindy and Dave got married shortly after graduation and Dave went on to the University of Washington School of Law.

Combining his Native American interest with his law degree, Dave became one of the foremost experts on everything related to gaming on Indian reservations. As his practice was really taking off, one of the Washington tribes approached Dave about a casino/hotel/spa they wanted to build on their reservation. Dave outlined the legal work that had to be performed for the massive project and presented them with a proposal that included his fees of almost $200,000. This was way above their budget. Even if they taxed the entire reservation, they could probably not round up more than $50,000 for legal fees. The tribal chiefs drafted a plan that included a payment to Dave of only $20,000.

Dave reviewed the plan and told the chiefs it was destined to fail. He pitched them a compromise: he would take no upfront money for any of his legal services but would keep track of his hours and agree to perform at least $200,000 worth of legal work. In exchange, Dave would get five percent of all casino profits for the next twenty years. If the casino failed, he'd collect a mere $10,000 for his efforts, half of what the chiefs were already offering.

The chiefs assented.

Within a year, Dave received his first check for $865,000.

The next fourteen annual checks were in that same very lucrative neighborhood.

While Dave had been attending law school and trying to establish his practice, Cindy worked as a dental assistant. But once they started cashing those big casino checks, Cindy's career as a dental hygienist was over. She stayed home and raised their only daughter, Chelsea. In her spare time, Cindy did the books for Dave.

Dave's practice revolved around the Indian reservation. He loved spending time on the reservation, learning more about the culture that had so fascinated him as a child. But as he grew closer to the Native Americans who lived on the reservation, Dave began hanging out in the casino, drinking with the high rollers, and partying with the entertainers and prostitutes (who were sometimes one in the same). A large guy with a barrel chest, Dave could put down quite a few beers at a time. Those few beers eventually became two six packs a night.

That life started to take its toll. He had to employ all his legal wiles to get out of three DWI's. His work suffered.

The tribal elders were disgusted and notified him they were going to terminate his agreement. Dave filed a lawsuit, but the tribe retained a Seattle litigator who succeeded in enforcing the morals clause in Dave's contract. It was really no contest.

Even after his disastrous fall from grace, Dave could not walk away from the bottle. His depression worsened by the day and it took a toll on his face and his body. Throughout it all, everyone who knew them was amazed by Cindy and how she maintained her outgoing demeanor in the face of all that was going on. At home, she was just grateful that Dave never became abusive to her or to Chelsea. But one steamy July night, what little semblance of normalcy still remained in their lives was shattered by a single shot from the .44 Magnum Dave kept in his bedside drawer. In a millisecond, Cindy's and Chelsea's lives were obliterated by a 240-gram piece of semi-jacketed hollow-point lead Dave lodged in his right temple.

Chelsea had been scheduled to start classes at Gonzaga University just two months later, but the family quickly scrambled. Putting their Washington state home on the market (although there was not much demand for a house that had borne witness to a violent suicide in the bedroom suite), they moved back to south Florida. Cindy had known the pain of losing her mother when she was just thirteen, and now had to endure the pain of losing her husband when she was forty-one.

Going away to college and getting a fresh start would be the best thing for Chelsea, and Cindy was determined to make that happen. Cindy and Chelsea decided to expunge any connection to Washington from their lives. Chelsea gave up her scholarship at Gonzaga and applied to schools in Florida. Once again, Uncle Liam assumed a paternal role. When she least expected it, and only a week after she had submitted her application, Chelsea received a full scholarship from the University of Miami. On the first day of freshman orientation, Cindy drove Chelsea to the campus and saw the large bronze letters adorning the façade of the Liam Perlmutter School of Engineering. She smiled, knowing that Chelsea's scholarship to Hurricane Nation was not just an arbitrary decision by the admissions committee.

Liam and Danielle spent a good deal of time with Cindy, helping her through this difficult time with their presence and encouragement. Cindy and Chelsea dined at the Perlmutter house almost every night that August, and Liam and Danielle were terrific, cheerily introducing them into Jupiter's social life.

Although Liam was eminently wealthy, Cindy didn't need his money. From his percentage of revenue from the tribal nation, Dave had received close to $1 million a year for fifteen years. They had lived sparsely, with Dave running his law firm out of a restored trailer – a double wide, Cindy always reminded people. Vacations were infrequent and their spending quite reasonable: Cindy was more comfortable in denim than diamonds. Besides, there were not many events in Renton, Washington, that required evening gowns. They had enjoyed the trappings of an upper-middle-class suburban family but had lived within their means. And thanks to Cindy's solid investments during a bull market, she now possessed an investment account worth over $30 million.

Two weeks after Chelsea began her studies at the university, Cindy met Liam for dinner at his club, the Palm Beach Yacht Club. Before the meal, they took a stroll on the docks, eyeing the many beautiful yachts bobbing against the greying, gull-covered buoys that protected those exquisite fiberglass surfaces from the splintering posts sunk in the muck decades earlier. There were so many beautiful sailboats and fishing boats, but Cindy was most attracted to the luxury yachts, especially those with majestic upper-level navigation bridges.

Sensing her interest, Liam regaled her with a discourse

on all the different types of yacht bridges – fly bridges, sedan bridges, sport bridges.

"How wonderful it would be to sail away on one of these!" It just came out of Cindy, unexpectedly. She laughed at herself, but was caught up in the moment, the fantasy. "To just go whenever you wanted, wherever you wanted, sail away! I'd hire a captain, and he could bring his wife – to look after the captain," she laughed again. "God. To just go...." After all, Chelsea was now safely entrenched in her new college life, in her dorm and making new friends at a furious pace and Cindy had no real roots in south Florida, not since she had left there for college in the Pacific Northwest twenty-five years earlier. Why not? Why not just sail away, let all the stress and grief and disappointment just vanish in the water behind her, her face in the sun?

The fantasy didn't fade at dinner. Cindy pressed more and more, peppering Liam with question after question on the finer points of yacht ownership. Because Liam had known Cindy since she was a child, he knew she did not have a proclivity for anything technical and owning a boat surely would require a certain amount of technical discipline. He just couldn't see her being happy with all the headaches of owning and running a yacht.

Precipitously, during their entrees, his mind did a 180° pivot. Why not introduce Cindy to the concept of Eva's yacht? Then Cindy could let someone else worry about fuel, port fees, all day-to-day challenges of yacht ownership – and she could just "sail away" as she said. With $30 million in assets, she certainly was on the favorable side of the scales for membership into Eva's boating fraternity. Liam's only concern was Cindy's age – at forty-four, she would be the youngest of the owners on the ship. But her usefulness and vitality could be an asset, and who knows, she might even find a new love on the ship. So, he slowly began describing the concept to Cindy.

She loved it. "Ha! This sounds a lot better than being the admiral of my own navy," she agreed, delighted.

Cindy Miller, through Liam, invested $6 million to buy what she called a "starter" luxury suite onboard Eva's vessel.

# CHAPTER TWENTY-SIX

It was late in the afternoon on an overcast day at LaGuardia Airport as Carly Burke anxiously waited for her friend, Michelle Poverman, to arrive on American Airlines flight 1754 from Wichita. Carly had arranged to take Friday off from Bergman Troutman so she could take Michelle on a tour around the city. When she asked Harris's consent for the free time, he sat back in his chair and engaged Carly in a bit of an unsolicited avuncular cross-examination about her plans.

"So exactly what are the highlights of the City you intend to show your friend?" inquired Harris, innocently enough – although with Harris, nothing was ever really innocent.

Carly had spent hours researching the top tourist attractions in Manhattan. As she was doing all this prep work, it became embarrassingly clear to her that she had not made the most of her own time in the City.

"I thought we'd begin with the Statue of Liberty. Then, the Empire State Building, and take a walk up Fifth Avenue, past Tiffany's and Trump Tower to Central Park. For lunch, I'm thinking of taking her somewhere downtown, somewhere chic."

Harris grinned. "Do you mind if I offer you a suggestion for your first day? Then, you can take it from there." Without even waiting for a response, he forged forward. "I never take people to the Statue of Liberty," he said authoritatively. "There is a much better alternative – and one I'm sure you will find more cost-effective. Take the ferry from Battery Park to Staten Island. First of all, it's free. Second, there are no lines or tickets needed. But most importantly, it sails right by the Statue of Liberty and you can get all those amazing photographs everyone wants to have. Then, when you arrive at Staten Island, you simply walk to the other side of the terminal and take the ferry right back to Manhattan. Once again, you get a terrific view of the lower Manhattan skyline and the Statue of Liberty.

"Once you're back in lower Manhattan, walk by Clinton Castle. Contrary to what most uninformed tourists think, it was not named in honor of our most recently impeached president. No, it was named after DeWitt Clinton, former mayor, and then governor of New York. So much wonderful history down there you can tell your friend about. Now, you do know that whole area by Battery Park was developed around 1808 in preparation for America's declaration of war against Great Britain in 1812, don't you? The name Battery Park is derived from the fortress and battery that were constructed there to fight the British. Twenty-eight cannons in place and they could project a cannon ball over a mile and a half!"

Carly was able to ignore Harris's condescension and actually appreciate the guidance. Well, ignore to a degree. She could do without the comments like "Now you do know..." but she knew he couldn't help himself.

"Then, take a walk up Broadway to the Charging Bull statue outside Bowling Green. Many people think it has something to do with Merrill Lynch. And others think it's been there forever. But I'll tell you the real story. It appeared one night in 1987, after the stock market crash of that year. It was designed and created by a fellow named Arturo Di Modica and delivered to the city as a gift. You should also know that most art displays in the city remain present for only one year, by city ordinance. But since that one has been there for over thirty years now, it's fair to surmise that it is a permanent exhibit."

Carly opened the cover of her legal pad and began to take some succinct notes.

"Next, walk up Broadway and then slowly start to make your way northeast. City Hall Park is located between Broadway, Park Row, and Chambers Street."

Carly smiled at Harris's misuse of the word "between," when "among" was the proper idiom. He didn't make many mistakes, so Carly was pleased to have noticed this one. But she didn't dare interrupt him.

"It was built at the same time Battery Park and Clinton Castle were constructed. So it cannot be confused with New York's original City Hall, which was the seat of the first United States federal government following the conclusion of the Revolutionary War. From there, keep walking northeast until you get to the legendary federal courthouse of the United States District Court for the Southern District of New York, at 40 Centre Street. Some of New York's most famous criminals have been prosecuted in that building, including John Gotti, Martha Stewart, and Julius and Ethel Rosenberg."

Carly got a kick out of the way Harris snuck Martha Stewart in there in between a mafia don and communist spies.

"Immediately across the street is New York State Supreme Court house at 60 Centre Street. You'll recognize the facade of the building from *Law & Order* and *Kojak*, but that probably pre-dates you. The movies that were filmed there are legendary including *The Godfather, Goodfellas* and *Wall Street*. In fact, if you want to go back to the black-and-white days, *12 Angry Men* and *Miracle on 34th Street* were filmed there, too." Carly was relieved that Harris did not take this opportunity to regale her with stories of his great legal conquests in either of those courthouses.

"Next, walk behind the courthouse and you'll see a playground. Cross the playground and you will be in Chinatown. One of my favorite restaurants there is Ho Wop, a hole in the wall. There's an upstairs Ho Wop and a downstairs Ho Wop. Go to the upstairs one. It looks like a hole in the wall, but they probably have the most authentic Chinese food in New York. If you go to China, of course, you'll see that the food there doesn't even resemble what we call Chinese food in America. But that's a subject for another day."

Here we go again, Carly thought, he just can't help himself. Yes, I get that you've been to China. Big friggin' deal.

"Order the hot-and-sour soup. It's the best you'll ever have. They make it with a tomato base and they bring a large bucket of it to the table, so you serve yourselves. Everything you get there is amazing, but they have some special daily delicacies. I won't bore you with my favorites because everyone has his own taste, but you won't go wrong there."

Harris drew a breath. Carly began to close her notepad but then Harris exhaled. "If you want to have some fun with your friend, do what I do. When the check comes, and she wants to pick it up, or share it, insist that you pay the whole thing. It will be a very inexpensive meal, trust me. Tell her that she can even things out by buying you dessert.

"Then, walk through Chinatown, where you'll see all the Chinese butchers and vegetable shops. You'll see that, in the butcher shops, the ducks are hanging by their necks. Those with the longest necks have been hanging the longest, an inside tip in case you are going to make your own Peking duck at home." Harris winked and Carly smiled. That was actually funny.

"When you get through Chinatown, you'll find yourself in Little Italy. Get to Ferrara and you'll have the best desserts of your life. It's on Grand Street between Mulberry and Mott Streets and it's been there since the 1800s. They have the most delicious cannolis..."

"I love cannolis," Carly offered.

Harris continued, ignoring the interruption without so much as a pause, "... but my absolute favorite is the *baba au rhum*. They're brioche pastries soaked in rum. I used to tell my kids they would get drunk from eating them. That only caused them to want more, making them sick, not drunk. When you each get a pastry, perhaps some cookies, and a couple of espressos, the bill will be more than you will have paid for lunch at Ho Wop. By that time, it should be after 3 and you'll both just want to nap, especially if you are planning some ... nocturnal festivities."

Who the hell talks like that? Carly thought. *Nocturnal festivities*?

"What *are* you going to do in the evening?" Harris inquired.

"Well, I really enjoyed that meal at Smith and Wollensky's, so I thought I would take Michelle there for dinner," Carly lied. Marcia had given her the names of some far more lively and hip restaurants down in the Meatpacking District, but Carly took this opportunity to flatter Harris.

"Superb choice," he chuckled, approvingly. "And then?"

"I thought we might go out downtown and see what's going on," Carly replied, trying to remain as obtuse as possible.

"Well, if you're going to go anywhere mainstream, you have to make plans in advance. You have to get your name on a promoter's list just to get in the door of any of the more intriguing clubs."

Thanks to Marcia, Carly already knew this, but she didn't know how to respond without seeming like she didn't know what she was doing. "I think we're all set with that," Carly mumbled, hoping that would end the inquiry. There was a line out there somewhere Harris would not cross for fear it would seem he was involving himself in Carly's personal matters. Or so Carly hoped.

"Oh, how is that?" Harris continued.

Shit, thought Carly. That was fast – apparently that line didn't exist! What do I do now?

"I think we are all set with that."

"You keep saying you're 'all set,'" Harris, pushed further. "What do you mean? I would hate to see you taken advantage of by someone who promises you something and can't deliver it. Who's getting you 'all set'?"

If anyone is considering taking advantage of someone it would be this probing, fat bastard, thought Carly.

"One of my friends." She didn't want to betray Marcia as her club source.

"Good for you. Smart girl," said Harris, every bit as patronizing as Carly could expect. She bristled. Carly reserved the term "girl" for young ladies under fifteen years of age. She was a twenty-nine-year-old woman, preparing to go out and party like a woman, condoms safely tucked in the zipped pocket of her purse.

"So, where are you going," Harris continued, unwilling to abort the line of inquiry. Carly caught herself crossing and re-crossing her legs repeatedly. She hoped he wouldn't notice the moon-shaped sweat stains forming under the arms of her Worthington sleeveless, chartreuse blouse. This is getting uncomfortable, she mused. How much more is he going to ask, for God's sake? It's none of his fucking business.

"I forgot the exact name of the place," Carly muttered, trying to dodge any further interrogation.

"Is it downtown?" Harris cross-examined.

"I think so," Carly responded, the reluctant witness.

"Hmmm. Cielo? Gaslight? Bijoux? Do any of those sound familiar?"

Carly truly did not remember the name of the clubs

Marcia had mentioned. But what she found most disturbing, was that Harris knew the names of all the hottest downtown clubs. He was almost sixty years old, highly unattractive and, more than anything else, married!

This is getting gross, Carly thought. I need to get out of here.

"I really don't remember. I can let you know on Monday, after we see where we end up," she offered, mustering a big smile. "But back to my original question, would it be all right if I took Friday off to show Michelle around town? You've given me such great suggestions about lower Manhattan, I'm anxious to try those out for myself." Carly figured flattery was probably the best way of getting out of Harris's office.

"Certainly, Carly. That would be fine with me. Just be sure to tell Miranda so she knows not to expect you." Miranda LeMaire was the paralegal supervisor and she kept track of the comings and goings of all her assigned. "And have fun – wherever you end up."

It took Carly about four seconds to close her legal pad, exit the large Senator Rayburn guest chair, and stride the length of Harris's office to escape.

In Terminal B of LaGuardia Airport, the ancient loudspeaker crackled with inaudible information about an inbound flight and the attendant baggage-carousel number. Carly was not at all impressed with the anything about LaGuardia. For such a large city, New York had a really crappy airport, she thought. She hadn't used JFK or Newark but had flown in and out of LaGuardia several times. Even our little Eisenhower

Airport in Wichita is ten times better than this, she concluded. Right. The airport was always filthy, understaffed, and hadn't really changed much in decades. It showed its age and wear.

Carly received a text: "Landed! Where 2 meet?" It was Michelle.

"Bottom of stairs," Carly texted back.

"K. Let me get my suitcase first."

Suitcase? Carly wondered why Michelle had packed a bag if she was only going to be in New York for three days. Why not just a carry-on? She spotted Michelle walking down the stairs, sporting a Ralph Lauren blazer over a crisp white blouse, matched with a floral jacquard skirt Carly recognized from Von Maur in Wichita. Michelle looked radiant and excited, ready to conquer the big city.

They laughed, hugged, and greeted each other with a sincere embrace and friendly kiss.

"I can't believe you're here," Carly laughed.

"Neither can I."

"Let's get your bag and get out of here." They made their way to the baggage carousel and were pleased Michelle was able to quickly identify a small red Samsonite bag that tumbled down the chute. "That's mine," she claimed. Carly grabbed it and took a step towards the exit, anxious to get a taxi and head into Manhattan.

"Wait, there's another one," Michelle said.

Carly looked at her, tilted her head, smiled broadly. "Seriously?"

Michelle tried to hide the sheepish grin on her face. "I

didn't know what to pack."

"So, what, you packed everything?" They both laughed.

After they gathered Michelle's second bag, appreciably larger than the first, they grabbed a taxi to Carly's apartment on East 85th Street and Second Avenue. They chatted incessantly about Carly's experience in New York, and Tom Jackson, a young American Studies professor at Kansas State University they both thought was so cute when they were enrolled there. Michelle was dating him now.

# CHAPTER TWENTY-SEVEN

In her Manhattan apartment on a Saturday morning, Melanie Hunter awoke alone and feeling scorned. Mario Garramone enjoyed toying with her in the office and consuming the fruits of her feminine nectar while they traveled together. Sure, he was going to make her his "special associate," whatever that meant, and she was going to be the lead junior banker on the EuroHoldings matters. But right now, he was enjoying the weekend, frolicking in the Hamptons with his perky little wife and two perfect daughters while she was sitting alone in her apartment.

Even Melanie's roommate, Marcia Coleman, wasn't there that morning. Marcia had been invited to a party at the Yale Club where the assembled Yalies had become inebriated. At their insistence, the party continued into the night and migrated to the sexy and salacious Cellar Bar beneath the Bryant Park Hotel a few blocks away. Marcia had shot Melanie a text inviting her to join the gaggle of young, professional wannabe wives, but Melanie was already in her pajamas, deep into her third episode of *Game of Thrones*. She was not about to get up, apply her war paint, pour herself into some skin tight something or other and summon up smiles and affability before trying to find a taxi. No, this night belonged to Melanie's loneliness.

With Marcia having found love on Friday night, or at least someone who was successful at getting into her pants, Melanie was alone to roam the apartment Saturday morning. She emerged from her bedroom and walked down the narrow hallway that forced her to turn left into the white kitchen. Lazily she inserted a Nespresso pod in the machine and pushed the button to dispense her daily dose of jolt. Her NBC Experience souvenir cup filled, she sauntered into their spacious living room, now full of light thanks to its southern exposure and the bright illumination from the morning sun.

All the furniture in the apartment was white, with like-new leather Saarinen couches and executive side chairs that commanded attention. A glass Platner dining table doubled as an office.

Although she didn't (necessarily) suffer from OCD, Melanie was not fond of the stacks of papers Marcia scattered all over the apartment. Today, Melanie was greeted by four stacks of papers Marcia had left spread across their dining-room table. Sighing heavily, Melanie scooped up the papers and cradled them with her right hand, her coffee in her left. Walking into Marcia's bedroom she stumbled over a pair of Manolo Blahniks, lost her balance, and dropped the papers.

She bent down to pick up the mess she had made. She had a rough sense of which papers belonged in which pile, but she could not be certain. It was not her fault, she reasoned. Marcia should never have left them on the dining room table in the first place. Sorting through the papers, Melanie noticed a familiar name on a PowerPoint. Curious, she flipped the pages and saw the same name, EuroHoldings, on many of the pages. EuroHoldings? That was Mario's biggest client. What did Marcia have to do with it? Why was it in Marcia's papers? Why was it being compared to Boeing? Antitrust investigation? Price fixing? Anticompetitive behavior? Did Mario know about this? And again, what did it all have to do with Boeing? It didn't make much sense to Melanie.

She tried to put it together in her head but dismissed it – Marcia's papers had caused her enough aggravation for one morning. Besides, she had better things to worry about on a Saturday morning. She was supposed to get her hair done at 1 at Polaris Studio and it was pouring. Even if she took a taxi and brought an umbrella, her hair would be ruined by the time she got back to the apartment. Exasperated, Melanie stacked the papers in two piles and turned her thoughts to what she was going to wear and what time she was going to summon an Uber.

She knew what she had seen but had no idea what it signified.

# CHAPTER TWENTY-EIGHT

Seated in her grey suede Arne Jacobsen swivel desk chair staring out the 16-foot windows of her General Motors Building office, Eva Lampedusa studied the glistening brown bodies lounging on Central Park's Sheep Meadow and wondered just who these people were. They were there every day, hundreds of them. Young, able-bodied twenty-somethings with their blankets, towels, lunches, and Frisbees, content to fritter away the meatiest hours of the day listening to their iPhones, reading, eating, and just lounging.

Every afternoon, with a degree of deniable envy, Eva wondered how they could afford to live in the most expensive city in America and not have to work. They couldn't all be trust-fund brats – or wealthy divorcees who had served their time, now paroled from their marriages with multi-million-dollar exit bonuses. She decided they were all unemployed actors, killing time until their next audition. Or waiters, enjoying their leisure time before their restaurants opened at 6:00 p.m. She scrutinized them every day. Sometimes she wished she were that carefree.

Eva was feeling bullish about her progress raising the

money needed for her ship. But she was keen to keep the pressure on, hopefully securing more than she actually needed to purchase the ship. Some of the initial investors suggested they could reduce the number of hotel-type rooms on the ship to make it more exclusive. However, Eva understood that those visitor flats were a necessary evil: necessary to supplement the ship's maintenance expenses, but evil in that it would introduce a transient element – outsiders – to the ship. That idea became less desirable every time Eva thought of it. Liam Perlmutter had been right, and Eva knew it.

She opened her top left drawer to review her crib note of potential investors. She hadn't yet spoken with Mario Garramone. She put a call into him last week, but his assistant said he was in Greece working on a deal.

Eva had met Mario about ten years earlier, when she was dating Mario's brother Eduardo. Eva and Eduardo dated for about nine months before Eva ended it. Even as she broke Eduardo's heart (that's what Eduardo said), Eva did it in the classiest, most considerate way possible. It had been the right time – she was concerned that Eduardo was preparing to propose, and she wanted to nip it in the bud.

Eva had gotten to know Mario and Janice well. She had spent numerous weekends with Eduardo, at the Garramones' Hamptons estate, in their "Williamsburg Suite," a guest suite named after all the Revolutionary War artifacts from Williamsburg, Virginia, adorning the walls. Mario and Eduardo's mother had lived in Williamsburg for a few years before she passed away, and every time the boys visited her, they collected a few trinkets of Revolutionary history.

Eva was an accomplished golfer (not Eduardo's game), so Mario invited Eva to play at the Parkview Club on several occasions. Eva carried a 9 handicap, having been bitten by the golf bug when her father introduced her to the game back in Colombia. Mario claimed to possess a 15 handicap, when he was closer to an 11. He routinely "forgot" to report his lowest scores; doing so would have lowered his handicap and he wouldn't have been able to swindle his cronies out of their weekend wagers so easily. Much to his chagrin, Eva beat Mario every time they played. And she did so with a smile.

It didn't take Eva long to discern Mario's chauvinistic ways. She routinely caught him gawking at her, checking out her long legs in her golf skirt, or her perfect curves in a bathing suit at the pool. Whenever the four of them went out to dinner, Mario consistently ogled Eva, making her quite uncomfortable. After all, she was dating his brother and she wanted to look good for Eduardo. Her bathing suits were indeed seductively cut to display her mind-boggling body, and her cocktail wear was intentionally beguiling and provocative. But that was for Eduardo, not Mario. Mario was just a collateral beneficiary and that irritated Eva.

Mario had the good sense never to flirt with Eva, but that was mostly out of respect for, and fear of, his brother. Aside from feasting with his eyes, Mario had behaved himself with Eva. In fact, after Eva and Eduardo broke up, Mario and Janice had Eva to their Manhattan apartment several times for dinner, and Mario had been a charming and hospitable host. For someone who had no children, Eva was fond of her friends' children and was especially enamored of Jessica and Roxanne. She offered to mentor them and help them with letters of recommendation.

Eva respected those who had achieved professional success, especially in New York, where it was so hard to come by. Mario was always on *Crain's New York Business'* lists of dealmakers of the month, and he was featured in *Bloomberg* and *Wall Street Journal* articles on a regular basis. It was clear that Mario had a seat at the big-boys' table and he was earning big-boy compensation. He was living high on the hog with his flamboyant Hamptons lifestyle, for sure, but he still had to be banking millions a year. Besides, Eva found Janice to be a refreshing and brainy conversationalist. Janice had put her NYU MBA to work for six years at Solomon Brothers and, even after she decided to stay home to raise Roxanne and Jessica, Janice kept current on global finances and politics. They were only three years apart and Eva, although herself amazingly fit and nubile, envied Janice's body. Whenever Eva stayed at the Garramones' Hamptons estate, Eva would insist that she accompany Janice to Soul Cycle, or on a long hike, or anything else Janice was doing to stay in such great shape. Together, they were a great sight – two Aphrodite-like figures, turning every male head in the Hamptons.

As Eva envisioned Mario ponying up the money for a luxury suite on her ship, she also envisioned spending quality time with Janice. In fact, she thought Janice Garramone and Becky Hirschfeld had quite a bit in common and the three of them could become good friends. In all likelihood, Mario and Harris would probably be chained to their desks back in New York and their wives would be free to join Eva on board and on trips exploring the Greek islands, hiking through Vietnamese villages, and kayaking in Peru. Eva was as interested in weaving a pleasing intellectual and social fabric for her ship as she was in landing the funds necessary to pay for it all. She picked up the handset on her sleek, black Alcatel desk telephone and dialed Mario Garramone's office number.

"Mario, Eva here."

"Well, my dear, how are you? What legal problems are you drumming up for some poor, unsuspecting bastard these days?"

"Ah, Mario, ever the cynic. And why are you answering your own phone these days? Have there been cutbacks at the bank?" Eva and Mario enjoyed ribbing each other, it was safer than allowing him to delve into anything personal.

"No, I saw your name pop up and immediately remembered that I owed you a call."

"How very lovely of you. I heard you were traipsing around Greece recently. Were you just sampling olives and octopus, or were you actually furthering bank business?"

"Eva, you never change, do you?" Mario teased, deflecting the question.

"No, I'm afraid I don't. What you see is what you get."

Mario leered, twisting Eva's clichéd phrase into his personal fantasy. He would love to get a piece of what he saw on Eva, but he knew that would never happen. He wanted badly to make a pass at Eva, but she intimidated him. In some ways, he was more afraid of her than he had been of Eduardo when his brother and Eva were dating. As much as it frustrated him, it was still hands-off with Eva.

"To what do I owe the pleasure?"

"Funny you should use that word Mario. Pleasure is precisely what I'm calling you about."

She wasn't making it easier. Just the sound of her voice got him hard.

"Oh really?" responded Mario, in his deepest, most curious voice.

"I'm going to ignore that tone in your voice, you old lech. You're too old for that kind of pleasure anyway." Before Mario could respond, Eva continued. "I'm buying a boat and I want you to be a part of it. Now before you say anything, let me tell you all about it."

For the next 20 minutes, Eva expounded upon her project. Mario listened patiently. Eva knew she was gaining traction with him.

"Sounds like you've really thought this thing through. But what about you? What about your life in New York? What about your law partners who anxiously await whatever crumbs you throw them, what do they say about all this?"

"First, its none of their business. I'm a big girl and I can do what I please. Second, I've busted my ass in this town for almost thirty years. I've made a lot of money for myself, and I've made a lot of money for everyone else. I don't owe anyone anything. I owe myself the opportunity to enjoy whatever lifestyle I want."

Eva sounded adamant and Mario knew better than to run into a buzz saw. Addressing things another way, he asked, "Why don't you just take a long-term rental in the Presidential Suite of a Celebrity cruise ship? Or one of the more elite ones, like Silver Seas?"

"I thought my skills as an orator and persuader were better than they apparently are today. Or you just weren't paying attention, my dear Mario. A cruise ship hosts thousands of people every week. Many of them are not as sophisticated as you are, my dear. And on some of those massive ships, the atmosphere can be like a Sandals or Club Med. Don't get me wrong – some people love it and it's a great vacation opportunity for them. This ship I'm putting together would only travel with a couple of hundred. And we will *own* the ship, so we can decorate the luxury suites however we like, leave our clothes in the luxury suites, and come and go as we please. Think of it the same as you do that marvelous apartment of yours on Park Avenue and 84th Street. You can live in it every day of the year, just come on weekends, or stay for a month or two whenever you please. You can leave the office on a Wednesday afternoon, fly to Singapore, and sail through Indonesia for a few weeks. Whenever you feel like it, you pack your briefcase back up, jump on an airplane, and fly back to New York."

"Would we be able to transact business on the ship?"

"Business functions, yes. We'll have free Internet and telephone service wherever we are in the world. Probably videoconferencing, too. But if you're talking about conducting business among suite owners ... The entire point is enjoyment and relaxation. I don't want the suite owners to feel they are prey for some smart, sophisticated, handsome New York banker wolf like you. That wouldn't make it fun at all."

She was blatant, but Mario couldn't help but be delighted by the flirting. Should he follow that path? Were moments like these an opening? The image of her in a bikini aside a shipboard pool filled his head. "How are you…" He stopped. His voice was too husky. He cleared his throat. "How are you going to arrange for free telephone service?"

Good one Mario, he thought. Way to ride the moment.

"Well, it wouldn't be free, per se. Like many of the other expenses on the ship, it would be subsumed in your quarterly condo-association cost."

The moment was gone. He knew it. Probably just as well, he thought, allowing himself one more image of her in a bikini, walking away. Great ass, he remembered.

"What about food and beverage expenses," asked Mario. "Are they included in the condo association charges as well?"

"No, there will be a food and beverage minimum levied against every owner, the same as you pay at your fancy Parkview Club – that club atmosphere, that's what we'll be cultivating on the ship. There will be a very strict dress code and rules of conduct…"

Mario could swear she slowed down as she hit the words "Strict. Dress. Code." He closed his eyes. She was back, but now in black boots and a black-lace bustier, standing over him…

"…maybe you can even help us out by sharing some of the regulations and bylaws from your precious Parkview Club."

"Yes, yes, of course. Can you tell me more about the 'rules of conduct'?"

Tell me the rules, Eva…

Explaining all the details and minutia about the ship was getting tiresome for Eva by now. God, they're all alike, she thought. But, if I'm asking for millions of dollars, I suppose it's only right that they be free to ask as many questions as they like.

She elaborated some more on the dress code and rules of conduct. She couldn't quite tell, but it was like Mario was listening intently but not really listening at the same time. She needed to snap him into focus. "So," she summed up, her voice firm and precise, "your thoughts?"

Mario got a jolt, like he'd been caught by Eva. He was embarrassed and thrilled at the same time. "It's an interesting concept, that's for sure. And Lord knows I'd like to get away from the City throughout the year."

The sex part of his brain shut down, the business part ramped up. I could entertain the bank's clients on the ship, he thought. Then I could write off a considerable amount as IRS-approved travel and entertainment. Or better yet, I might just be able to have the bank reimburse me for the money...

Mario also thought about Melanie Hunter and how impressed she would be jetting to his luxury suite on his super yacht. And there would be plenty more Melanie Hunters. He could entertain them in privacy away from New York and away from Janice, his daughters, and his office. How wonderful he imagined this could be. Would Janice even have to know about it? He could disguise his trips to the yacht as business trips. He'd explain that he would occasionally have to be resident overseas to help his bank. With seamless Internet and telephone service, how would she ever know? He already traveled extensively, so it wouldn't really be that big a difference to Janice. Eva would have her friends on, too, and if they looked anything like Eva, this floating paradise could become his floating brothel.

"Eva, I'm a banker. Eventually I have to ask – how much does all this cost?" Mario's tone was firm, but friendly.

Eva paused briefly before responding. She liked Mario and wanted him to be part of the community. Besides, all the owners would eventually know how much each had paid for his luxury suite. She couldn't really gouge him the way she had Harris.

"For the size of the luxury suite you'd want, $20 million gets it done. Of course, there are bigger ones but, frankly, I don't think you need anything that size. There are smaller luxury suites, all the way down to the $8 million range. But I don't think one of those befits a man of your so highly regarded stature," she ribbed him.

"Eva, I think I'm going to do this," Mario exclaimed boldly. "I'll need until the end of the week to look at a few things, but don't give away my luxury suite just yet."

Eva felt relieved. Another pitch, another close.

Damn,       I'm       good,       she       thought.

# CHAPTER TWENTY-NINE

Once the Garramones returned to the city from the Hamptons and began their back-to-school fall routine, Rolando cleaned up from the Labor Day weekend festivities. Well, Rolando didn't really clean anything himself. He waited for Josephine to come at 9:00 Tuesday morning. A thirty-nine-year-old Mexican divorcee who looked at least ten years older, she would change all the linens, do the laundry, refresh the bathrooms, wash the floors – especially the kitchen and dining areas where there were sticky patches from spilled mojitos – and generally tidy the house. Josephine came two days a week when the family was not in residence. When they were there, she came every day. Janice liked to have the house maintained in pristine fashion.

Josephine originally worked for Janice's friend, Mindy Davis but after Mindy's divorce, she did not have as much need for Josephine and Mindy cut her back to one day a week, Fridays. Janice took Josephine. All went fine at first; Janice was thrilled with her diligent work ethic. But the more Josephine accomplished, the more it became apparent to Janice that

Rolando was a slacker. Heavily compensated, he was nothing more than a referral source in a network of cronyism, and an odd pal of Mario's. Josephine appeared to do all the work. Rolando gradually became aware of Janice's fondness for Josephine, and Janice's increasingly cold shoulder towards him. He started to worry about his job. He was no idiot, that's for sure. One week, when the Garramones were in New York, Rolando approached Josephine and hinted that, as the man with oversight responsibilities for the house, he might need to reduce her hours. Josephine was devastated. She was living paycheck to paycheck – or cash to cash – as it was. Rolando allowed Josephine to operate under this threat of intimidation for the next several days before finally using the situation to his full advantage.

On Thursday afternoon, following Labor Day weekend, Rolando told Josephine he would need her help with some special projects the following day. He knew very well Friday was the only day Josephine still worked for Mindy Davis, and there was no way she could shirk that responsibility, especially with Mindy having guests coming for the weekend. Josephine explained all this to Rolando and asked if her daughter, Maria, could work instead. Rolando had met Maria, a sixteen-year-old senior at Hampton Bays Senior High, on several occasions and he found her to be most attractive, with an appreciably mature figure for her age. Rolando immediately hatched a fantasy that quickly became a plan. He told Josephine that Maria would be a suitable substitute but that they had to perform a deep cleaning of the pool on Friday – Maria should bring a bathing suit.

The next day, after Maria had labored through her

morning tasks and Rolando had luxuriated with his morning coffee, he told her to meet him by the pool in 20 minutes. She did – in a shocking red bikini that accentuated her bronze skin and ample breasts. She didn't have many bathing suits to choose from, and that's what sixteen-year-old Hampton girls wore anyway. They didn't exactly traffic in matronly. Rolando could barely contain his excitement – he didn't even try. He hungrily eyed every inch of her firm, dark body. Maria was a Latin beauty in every sense of the word. Not only was she abundantly endowed, but she had long, black hair that draped down her back, straight as a curtain of silk. Her eyes were large and dark, like two perfectly configured balls of shiny obsidian.

Rolando produced two wire brushes and explained that they would have to get in the pool and brush the algae ring off the water line around the circumference. This was necessary before closing the pool for the fall and winter. He threw two thick foam pool mattresses into the water – floating work stations – and turned on the outdoor stereo. Brazilian music, Maria's favorite.

Rolando could be very charming, and it was this charm that had saved him on more than one occasion. As they chatted and joked while they worked, Maria teased that the job could go much better with a cold beer. That was all the opening Rolando needed. After waiting a consciously calibrated few seconds, he agreed and raised her bid: getting high would make the work even more fun. When Maria agreed, Rolando pounced on the idea. He disappeared and came back holding the thickest blunt Maria had ever seen. She laughed innocently as Rolando lit it and passed it to her.

They floated on the pool mattresses for a while and did scrape some algae off the pool walls. Within the hour, Maria's red bikini lay on the floor of Rolando's bedroom as he entered her again and again, both laughing, moaning, and screaming with pleasure and ecstasy. Rolando had gotten exactly what he wanted.

Hours later, after they had each been completely satisfied, numerous times, Maria dragged herself out of Rolando's bed, grabbed a quick shower, and headed out to the driveway where she had parked her 2002 Honda Civic. The effects of the pot had totally worn off, but she was buzzing with an intense post-sex high. She thought about going back upstairs, back to Rolando's bed, back to Rolando's powerful arms – but the sun was fading. Her mother would be suspicious, so she declined another smoke and another orgasm.

Rolando was completely pleased with himself. His total satisfaction with screwing a pretty young thing lingered in waves, and he relished the moment. In the moment, there was just pleasure – no thought of the future, no thought of the potential consequences of his seduction.

Consequences – what consequences? For example, Maria could tell her mother that Rolando had plied her with drugs. What could Josephine do with that? It would give her terrific leverage over Rolando if he ever tried to cut her hours. Worse, if Maria ever told their secret, Rolando could be arrested and charged with statutory rape of a minor. It was a big risk. But in the moment, none of that mattered. In the moment Rolando was as smug as the Cheshire Cat.

After Maria left, Rolando went about his usual routine, striding through the house and making sure things were in order. The house was in a state of disarray; not a lot had gotten done that day. The bathrooms still needed to be tidied, garbage cans emptied. Rolando wasn't about to do any of that, but he was keen to make a task list so he could reach out to his squadron of immigrant friends.

In the master bedroom, he noticed that the bracket holding one side of the bookshelves had become disengaged from the wall. We'll need a carpenter to remount the whole thing, he thought. Looking out the window, he noticed a massive yellow-jacket nest in one of the branches right outside the bedroom window. If the family opened the window, the bedroom would surely be lousy with yellow jackets within minutes. That's a call to the exterminator.

Rolando was aware of his weaknesses, and a sterling memory was not among his strengths. It was even more clouded after smoking dope. He knew he needed to make a list. Not seeing any paper on the desk, he reached into the garbage can, and grabbed a piece of discarded stationary. On the back he wrote: Juan/bookcase, Eddie/yellow-jacket nest. He tucked the paper into the back pocket of his jeans and went about the rest of his house tour.

After he whipped up a black-bean burrito for dinner and replayed in his mind the highlights of his afternoon conquest, it was time to call his friends to set some appointments. He removed the crumpled paper from his pocket and set it on his desk. For the first time he looked at the paper's other side. There, in Janice's clear handwriting, was the outline of a list of the Garramones' assets, with dollar numbers ascribed to each one. The names of two men and a woman were scribbled at the bottom of the page. Ordinarily, Rolando would not have known any of these names, or who these people were, but one of them, Frank Saltieri, was the employer of his friend in neighboring Quogue, and Rolando knew Mr. Saltieri to be Long Island's most famous and ruthless matrimonial lawyer. He had no idea who the other man was, Mitchell Goldblatt, or the woman, Melanie Hunter, but he definitely knew Saltieri's name. Rolando might not have been the smartest man in the county, but upon discovering a list of assets and the name of a divorce lawyer, he smelled trouble.

His cushy job might melt away like an ice pop at a county fair in August if the family split up, he thought to himself.

If Mr. Garramone didn't know about this, Rolando surely would curry favor by bringing it to his attention. Between the explosive afternoon with Maria, and the discovery of this smoking gun, Rolando's adrenaline was pumping like crazy.

It had been a big day. He lit another joint and tucked himself into bed.

# CHAPTER THIRTY

ank Blaser entered the Garramones' 1930s-era apartment building on Park Avenue and East 84th Street ready to get to work with Roxanne. A few minutes after Jose the doorman called upstairs, and with her hair neatly bunched on top of her head, Janice first set her eyes on Hank: a 6'3" Adonis, just as the Spence mother had described. The Spence mom had left out a few details: his perfectly sculpted biceps, more than evident under the short sleeves of his white Garth Brooks Live in Dallas tee shirt. Nor did she mention his fabulous wingspan, the chiseled deltoids and lats. And just behind the large blue G on his shirt were Hank's enviable abs and obliques. A modern-day Hercules. Even more enticing were his Caribbean-blue eyes and his golden locks. The total package looked like something out of a Bjorn Borg underwear ad. Janice stifled a gasp – he was *that* gorgeous.

"Ms. Garramone?" He knew it was her, he was just asking to be polite.

"Yes. Hank?" blurted out Janice. She immediately felt self-conscious, like a school girl. "Nice to see you," she continued.

It was nice to see him, that's for sure, she thought.

"C'mon in and I'll fetch Roxanne." Janice said, leading Hank to the dining room table. "Rox, Mr. Blaser's here."

"Please, call me Hank," he said.

A few seconds later, Roxanne and her mother appeared in the hallway leading from the girls' bedrooms. Roxanne looked bored. But once she got a glimpse of Hank, she stood up a little straighter, puffed her small chest out a bit higher, and tried her best to conceal the tingling sensation that was pulsating throughout her body. Hank caught it all. He noticed, too, that Janice had pulled her own hair back off her face in the few moments she had disappeared down the hall to fetch Roxanne.

"Nice to meet you," offered Hank, thrusting out his enormous paw.

"You, too," stammered Roxanne, already thinking of a clever tagline to add to her Instagram story as soon as she could sneak into the bathroom and update her posting.

"Your mother's told me a lot about you. I'm anxious to begin."

So am I, thought Roxanne.

So am I, thought Janice.

For the next 60 minutes, as they sat at the dining room table, Hank outlined for Roxanne his plan of attack for SAT preparation, got to know Roxanne generally, and started her on some math problems and test-taking games. Throughout, Janice hovered in the background, fussing from the kitchen to the living room, necessitating several passes through the dining room. Twice Janice asked whether she could bring them anything to drink, or some fruit. The second time, Roxanne rolled her eyes in a way that said: "Really? Aren't you going to leave us alone?" Although she found Hank gorgeous, Roxanne was a diligent student and she was presently more concerned about getting the best test-preparation assistance available. She was oblivious to her mother's degree of interest in Hank.

As a mother, Janice was interested in judging the level of Hank's proficiency to make sure her daughter was getting the best service available and that her money was being well spent. As a woman, she was just mesmerized by this breathtaking specimen at her dining room table. How could she eat supper at that same place without thinking of him? Thinking of those amazing arms. Of those eyes. Of that infectious laugh. Why couldn't she be the one studying for the SAT? He was wasted on Roxanne.

She knew it was strange that she was so consumed with visions of this boy she had just met. It made no sense. But that letter couldn't be erased from her mind. *"Special position on his staff. Trip to Miami Beach later this month."* That whore, Melanie. Mario was having his fun in the flesh. Why couldn't she indulge her fantasies, as long as she didn't act on them? Her thoughts were hot, but harmless. Mario's had been gross, and harmful. There was a difference, she reasoned. A big difference.

As the first tutoring session drew to a close, Janice led Hank to the door of the apartment and explained her desire to have Cara English join the SAT-prep undertaking, with Hank tutoring Roxanne and Cara together. "Well, I'll consider that," Hank said, "but I'd need to meet Cara first – and there'd be an additional charge."

Janice's well-plucked, light brown, eyebrows rose a tad. Hank assured her. "I don't mean it would be double, just a nominal increase... I mean, I've never structured anything like this before... would an extra $200 be fair?" Janice smiled. The boy was gorgeous and reasonable. She assented to the conditions.

Roxanne and Hank had already gone over their respective schedules and made plans for their next two prep meetings. Janice agreed to contact Gillian English to tell Cara about the planned dates so they would all be on the same page and could begin working together in earnest at the next session. But after this, Janice was content to leave the scheduling to the girls and Hank, as much as she would have liked to remain involved in the discussions with this man-boy.

# CHAPTER THIRTY-ONE

Eva walked twelve blocks downtown to meet with her financial advisor, Matthew Harrison of AXA Equitable, at his offices at 1290 Avenue of the Americas. No self-respecting New Yorker called it "Avenue of the Americas" though; it was 6th Avenue. In fact, calling it Avenue of the Americas was a screaming signal to every yellow-cab driver in the fleet that you were a tourist and could be taken for a ride.

Eva was brilliant in almost all things, but she appreciated having professional help with her investments. She first met Matt at the campus bar, The Mug, when they were sophomores at Vassar. Matt had a few things going for him. He was one of the few male students in his class – Vassar had only gone coed a few years earlier. He was also tall, handsome, and athletic. He had been set to attend Amherst as a member of the crew team, but he separated his shoulder during senior year of high school. His mother had been a Vassar girl and was now on the board of the school, so there was some maternal pressure for him to attend that legendary and legacy Poughkeepsie institution.

Eva and Matt became quite close during that sophomore

year. Surprisingly to most of their friends, they never dated, leading some to believe, incorrectly, that Matt was gay. They were probably two of the best-looking students on campus, and both were leaders in their fields of study and extracurricular organizations. Eva was one of the editors of *The Miscellany News*, one of the oldest college weekly newspapers in the country. Matt was the leader of Matthew's Minstrels, an a cappella group named not after him, but after the college's founder, Matthew Vassar.

They had a break in their friendship when Eva went to St. Petersburg, Russia, to study abroad her junior year, while Matthew opted for an easier program in London. Still, they remained close, and Matt even visited Eva in Russia during Easter break.

Eva obtained a double major in political science and English, while Matthew focused his studies on business and economics. They both ended up in New York for graduate school, with Eva at NYU and Matt earning an MBA at Columbia. They each developed their own set of New York friends. Matt's were conservative, William F. Buckley-type political and economic junkies, while Eva's posse was more creative and Bohemian, favoring the underground clubs and party scene of the West Village. Sometimes months passed when Matt and Eva had no contact whatsoever, but their bonds were fast, and they knew the other would always be there.

As Eva and Matt began to achieve success in life, they found themselves back in touch and relying on each other's professional advice. Before settling in at AXA, Matt had made a few other stops in the financial world. Every time he got an employment agreement or a resignation package, he would have Eva read it. With laser-like focus, she zeroed in on the non-compete clauses and the non-disclosure provisions, twice saving Matt from what would have been serious mistakes.

As Eva rose through the cutthroat associate ranks of Wilson Everson, she collected ever larger bonuses each year. On Matt's advice, Eva invested those large bonuses every year in life insurance policies. Matt loved life insurance as an investment, telling Eva it was a well-kept secret among the ultra-wealthy, not simply to provide cash to your beneficiaries when you die, but to direct premium payments among a wide array of investment options, yielding strong returns through strategic investment in equity and bond portfolios. Best of all, all the investment income was tax deferred until the owner of the policy reached sixty-five.

After greeting each other in the luxurious 38th floor sky lobby, Matt and Eva strolled to Matt's office. There were no corner offices at AXA because the philosophy was not opulence, but hard work. Matthew Harrison was one of the largest producers among the two-hundred-and-thirty-eight agents in AXA's New York platform, but you'd never know it by his austere office.

Matt was wearing well-fitted, flat front Ralph Lauren khaki pants and an unusually colorful Paul Stuart shirt – pink, with light blue under cuffs which were exposed when the cuffs were rolled back in the same manner as the mannequin in the window of Paul Stuart's flagship store on Madison Avenue and 45th Street. His Vineyard Vines canvas white-trimmed belt incorporated both pink and light blue and displayed a series of nautical flags. Eva enjoyed the irony of the nautical motif. To compensate for the informality of his belt and khakis, Matthew sported $295 brown Deerfield tassel wingtip Johnston Murphy shoes, with a naval aviator's shine.

They began with a summary of the performance of Eva's accounts. By this point in her career, Eva was not simply amassing money through large bonuses; her total annual compensation had been in the $10 million range each of the past eight years. And although she bestowed some of her earnings on her friends through the decadent jaunts she organized, Eva invested most of her earnings through Matt. Friendship was very important to Eva, but it was Matt's success as an investment guru that brought Eva back to him every year. In fact, she recommended Matt to many of her partners and clients. Consequently, Matt had created a nice little cottage industry from the praises of Eva Lampedusa. Matt rewarded Eva by charging her the lowest management fees allowed by AXA's international regulations, but he still made over $300,000 a year just through his fees on the investments of Eva and her partners.

"Year-to-date you're up 11.7 percent, which is extraordinary this year," Matthew explained. "The S&P 500 is up 4.9 percent on the year, and even the Russell 2000 is up only 5.8 percent. Because we have a fair amount of your money invested in the Asian markets, we need to look at the MSCI EAFE, and even that index is only at 6.3% this year. It would have been much stronger, but for all the unrest in China that's creating market instability."

Whenever Matt got serious about explaining what he was best at, Eva was impressed. He was even kind of sexy doing it. Most importantly, he made money for her. As a little girl, Eva remembered hearing her father repeatedly remind her, "It's not what you earn, it's what you keep." She had done a remarkable job investing the majority of her income over the past twenty-some years, and Matt had done an even better job managing it for her.

Matt concluded the review, asking "Okay, any big changes in your financial picture coming up I can help you with – anything I should know about?"

"Well my dear, there's this boat . . ." Eva began. She detailed the entire financial arrangement for Matthew and explained how much money she had to raise over the next three weeks. His reaction was mixed. He asked many questions as she explained the deal she had negotiated with both the Sheik and Mitsubishi Marine. Matt was a boater himself, although his passion and budget were limited to his 2015 Sea Ray 280 Sundancer that he kept in his slip at the Glen Cove Yacht Club, a fairly pedestrian boat in a working-class boating club.

"I have to tell you that from a financial perspective, this makes absolutely no sense. More importantly, it could destroy everything you've worked for your whole career." Matthew was speaking as an objective investment advisor and as a friend. "Lemme get this right. You're planning to invest unheard of sums in a venture you really don't even understand yourself yet, having no cogent structure, with a bunch of people with nothing in common but their enormous wealth and connection to you? Oh, and after you sink in all this money, you're going to have continuing expenses of millions of dollars a year? Did I get all that right?" asked Matthew, becoming more bewildered and concerned by the minute. He was even growing agitated that the meticulous work he had performed for Eva all those years was about to go up in smoke – or down in kelp, as the case may be.

"Exactly," replied Eva, her expression unwavering.

"I mean, it sounds wonderful, like an amazing adventure, but you could wind up bankrupt if this rolls the wrong way. I can't let you make this big a mistake. Have you discussed this with your dad?" Matthew had met Eva's father on several occasions dating back to their graduation from Vassar. He knew how close Eva was to her father. But he had never invoked Eve's father's name in connection with her decisions. She was a grown woman, making millions of dollars a year, with a sensational reputation as one of the leading lawyers in the United States. But this was not just any decision – this was a $300 million decision with potentially fatal consequences.

Eva laughed. "I would have been disappointed in you if you didn't try to talk me out of it. But I'm doing this, Matthew. It's a dream. It's my dream."

"Eva, it's your life, of course. But from an investment standpoint, this doesn't make sense. It borders on being financially irresponsible. Hell no, it doesn't border on it – it's just... God, it's just dumb! I know the next thing I should say is that if this is what you really want to do, you should do it. But come on, Eva! You're talking about investing all of your life savings in this escapade."

"Matt, I love you dearly – always have and always will – and I value your financial shrewdness, but this decision has already been made, and I'm doing this. All I need from you is a way to liquidate $80 million from my portfolio by October 15th." Eva's face was as determined as Matthew had ever seen. He realized there would be no talking Eva out of it.

"How do you figure $80 million?" he asked, resigned to the fact this transaction was going to transpire and not wanting to fracture their friendship over it.

"Well, this is how I figure it. Lorraine Williams is going to be the largest investor. She's already committed $100 million. Harris Hirschfeld over at Bergman Troutman will be in for $30 million."

"Wow, how'd you get that cheap bastard to put up so much cash?"

"That was the easy part. And fun too. I appealed to his vanity and ego, both of which are colossal targets. I told him that all the big financial hitters would be on board and he assumed he would end up farming millions of dollars of business from them."

"Is that what you told him? And that got it done?"

"I didn't *tell* him that at all. I just told him who would be on the ship and that my practice is going gangbusters. He drew the conclusion himself, inaccurate as it may be. Oh, and he figured that while I'm away, he would steal my clients. I'm sure he thought of that too."

"Why inaccurate?" Matthew asked. "That sounds pretty logical to me."

"Because, my dear friend, I'm not looking at this ship as a

way to mine for clients. This is a lifestyle change for me, and for all of us. The goal is for us to be able to shed our terrestrial identities, let down our hair, and be ourselves while on board. There should be no sales pitches among the owners. And besides, I can continue to service my clients while I'm on board. I always manage to do it when I take the girls on yachting trips – this will be even better since I'm buying the best technical equipment in the world."

Eva continued. "Marc Romanello, Mario Garramone and Liam Perlmutter are each good for $20 million apiece. With Lorraine, Harris, Marc, Mario and Liam all together, we're at $190 million. If I buy a $20 million luxury suite, we get to $210 million. That leaves me $60 short of the total $270 I need. So, I need $80 million – $60 million for the overall bid and $20 million for my suite."

"Okay, but if you are going to put up all that money, why not buy a bigger luxury suite for yourself? Instead of putting so much cash into the general purchase of the ship, allocate more of it towards the purchase of your individual luxury suite. Instead of buying a $20 million share, buy an $80 million share. Then, you allocate the ownership among all your fellow owners, assigning shares based on either square footage or the monetary contribution."

Eva sat back assessing Matt's suggestion. She tried to challenge it in her mind, gaming different arguments against that idea, as she did with her clients' cases for so many years. How could she have missed this? She had been so concerned trying to raise the capital and explain the concept to her friends, she had gotten lost in the weeds, something that rarely happened to Eva. "You're a fucking genius. Of course, that makes perfect sense," squealed Eva, with all the enthusiasm of a sixteen-year-old newly elected homecoming queen.

"Of course it does, or I wouldn't have suggested it," Matt agreed, just smugly enough to be charming. "You don't pay me for stupid ideas. You pay me to manage your money, and sometimes that means managing you, Miss Lampedusa. We're a team. You come to me with your ideas and I transform them into reality."

Eva smiled. "I think you just earned yourself a week in one of our nicer visitor flats on the ship."

"Visitor flats? I want to stay in one of those fancy luxury suites."

"Well, unless you're going to convince one of my friends to lend you their luxury suite, it'll be a visitor flat for you."

"I just transformed your luxury suite into one of the two most expensive on the ship, there must be a guest bedroom in there with my name on it."

"Matthew, Matthew, Matthew, how long has it been that we've talked about shacking up together? It hasn't happened in twenty-one years, and it's not about to happen now." Eva enjoyed playing with Matt, now that the business meeting was over. She even crossed her legs so that the slit in her orange floral YSL skirt opened towards Matthew, giving him a full view of her shapely leg, not too far below where her underwear should have been. His eyes immediately dropped to her taut thighs, as she fully expected they would. But then he caught himself and jiggled his focus back to reality. She smiled. He choked.

"Tell me again – when do you need this money?"

"October 16th. But since I'm wiring most of it to Mitsubishi's office in Japan, I would like to get it there the morning of the 15th. I don't want to become embroiled in a dispute about whether it was paid on October 16, New York time, or October 16, Tokyo time. And the other part, the $50 million, gets wired to the Sheik that same day. As great an investor as you are, I can't imagine that twenty-four hours will make such a meaningful difference in my account."

Matthew smiled. Although $80 million of funds under his management umbrella was walking out the door, his friendship with Eva remained intact and he had provided her with sound financial advice. Moreover, with all her rich, hot shot friends on the ship, Eva might just pimp Matt's investment excellence to a few of them. And there wouldn't be anything wrong with that, he reasoned.

# CHAPTER THIRTY-TWO

L ater that day, the Garramones drove back out to the Hamptons for the first post-Labor Day weekend of the summer. It was around this time every summer, after the girls had gone back to school, that the Garramones' trips to the Hamptons became less frequent. From every weekend to every other weekend, then by middle of October, they would be down to once a month, scheduling their visits to coincide with friends' birthday parties or events at the Parkview Club. By then, most of the shops on Hill Street would be closed for the season, shuttered until the trees had once again filled themselves with the new growth of spring, private schools in the city were released for summer vacation, and the lifeguards were back in their legendary (and still classic) white wooden towers.

But this September weekend the sun was still shining brightly, the stores still open and the Garramones' friends were still squeezing out the last drops of summer fun. Pat Monahan had arranged to fit into Mario's foursome for Sunday morning. Mindy Davis and Gillian McNulty were taking a "power walk" and had invited Janice to join them.

Power walking was an upper crust way of turning the simple act of putting one foot in front of the other into a putative sporting event. The women of Southampton believed that by simply describing a brisk walk with the word "power," it somehow elevated the mundane to an athletic endeavor. Then, after walking scarcely half a mile, they would all compress themselves into the Golden Pear where any calories they might have burned off were quickly restored by the macchiato and blueberry muffins they consumed.

In between mouthfuls of muffins, all news items were covered: their children's academic prowess, their recent sartorial acquisitions, the latest efforts of the Army Corps of Engineers to rehabilitate the precious sand dunes along Dune Road, or intimate gossip about their fellow blue-blooders' latest separations and divorces. It was this last subject that riled the women more than anything else. No sport was as rewarding as discussing the marital failure of someone in their little clique. It was uncanny how these women could revel in the sufferings of their friends, but they did. They gnawed on each other's misfortunes like seagulls picking at the carcasses of the bluefish that had been washed ashore just a few blocks to the east. And both stank.

While Janice chin-wagged with her cronies, Roxanne and Jessica remained asleep. Another pot-filled party at Ben's Den, a weekly Friday night happenstance whenever the rich kids of the Hamptons were assembled, had deprived them of their vitality, as well as a few brain cells and some of their honor.

Careful not to wake his daughters from their beauty sleep

and clad in blue and white seersucker shorts a full week past the Labor Day deadline arbitrarily deemed appropriate by the fashion disciples, Mario descended the center staircase. He entered the kitchen where Rolando was busy slicing and dicing vegetables with impressive precision while Brazilian folk music played softly in the background. The dining room table was set for one: *The New York Times* folded perfectly in half on a yellow and blue hand painted Mexican ceramic plate.

"Good morning, Mario," Rolando greeted him warmly. Mario had long ago insisted that Rolando call him and Janice by their first names; he hated formality in the house. He was surrounded by enough stiffs at the bank and the Parkview Club and he abhorred unnecessarily formal behavior in his home. Of course, when the Garramones entertained, it was always, "How may I assist you, Mrs. Garramone?" and "Is there anything more I can bring you, Mr. Garramone?" but when it was just the family, things were appreciably more relaxed.

"Good morning, Rolando. What's going on today? Where is everyone? The girls are still sleeping?" he asked, knowing full well they were.

Rolando just smiled and rolled his eyes. If his daughters ever got up before noon it would be such a shock for Mario, he might have needed cardiac intervention.

"What's that I smell?"

"Fresh avocados, onions and garlic," explained Rolando.

"Not together, I hope," replied Mario, smiling.

"No, not together. But they'd all go together quite well in an omelet, if you like." Rolando's omelets were the freshest, fluffiest and tastiest omelets in all of Southampton.

"Throw in some mushrooms and peppers and you've got a sale," beamed Mario. He wandered out of the kitchen and plopped into his seat at the near end of the enormous, nineteenth century chestnut dining room table that seated sixteen when the social mavens of Southampton were over for nattering and gossiping, otherwise known as dinner.

He opened the *Times* and scanned the front-page article about Nancy Pelosi chastising Donald Trump for skirting the edges of ethical boundaries. Skimming the rest of the news – bad job growth numbers, another terrorist attack in Syria, rising national debt – was no fun. The depressing news infected Mario's mood. It was all as welcome as a Lyme-carrying deer tick. Time enough for all that solemn real-world stuff back in the city.

Turning to the sports page, his mood abruptly brightened. An avowed Mets fan, Mario was delighted by the Yankees' September swoon. His beloved orange and blue Queens boys had themselves faded already – and misery loves company.

Rolando pranced into the dining room bearing Mario's omelet and another gift, although not a welcome one – news of the scrap paper he had found in Janice's garbage can. He placed the silver rimmed plate in front of his boss and shuffled his feet nervously. He wanted to tell Mario what he had discovered but could not slow the rush of anxiety charging through his brain. Rolando never sat with Mario when Mario ate, and this was not the opportune first time for that. He mumbled something about pink Himalayan sea salt and some sort of pepper from Sri Lanka he intended to procure from Citarella later that afternoon as he retreated from the dining room, sweating like an unprepared, nervous fat boy at a spelling bee.

After he finished breakfast, Mario walked his dish into the kitchen. It was the way he was raised, he always brought his own dishes back into the kitchen. Rolando puttered about the outsized kitchen nervously, fastidiously picking up little things and putting them into drawers. He didn't make eye contact with Mario.

"Is everything all right, Rolando?" Mario asked. Often, when Rolando had problems, he shared them with Mario. Mario took pride in his knack for giving good advice.

"I'm fine. I mean there's nothing wrong with *me*," he said.

"Well, what is it then? Is one of your friends in trouble?"

"Can we talk?" At this point, Rolando's mouth was racing three times faster than his brain. "I mean, there's something I want you to know. I mean, there's something I should probably tell you. It's like this. Well, how do I say ... I saw something, and I don't know ... I'm just ..."

"For God's sake, Rolando, just spit it out."

"I saw something. I found something. I found a piece of paper."

"And?" Mario asked, becoming increasingly agitated.

Rolando drew in a deep breath and composed himself. "I found a piece of paper in Janice's garbage can. I wasn't snooping or anything like that. I needed to write something down and I didn't have any paper. So, I went in the garbage can." His voice was once again becoming progressively more animated. "Anyway, when I looked at it, I noticed there was writing on the other side."

"And?" pleaded Mario, growing increasingly uncomfortable.

"And it was Janice's handwriting. It talked about this house, the New York apartment and bank accounts. And it had Mr. Saltieri's name on it. Frank Saltieri from over on ..."

"I know where Frank lives, Rolando. What on earth does he have to do with any of this?"

"His name was on the paper. The paper I found."

"What paper? Where did you say ... Never mind – do you still have it?"

"Yeah, lemme go get it." Rolando almost fell as he galloped out of the kitchen and sprinted up the stairs to his little room on the far side of the third floor. There, tucked neatly under this desk blotter, was the note that had cost him more than a significant amount of sleep the past few nights. Rolando clutched the paper tightly as if it were his prize possession. He flew down the stairs, two at a time. He was titillated and excited, though he didn't know exactly why. Drenched from perspiration, he was Rolando being Rolando, almost experiencing orgasm through chaos.

Slowing himself to a canter, he handed Mario the note, a bit more wrinkled and a lot moister than it had been sixty seconds earlier.

As he had left his reading glasses in the dining room, Mario squinted at Janice's unmistakable handwriting. Sure enough, there was a complete list of their marital assets. Mario was stricken with a sharp pang of insignificance as his entire net worth – his life – had been reduced to scratchings on a 5 x7 piece of paper. It was all there – 993 Park Avenue, 2 Captain's Neck

Lane in Southampton, the small winter weekend-getaway apartment at 200 Ocean Trail Drive in Jupiter, Florida. Also: bank accounts, brokerage accounts and other assorted holdings. Why would she do this?

He studied the page intently, finding Mitchell Goldblatt's name alongside Frank Saltieri's. He had no idea who this Goldblatt character was but there was no mistaking the starkness of the other name – Frank Saltieri. His name was legendary among the Hamptons' well-heeled, maritally-challenged aristocracy. He was a shark, a famously aggressive, bellicose, take-no-prisoners divorce lawyer whose mere name on a court filing could materially alter the strategy of opposing counsel. A nasty bastard who was thrown out of the Quogue Golf Club because he was having an affair with a woman he was representing in her divorce action.

Mario scanned the page further. He stopped, numb. There it was, written in his wife's charming, feminine hand – Melanie Hunter. He was stunned. Beyond stunned. He was totally dumbfounded. How did his wife even know that name? Melanie Hunter – this was his secret weapon at work, his concubine – why was her name on this same sheet of paper? Melanie Hunter – she had nothing to do with his assets or Frank Saltieri. Why was her name here? In seconds, Mario felt as though sweat was streaming out of every pore of his head. How did Janice know that name, and what could she know? What did she know?

Mario snatched the paper off the counter abruptly and stormed upstairs to his bedroom. He switched on his MacBook Pro and entered the name Mitchell Goldblatt. Within seconds, although it seemed like a week, the screen filled with citations to Goldblatt, Haddad & Stein, matrimonial lawyers. Goldblatt himself was something of a big deal because he had chaired the American Bar Association's Section on Matrimonial Law only two years earlier. Shit, this can't be good, Mario thought. And Melanie Hunter. That gnawed at him more than anything else. That just wouldn't go away. There it was – in Janice's cold, stylish, blue cursive.

As much as Mario's wanted to, he could not deny the obvious. Janice must have heard something about Mario's fling with Melanie Hunter in London or Greece. She *had* to know. There was no other explanation. Melanie Hunter's name, the assets, the divorce lawyers. Fuck, this was bad. Really bad. Not only did she know about Melanie, but she was already gaming her next step. The last time Janice caught Mario having an affair, she warned him there would be no more second – or third as the case was – chances.

Mario's mind flooded with more thoughts, concerns, and strategies than he could keep up with. What should he say when she returned from her walk? How should he act towards her? Should he let on that he knew something? Was it better to play it cool and avoid the subject, or address it head-on? Who else had she told? Did anyone at the club know? Did the girls know? Had she already contacted one of these lawyers? Whom should he retain? Should he call Saltieri or Goldblatt and retain them just to keep her away from them? He had a friend, Harvey Jacobs, who had done just that five years earlier. He retained five of the top divorce lawyers in New York, paying each one a minimal retainer of a few thousand dollars, just so they would be conflicted out of representing his wife.

Mario wanted a drink. He never drank during the day, but today was different. Shit, it was only 10:30 in the morning. He couldn't drink now. He had to be strong. He had to think. He had to act.

"Dad, are you in there?" came the voice from outside his closed bedroom door. It was Jessica. She was never up this early. Why today?

"Sure, honey, c'mon in."

"Rox and I want to know if we can drive to Montauk today."

"Sure."

Jessica was surprised. Her father always had a million probing questions whenever the girls wanted to go out. It was not that Mario was overly inquisitive, but he was a protective parent and a seasoned litigator. He usually wanted to know where they were going, who they were going to be with, when they would be back, whose car they were taking, all the details. But Jessica was no dummy. She had asked and gotten the answer. No need to stick around any longer for her father to ask questions or, even worse, change his mind. Don't sell past the sale, she thought to herself.

Mario wasn't totally unaware of what he was doing. He had instinctively reasoned it would be better for the girls not to be in the house when Janice came home. Ten minutes later, he heard the purr of Roxanne's Mazda pulling out of the driveway.

Mario felt nauseous and his chest was growing tight. His

daily Nexium regime was not working. He looked in the medicine cabinet for Pepto Bismol. Damn, it had expired six months earlier. So he took twice the amount of that disgusting pink syrup than indicated on the label. He sat in his chair bewildered, numb and sweating. He couldn't process what to do next. He thought of the girls and their reaction when they found out their parents were divorcing.

And how would this affect him at the bank? The CEO position? Would a divorce have any impact on the supposedly inevitable promotion? He quickly convinced himself that it wouldn't – Frank Huggins, the current CEO, was on his third wife, and his last divorce had kept the gossip pages in the New York press busy for months. He would just have to keep it low key, and that probably meant not mounting much of a fight. So, capitulate and settle with Janice. That would definitely have a better shot at not attracting any media attention than if he engaged one of those divorce monsters to unleash holy hell on Janice.

Besides, what had she done wrong? Nothing. She had given up her career and resigned from her job at Solomon Brothers to stay home and raise their two daughters. She had been an exemplary mother, the kind any man would want to raise his children. He had no reason to believe she had ever been unfaithful or had violated her marriage vows in any way. So how would he mount an attack? It repulsed him to consider how one of these courthouse leviathans might bring pain to Janice. No, she didn't deserve it. I screwed up, Mario thought, and I'll have to pay for it.

He heard the electronic beep indicating someone had opened the front door. It was Janice.

He considered going downstairs to meet her. But he waited. He really had no idea what to say to her, but he knew he had to say something. His personality would not allow this elephant to roam the room unrestricted. It had to be met, addressed and dealt with.

Janice had enjoyed a nice power-walking session with her friends, including Mindy Davis, who had shared her own divorce story with Janice a week ago. Halfway through their walk, Mindy and Janice scooted ahead of the rest of the ladies.

"So?" Mindy lowered her voice, so the others couldn't hear. "How'd he take it?"

Janice stalled. "Take what?"

"When you lowered the boom?"

Sheepishly, Janice admitted, "I haven't said anything yet. He doesn't know I know." Mindy spent the next 20 minutes coaching Janice.

Janice climbed the stairs to their bedroom. She felt sick. She still didn't know what she was going to say to him. But she knew the time had come.

When Janice reached the room, Mario was sitting at his desk chair. He swiveled around to face her.

For the next two hours, Mario offered humbling apology after apology, admitting everything. He promised to make the separation as painless and fair as possible. Tears filled his eyes as he confessed and said all the right things that would allow Janice to hold her head high.

As Janice listened, it was as if she was experiencing an out-of-body encounter. Mario confessed that he had been screwing this Melanie Hunter person in his bank. The Greek deal had been canceled when they were in London, but they nevertheless went to Athens to frolic on the beach, he admitted. Without prompting, he told her that they were planning to go to Miami Beach in a month, but now swore that he would cancel that trip. Janice knew about the trip already. It was in the note.

Janice didn't want an acrimonious divorce. More than anything, she wanted to save her daughters and herself that ignominy. As Mario continued to cry and confess his cheating ways, Janice began to wonder if divorcing at all, and the destruction of their family home, was really the best for everyone. Roxanne was about to begin her senior year of high school and Jessica was only two years behind. Wouldn't it be better for them if Janice stuck out the marriage for just two more years so the girls' last years of high school need not be turned upside down?

She listened as Mario begged her forgiveness. She hated him for what he had done, but it was complicated – he sounded so miserable, his contrition so complete. He was beginning to sound like the sincere and honorable man she had married twenty-one years earlier. And besides, she knew she would undoubtedly be able to extract some fantastic concessions from him in exchange for not publicly revealing his moral lapses. She was in the driver's seat, and that helped ease some of the pain.

Why should his screwup ruin what they both had worked to build – his becoming CEO of the bank, and all the prestige and income that went along with it. She too had been sitting quietly and planning for that eventuality. She too had skin in the game.

Other women confronted with the same situation had stuck it out and their children were better for it. Well, they all *said* that was the case. It's not like Mario and Janice were always together anyway. On the weekends, Mario was usually off playing golf or hanging out at the club with his buddies. Janice had her cadre of lady friends she spent most days with at the beach. And during the weeks Mario was always working – or screwing around while he was supposed to be working. They really didn't spend so much time together as a couple anyway.

In the span of those two hours, Janice's mindset had changed from wanting to leave the son of a bitch to be willing to give him a second chance.

This wasn't what Mario thought was going to happen. He was frightened about what Janice knew and he wanted to lay it all out on the table. He was so frightened, he was a lot more honest than he anticipated being. Because there had not been much time to think between Rolando showing him the note and Janice walking in, he hadn't really put together much of a strategy. So, he just talked – and talked, and talked. And the more he talked, and saw the tears streaming down Janice's face, the more he felt obligated to reveal. At one point, Mario wanted to end the conversation, or sweep it in a different direction, but he just kept talking, plowing ahead like a Catholic schoolgirl in the confessional the week before her first confirmation.

When it was all over, when he was spent, and he finally shut up, they cried, hugged and even smiled a bit. Mario was going to change his ways and Janice was going to forgive him. In a sense, it was a relief for them both. It would be a new beginning.

Half an hour later, Mario texted Melanie to confirm their trip to Miami.

# CHAPTER THIRTY-THREE

C arly Burke and Michelle Poverman had enjoyed a raucous weekend clubbing in New York. Thanks to Marcia Coleman, they had been able to get into two outrageous clubs in the Meatpacking District on Friday night. Although Marcia assured them nothing happens until 1:00 a.m., those two midwestern girls just refused to believe it. They got to Cielo at 10:00 p.m. Marcia had called Tony Grandelli, the bouncer, so the girls were escorted straight in – or so they thought. The "red carpet" list for the night hadn't been prepared yet, as it was so early. The ladies were allowed in because the joint was empty, and management was always happy to have two pretty, provocatively dressed women in the club. Sugar attracts bees, and bees spend money. Although generous, Marcia's call had been irrelevant.

There were two stockbrokers from Long Island, also way too early, sitting at the bar. They glommed onto Carly and Michelle and bought them drinks for a few hours. The girls were flattered and did the dullards the favor of dancing with them. One of them, a chubby fellow, had a few too many Ketel One mojitos and, eventually his right hand found itself squarely in the middle of Miss Poverman's ass while they were dancing. It had started behind her back, but then the meaty paw slunk to Michelle's hip, remaining just long enough to establish credibility, then on to the next move. His sweaty right hand dropped right onto her well exercised, perfectly rounded left cheek.

Because she had consumed three, or was it four, Cosmopolitans, it took her a few seconds to react. But when she did, it was firm and unequivocal. She grabbed his offending grappler and swung it out to the side, thrusting it downwards like it was a cockroach that had suddenly crawled up her leg. With both hands on his flabby, pendulous chest, she pushed him backwards. He would have slammed flat on his ass if he hadn't knocked into the other chubby stockbroker, who dropped his Corona, beer flying everywhere, all over Carly's shiny Jimmy Choos. That was enough of Cielo. Within ten minutes of Chunky Charlie's butt grab, Carly and Michelle were outside waiting for their Uber to arrive.

Their next stop was Purgatory, the hottest rooftop lounge in the city. The line downstairs consisted of over 100 anxious souls, each dressed more outrageously than the next in hopes of winning the bouncer's attention and entering this crazy world. This time, Marcia really did get them in. Not only had she submitted their names to the club earlier that afternoon, but she had entered the club herself about half an hour earlier and reminded the bouncer to expect her two "really good friends." Carly and Michelle didn't know that Marcia was inside. They never even saw her once they entered the pounding club, packed with bodies from Brooklyn and Queens, all trying to impress each other with fake tans, fake lips, fake hair extensions, fake eyelashes, fake boobs, and fake lives.

The scene was flamboyant and earsplitting and the cocktails they consumed made everything seem even more deafening. While Fergie was screeching about her lady lumps, Carly and Michelle spent 20 minutes at the bar trying to order a drink, then they decided it was time to leave. Michelle was tired from her trip and not at all used to headbanging music, intense crowds, and such obnoxious strutting. As they turned to plow their way through the crowd to the exit, Carly spotted something that stopped her in her tracks. Clear across the massive dance floor, in the darkest recess of the back of the room, near what appeared to be an entrance to some sort of inner sanctum, was Harris Hirschfeld.

No, it couldn't be him, she thought. That just didn't make sense. Carly immediately remembered how much he had probed her on where they were going that night. She was positive she never mentioned Purgatory. Positive. She didn't even know the name at that time. But why else would he be there? Was that really him?

She nudged Michelle to tell her, but the music and screaming dancers were so loud it was impossible. She took Michelle by the hand and pulled her through the mob of throbbing and bobbing bodies clinging to each other on the dance floor like praying mantises in flight, and marched straight for Harris. But when they got there, he was gone. He may have stolen into a private room at the back of the club. Or maybe he slipped onto the dance floor, lost among the hundreds of young couples who had just met and were already swearing their love and devotion to each other (at least for the night). Or he may not have been there at all.

The following Monday, Harris summoned Carly to his office.

"So, Ms. Burke, how was your weekend?" inquired Harris with mock formality.

"Great fun. I really enjoyed showing Michelle around the City. All your great suggestions about the Staten Island Ferry, Chinatown, and Little Italy were perfect. Thank you so much for that." Carly felt a bit queasy about complimenting Harris that much.

"Of course, Carly, of course. And how did that whole clubbing business work out for you? Were you able to get into any of the places you had in mind?"

"Yes," replied Carly, a little too curtly. She was curious about her bizarre Harris sighting (was that him?), but she also didn't want to get into a protracted discussion with him about where they went, who they were with, or anything else about the evening that was really none of his business.

"That's great. I hear stories about some people who wait on line for hours never to get in and that only gives them a terrible sense of the city."

"No, it was wonderful. Thanks for asking."

Harris changed the subject.

"Let me ask you this – have you any leads with regard to the leaking of that confidential information to the US Attorney's office?"

Carly was relieved to have the discussion turn back to business.

"Not really anything yet. I've been trying some creative ways of tracking down potential links, but I can't report anything yet."

"Have you spoken with our IT department to determine if they can track any of our lawyers' email accounts to see if they transmitted the material to the government?"

Carly was proud of herself that she had already thought of this and discounted it as an unlikely avenue for leads.

"I think that even the most technologically inexperienced lawyer or paralegal in the firm would know that any email can be traced to its sender's IP address." She knew she was right.

"Yes, now that you put it that way, I guess I'd have to agree with you. But you're on top of it, right?"

"Yes, sir," replied Carly in a staccato fashion, even snapping off a bit of a salute to Harris, who was only too pleased to raise his right hand to his own temple and return the feigned show of respect.

"Well, I'm sure Boeing and our respective firms are safe in your capable hands. Keep up the good work and let me know when you have something to share."

Carly arose from Senator Rayburn's chair and strode to the door.

Just as her hand touched the doorknob, Harris piped up. "Say, you never told me, what did you think of Cielo?"

Carly thought of the chunky stockbrokers.

"It was fine, I guess. Nothing special."

As soon as she pulled shut the large pine door of Harris's office behind her, a chilling thought raced through her mind. She froze. She had never told him they were going to Cielo. In fact, it wasn't until after she had left the office last Thursday afternoon that Marcia had texted her and told her about Cielo. How could he possibly know? Had she seen him in Cielo? No, that was Purgatory, she reassured herself with absolute certainty. Had he been in Cielo and then followed them to Purgatory? Wow, that would be creepy. More than creepy, that would be stalking. Visibly unsettled, Carly rode the elevator down three floors to her office.

She shut the door and called Michelle.

# CHAPTER THIRTY-FOUR

When she was a little girl, Eva was smitten with her father's hackneyed expressions, like "when it rains, it pours."

Eva remembered it came from the label on the Morton salt cannister her mother kept in the kitchen. The little girl in a yellow dress against a dark blue background, walking in the rain with an opened umbrella and holding a container of salt. With an umbrella in one hand, she was oblivious to the fact that the container of salt she clung to under her other arm was upside down, the salt pouring to the ground, as she was pelted by sheets of rain.

"When it rains, it pours," her father would say, cheerfully. This week had been no exception. After Eva had left Matt Harrison's office – achieving her goal of raising the $270 million – she received a few inquiries from friends of Lorraine Williams, Harris Hirschfeld, and Liam Perlmutter. Dr. Perlmutter had provided Eva's contact information to, as well as several more of his friends, Carmine Scantello and Cindy Miller, three of whom called her.

Lorraine's friends were Dr. Oliver Rasmussen, and his wife Heidi, of Johannesburg, South Africa. Eva had met Oliver on several occasions, both in South Africa and New York. He had been the chairman of First National Bank in Johannesburg and was well regarded in international accounting and banking circles. A jolly man, who, in his sixty-eight years had perfected the art of enjoying life. After earning his Ph.D. in accounting from the University of Cape Town, Oliver had made tens of millions of dollars, just a tiny bit more than he had spent. Now on his fifth wife, he had also developed an appreciation for private jets, large yachts, vacation homes, and fine scotch. Each one cost him significantly. He paid twice for everything, once when he bought it, the second time when a wife got it in the divorce. Wife number five, Heidi, was fifty-eight but looked younger. She was a petite, blonde and demure woman who didn't drink. Oliver, on the other hand, drank scotch daily – and plentifully. Everyone who knew them wondered how she was able to tolerate Oliver's bombastic personality. He was brash, loud, and had an opinion on just about everything, even if he had no idea what he was talking about. But he was really a rough looking teddy bear. Oliver didn't make friends easily but when he did, he was a friend for life.

Based on his conversations with Lorraine, Oliver had become fascinated by Eva's project. Oliver had recently sold his 110-foot yacht and was in the process of shopping for an even larger one. He enjoyed sailing though Cape Town's harbor as the self-proclaimed Poseidon of South Africa, but Oliver knew he was too old to mess around with the details of yacht ownership. If there was a way to leave those things to others to manage, Oliver was all for it. And he was an enormously social chap, far preferring the company of others to being alone. Oliver had yarns for any occasion, and it didn't take much of an occasion to get him to unspool them. Oliver's friends had heard the same anecdotes countless times, from his discussion with President Clinton about the importance of Asian trade initiatives to his arguments with Angela Merkel about keeping the European Union together.

Oliver was not a hard sell. He agreed to purchase a $12-million luxury suite for himself and Heidi. He wanted a presence on the ship.

The second contact Eva received was from Donna Bickford, an acquaintance of Karen Romanello. Like many women who lived in Westport, Donna was elfin and cute, sporting a lively bounce when she walked. She also had the ubiquitous blonde bob haircut of southeastern Connecticut. In almost every luxury car that drove along Post Road during the day, there was a thirty- or forty-something behind the wheel with the same blonde bob.

These Blonde Bobs filled the Stop & Shop during the mornings, the high school PTA meetings in the afternoons, and the country and golf clubs on weekends. For the most part, they were trophy wives who had been cute enough to attract their mates and pump out a few tow-headed kids and were now fully cognizant that if they slacked off in any way, by gaining a few pounds, or schlumping around in frumpy clothes, or just didn't put out regularly, they would be jettisoned in favor of another Bob. In fact, even if they did nothing wrong, sometimes their husbands would just find a new Bob more attractive than the one he had, and trade up (or down, if one were scoring by age).

Donna had been a victim of that herself. Tallying her marital history, Donna disregarded her brief marriage to Dave Edmundson, her high-school sweetheart at Westport Country Day. They had both gone to the University of Massachusetts' Worcester campus, but Dave transferred after one year to the University of Michigan, so he could enroll in the ROTC program and fly jets when he graduated. Donna and Dave maintained the long-distance relationship and married soon after Dave was commissioned a Midshipman, Third Class. The marriage had been a beautiful affair with both looking chaste and virginal in their matching white costumes: Donna in her mother's wedding dress; Dave, and all his groomsmen, in Navy dress whites. The groomsmen all held their sabers aloft, forming an arch over the happy married couple. A majestic, beautiful service.

Within six months, all hell had broken loose. Dave's commission was revoked. Assigned to Officer Candidate's School, he had been caught selling crack to an undercover military intelligence officer. When he returned home to Donna, now in Westbury, Connecticut, he deteriorated rapidly into alcoholism and started buying firearms. "A hobby," he explained.

Sensing that his boy wonder son-in-law was becoming a treacherous liability around his daughter, Donna's father imposed upon his pastor to intervene and influence Donna to accept that her marriage should meet the same fate as Dave' erstwhile military career. Marriage one was over.

It took only two years for Donna to fall eternally in love with Scott Kelly, a local real-estate star in Westport. Scott moved Donna into a spacious mansion in Westport where she had become one of the Bobs and dutifully produced two adorable girls. Scott and Donna were affectionately referred to as "Barbie" and "Ken" in their community, the All-American, smiling, happy, beautiful, and successful wunderkinds. They were extremely popular among the socialites in Westport and were content.

Scott was an outgoing fellow who loved to regale everyone with stories of his exploits as a high-school football star while he sold them expensive properties. Often one led seamlessly into the other. But leaks sprang from their little rowboat of love as Donna never quite shed the few extra pounds from her second pregnancy.

One day, during his midlife crisis, Scott insisted he need a new Mercedes convertible to properly project the image he needed to peddle high-end real estate to the Bobs and their deep-pocketed husbands. After much squabbling over their tight family budget, they agreed Scott could lease (not buy) an Audi (not Mercedes).

Scott went to the Audi dealer and fell in lust with a silver 8-speed shiftable, 2.0 T Premium Quattro convertible.

He also fell in lust with the Audi dealer, a tall redhead with shiftable speeds of her own.

Soon, that was the end of husband number two.

Don Bickford was Donna's latest and, she hoped, last husband. Don was a straightforward and well-respected executive with a hedge fund in Greenwich. Donna had no real appreciation for what a hedge fund was, or what it did. She knew a few important things about Don, however, and they all appealed to her. First, at 67, Don was thirteen years older than Donna, who was certainly not getting any more attractive, unless one found the early stages of a third chin and a gently protruding belly attractive. Don, with his silver hair and rugged good looks, on the other hand, was quite handsome and alluring for his age. He never touched drugs and was a trivial wine drinker, so he was way ahead of husband number one in that regard. He was mature, confident and relatively staid, which put him ahead of husband number two. And he was rich, very rich. So that didn't exactly turn Donna off. At this point in her life, she knew she had one last chance to marry the lottery ticket or she'd end up raising her girls in neglected Bridgeport, only a few actual miles from Westport but a social lifetime away.

Sure, Don was kind of boring, but boring men usually didn't stray too far.

Karen Romanello knew Donna through their daughters' school, Westport Country Day, Donna's alma mater. Donna's two daughters were enrolled there now, as was Karen's step-daughter. Karen's own daughter, Stacy, was enrolled in boarding school in Sydney. Both women played a significant role in the school's fund-raising efforts. They were two of the heaviest hitters, shaking down alumni and parents for maximum donations, keeping their precious prep school's endowment larger than many small private colleges.

Donna was relied upon for her contacts and connections with fellow alumnae, while Karen was revered for her strategic insight and sound business acumen. Perhaps because she had worked as General Counsel of Estee Lauder, and perhaps because she was beautiful and married to a handsome and successful retiring banker – and perhaps just because of her own self-awareness – Karen knew she was in a different league from Donna. Karen cringed when they would be lunching with a serious donor prospect and Donna's misuse of a phrase, or use of an ugly malaprop, would cost them the contribution. But they had worked closely over the years and that relationship spilled over into their personal lives. The two couples socialized regularly, and their husbands had become friends. Don Bickford and Marc Romanello were both highly successful and self-confident titans of the financial world. They got along well with each other.

Karen and Donna were lunching in early October, comparing notes about how the girls were enjoying the new school year. Karen could not hide her enthusiasm about Eva's boat. She practically glowed as she described the details to Donna. Donna brought the concept home to Don.

He thought it a fantastic idea and they committed to purchase a $10 million luxury suite.

# CHAPTER THIRTY-FIVE

aren Romanello was cruising along at 70 mph in her beige Lexus LX-570, relieved not to have any traffic on the southbound lanes of Route 7, just south of Danbury, Connecticut, when the Mark Levinson sound system vibrated with an incoming call. Her eyes darted to the LED screen in middle of the dashboard and she saw Eva Lampedusa's name.

"Hey Eva. How are you?"

"I'm terrific. How are things with you?"

Even though Karen and Eva had never been as close as Eva had been with Marc, both women were fond of each other and had longed to become closer friends. They sensed that Eva's ship might just afford the perfect opportunity for that to happen.

"Coming along. I reached my fundraising goal. Thank God for that. Now any additional funds I raise are pure gravy. But I'm not kidding myself — I know there'll be plenty of need for more money over the first few months, until we really get this thing up and rolling. What are you up to today?"

"Just driving back from Woodbury Commons," confessed Karen. True to her roots in the cosmetics and fashion industries,

Karen loved designer clothing but hated paying retail. It was something she had been trying to teach Marc's daughter, Nicole, for years now.

"Saks Off Fifth was having one of those 30 percent off things they always do, so that was reason enough for me to drive up there. But of course, once I was there, I ended up making a killing in St. John, Jimmy Choo, and La Perla," revealing her favorite dress, shoe, and lingerie shops.

"You have a few minutes to talk?" asked Eva.

"Unfortunately, I've got about an hour and a half."

"Good. Well, I won't take that long, but I wanted to pick your brain about something."

"Sure. Go ahead," invited Karen.

For the next 30 minutes, Eva and Karen discussed decorating and appointing the ship. They discussed design themes for the ship overall, as well as specific color, shape, texture, and decorating ideas for each of the restaurants, the health and wellness center, the lecture hall, hallways, and the grand entrance. Karen made suggestions as she drove, and Eva took copious notes.

"We need to work something out. You really should be compensated for all this great advice," Eva said.

"Nope! Some things we do for fun and for free," Karen laughed. "Besides, you're helping me kill this drive home. I've got another free labor idea for you from the Romanello family. As I'm sure you know, Marc's phasing out his work at Citibank and is looking to take on something new. Have you thought at all about the governing body of this ship and how it would all be run? He has more energy than anyone I know, and he'd love to sink his teeth into this. I just know it. And don't forget, he's a lawyer by training, even though he hates to admit it."

Eva had actually given a great deal of thought to the governance of the ship. She was concerned about how she would manage all the heavy hitters, all these powerhouses who had been so successful in their own industries and would undoubtedly want to take control of the direction of the ship. She would need some kind of covenant they would all have to sign outlining all the rules for decorum and civility. Even though she was a lawyer, she was a litigator. Corporate governance just wasn't her thing.

"I'm sure Marc would be great at it, but that's asking a lot of him. This isn't a matter of simply drafting a new form agreement that copies from many other corporate-form documents. Remember, nothing like this has been done before. Because we're all a little bit blind here, he'd have to invent this out of whole cloth. And that's a heavy ask."

"I'll ask him. He'd love it," offered Karen.

"Maybe wear some of that La Perla underwear when you ask him," Eva joked. "I'll tell you what, girlfriend. I'd be so relieved if Marc would really take that on. In fact, I'd be eternally grateful to both of you – to you for helping with the design of the interior space, and to Marc for all this legal bullshit."

"Nonsense, it'll be fun for both of us," replied Karen. She was totally positive Marc would sign on, no encouragement needed.

Eva was impressed. "First you got him to buy into this ship concept when I wasn't sure you guys would do it. Then you volunteer to help me with all the design stuff. Now you've got Marc pitching in. I wish I could clone you."

"It's our pleasure, I assure you." Karen knew how important Eva had been in Marc's life after his first wife died and, although Marc and Eva had drifted apart a bit when he married Karen, it was clear to Karen that they shared a deep friendship and a great deal of respect for one another.

"You know, I just thought of something that would work for everyone," Eva said. "Because you guys will be putting in all this extra time, and you won't take any money for it, I think that among the luxury suites in your class, you should get the biggest one."

"Eva, you're too much. But what do you mean in our class?"

Once again, Eva found herself describing the ownership structure in a bit more detail. She really didn't mind doing this because every time she explained the concept to someone new, or in greater detail, she crystallized the direction of her project in her own mind.

"Well, as I explained at the house, luxury suites will be different sizes. There will be a few huge ones, let's call those the Platinum luxury suites. I think there will only be two or three of those on the ship. Then, there'll be some that are a bit smaller than that and we'll call those the Golden luxury suites. The smaller ones are Silver, and the smallest are Bronze luxury suites. Then there are the hotel rooms, but we'll never call them that. We'll call them visitor flats. Those are critical to the ship, remember. That's going to be our revenue stream so we can keep our condo-association costs under control. You with me so far?"

"Yes." That all made perfect sense to Karen.

"Now, since it's a ship, it can't be absolutely symmetrical. Luxury suites closer to the bow would be a different shape from those in the stern."

"Oh, I get it," chimed Karen, grinding her teeth because of the intensifying brake lights on the highway ahead of her. This drive was going to take longer than she thought. "The luxury suites in the bow will be a little smaller than those in the stern."

"Well, that's not necessarily the case. Although the ship is narrower in the bow from one side to the other – from port to starboard – we can equalize luxury suite sizes by making them a little longer in the bow than in the stern, where the beam is widest. So the luxury suites in the stern are more rectangular, the ones in the bow a little more oddly shaped."

"What do you mean – the beam is widest?"

"The beam is the width of the ship," explained Eva. "You measure it at the widest point of the ship, usually closer to the stern. The wider the beam, the more stable the ship."

"Wow. You know a lot about ships, don't you? I think you're going to have to give all of us some sort of class or something on all this stuff," Karen joked, only half-kidding.

"Don't worry, it'll become second nature to you after only a week or two. You won't be using landlubber terms like left or right or front or back anymore. But because the ship is going to be luxurious, like a condo, we're not going to use traditional nautical terms like calling a kitchen a galley or calling a bathroom a head."

Karen had another revelation to share with Eva. "You know, Marc would kill me for telling you this, but we've been contemplating spending more time on the ship than just a few months a year." She paused, waiting for Eva's reaction, but Eva had none. Karen continued, "Now that Marc's children are in high school and Stacy is in London, and Marc is contemplating making this total break from Citibank, we may just pack up this big house in Southport and buy something smaller. Or maybe just get a condo in Florida."

"Florida?" Eva was genuinely surprised. "I've never heard either of you mention Florida before. Where'd this come from?"

"Well, we were thinking...actually, Marc came up with it. If we sell our Connecticut residence and buy a condo in Florida, we can spend most of our time on the ship and declare ourselves Florida residents so we can avoid paying state income tax. We could even just buy a smaller place in Connecticut as long as we don't spend more than six months a year here."

Eva knew that to be correct. "But you would sell that magnificent house?"

"Eva, it's a magnificent ship, too. We'd be exchanging a beautiful residence in Connecticut for a beautiful residence all over the world. What's wrong with that?" Karen was perplexed; Eva sounded less than enthusiastic. "We thought you'd be excited to hear that."

"I am. It's just that I can't believe you're going to sell that house." Eva was experiencing an odd sensation and it took her a few seconds to identify what it was. She was feeling stress and anxiety over the decision her best friend and his wife were making to jettison their home and follow her lead. What if the ship didn't turn out to be all Eva dreamed it could be? And what if the ship didn't turn out to be what Marc and Karen wanted it to be? Their house would be sold, and they would be stuck on the ship. Eva didn't know what to say in response.

"That's exciting," she offered feebly.

But Karen was distracted as she passed a white Subaru Outback on the left shoulder that appeared to have only three wheels. "Ah! That's what was holding us up. Okay, we're moving now … Okay, I'm just getting on the Merritt. What's the next step, and when do we get to see you next?" inquired Karen.

"I'm afraid there are so many balls in the air right now, I can't answer either of those questions. I'm on the phone with the shipyard every day, and I'm trying to make sure I get all the money in place to make the deposits on time and take possession."

"That sounds like fun – the taking possession part," exclaimed Karen, unable to hide the genuine excitement in her voice. "Will there be some sort of party?"

"You know, you're right. There needs to be something. Something special. A party. If you've never seen a large ship get launched out of a shipyard, it really is a sight to behold. They build these massive ships in a dry dock, which is just a dock without water, like a warehouse. When the ship is finished, they slowly flood the dry dock. The rush of water raises the ship off its keel blocks and, when the water level inside gets to the level outside, the large gate at the back of the dock is swung open and the ship is floated out. Then, a few tugboats pull up alongside and move the ship to the pier where they tie it up. It's really a cool thing to see."

"Well I think that calls for a party, that's for sure. We can all gather together and get to know each other while we're all experiencing this maiden launch together," Karen said, growing even more animated.

"I'm not sure that's exactly the time we should have the party," responded Eva. "Once the ship is floating and ready to go, the crew takes it out on a shakedown cruise. Usually, the engineers, and even the shipbuilder, have to tweak a few things to make sure everything is operating perfectly. It's not quite as easy as buying your BMW and driving it off the showroom floor."

"Well, when you actually take possession of the ship and get to drive it away, that's when we should have the party," asserted Karen.

Eva rolled her eyes. "You don't *drive* it away –" she began but caught herself. Eva only had a week to make sure no investors backed out, that there were no complications closing the deal. That had to be her focus, much as she might have wanted to continue chatting with Karen.

"That's a splendid idea. We simply must arrange a party when we take possession of the vessel. In fact, I'll even let you be in charge of that, too, since you're our decorator par excellence. We'll come up with some sort of theme, what do you think?"

Karen was in full organization mode, already auditioning party themes in her mind as she drove the last mile to her house.

"I think that's a terrific idea. All the owners should plan to spend one week together on the ship, so we can get to know each other."

"Yes, and that marvelous husband of yours can explain the rules of ship behavior to all of us at the same time."

Somehow having Marc explain to her the "rules of behavior" didn't sound like a lot of fun to Karen, but planning the party did.

# CHAPTER THIRTY-SIX

A week had passed since Mario and Janice began the new direction in their marriage. Once again, they were out at their Hamptons estate – the family's last visit before the cooler weather hit and their trips to Southampton became as rare as Mario telling the truth. Once again, Janice and her girlfriends were engaged in that modern-day sport that would never be included in the Olympics: powerwalking. Roxanne and Jessica slept late, and Mario got in an early morning round of golf at the Parkview Club. By 11, when Mario drove back to the house and strolled into the kitchen, Rolando was busy with a half bushel of apples strewn all over the large wooden table, preparing to bake apple pies for the weekend.

"Hey guy, whatcha up to?" inquired Mario, in a chummier-than-usual tone.

"Just baking some pies. And for dinner tonight, I'm making a pheasant dish, with some carrots and acorn squash. I thought the apple pie would be a great conclusion to the meal. Kind of an 'introduction to fall' dinner."

Janice had told Rolando that two couples would be joining

the family that night and one of the couples would be bringing their two daughters. Rolando was fixing dinner for ten; he was at his best when he was entertaining for large groups. To the outside world – or at least those outside the Hamptons elite – it appeared that Janice was one of the best supper entertainers in all Long Island. But everyone who was anyone in the Hamptons knew of Rolando's culinary expertise and that he was the one doing all the work.

"Do you have a free minute or will those apples rot?" asked Mario, sarcastically.

They sat across the table from each other, surrounded by three dozen Granny Smith apples and the waft of brown sugar and cinnamon, simmering ever so gently from a cast iron pan on the other side of the room. Slowly, Mario explained to Rolando the concept of Eva's ship and all its details. Rolando nodded appropriately and politely, but he wondered why Mario was sharing all this with him.

Rolando listened patiently for almost 30 minutes. Finally, his curiosity was peaked. "That sounds great, Mario, but why are you telling me all this?"

"Rolando, what would you think about becoming the executive chef for the ship?" Mario grinned with great self-satisfaction. He knew he was offering Rolando the opportunity of a lifetime.

Rolando didn't know what to say. He was not at all interested in working on a ship. It was the last thing in the world he wanted. But he couldn't just blurt that out, so he stalled. He asked about the whereabouts of the ship, how many days a year he would have to work, the pay scale, the accommodations, how many people would be under him, and who he would answer to. Mario answered each question as best he could. Rolando nodded politely, exhibiting just enough level of interest before the conversation petered out to a natural close.

The day progressed. Janice came back from her powerwalk and took her last drive of the year with the top down in her little Saab convertible. She spent the early afternoon with Mindy who, though supportive of the way she and Mario talked things out, expressed a certain wariness about the whole situation.

Jessica and Roxanne slept past noon, then drove over to the Parkview Club for the finals of the boys' 21-and-under tennis tournament. It was Fashion Week in Manhattan, and the girls looked like they had gotten lost at the beach on their way to the catwalk. They were a bit overdressed to watch a tennis match. But at the Parkview Club, they fit right in – they were not the only girls in the viewing stands with three-inch heels, miniskirts, hair extensions, and $2,000 purses.

They were there to watch the boys, and to be watched themselves. In fact, Jessica knew precious little about tennis. One of the boys playing, nineteen-year-old Chris Hurley, had graduated from Collegiate the previous year and was playing for Amherst that fall. Jessica had met Chris on several occasions over the past few summers and always thought he would be a wonderful conquest, despite their three-year age difference. Several other girls had the same desires ... and had acted on them, so Jessica's affair with Chris had to remain a purely mezzanine-level fantasy. Billy Doplinger, Jessica's other crush, was playing as well. If she couldn't arouse Chris' attention after the matches, Billy would do.

Roxanne wanted to watch the tennis, but sitting with Steven Seidman did make the tennis more exciting. They had continued to flirt after their little experience in Ben's Den. They enjoyed a few typical Hamptons-teen summer dates: movies, miniature golf, and bowling. If there was any girl in the Hamptons who was grounded and not obsessed with drugs or crazy parties, it was Roxanne Garramone.

Both girls were there as much to find out who was having the spiciest parties that night as they were to watch tennis. They succeeded.

At home, Mario had swum some laps and was relaxing by the pool. The gentle breeze across the pool patio this last week of September was still enough to chill his skin. Not the same feeling he had enjoyed exiting the pool just a week before. Soon enough, Larry, Rolando's friend from Ecuador, would be around with his crew to drain two feet of water from the pool, pump the remaining water with gallons of chlorine, roll the massive green tarp over the pool, and cover it for the winter. There was something gloomy and disconsolate about seeing the cover rolled onto the pool. It signaled fall. And winter.

In the kitchen, preparing the pheasants for roasting, Rolando considered everything Mario had presented to him. He had to admit, he was warming to it. The opportunity to travel the world, especially on someone else's dime, was intriguing. And, as executive chef, he would be a big shot. In fact, he probably wouldn't even have to dirty his hands in the kitchen. There would be sous chefs, chefs de cuisine, line cooks, pantry chefs, pastry chefs. He could stride the dining rooms in his toque and double-breasted chef's jacket and take credit for all the creative dishes the richest people in the world were enjoying. A heady thought.

Still, no matter how appealing that image was, he just couldn't see giving up an incredibly cushy job in the Hamptons to serve strangers on a ship somewhere on the other side of the planet. In the Hamptons, the Garramones barely came out to the house between October and May so the house was ostensibly his. On the ship, he would be responsible for the preparation and service of three meals a day for total strangers. In the Hamptons, Rolando had his own BMW and was treated like a rock star among the migrant workers. On the ship, he would just be one of a hundred employees.

Around 5, while the ladies were still out, Rolando brought Mario a glass of his favorite rishi mango iced tea at the pool. Mario invited Rolando to have a seat.

"Have you given any thought to our discussion?" he asked, although they hadn't really *discussed* anything – Mario had just rambled on about the ship and had offered to see about getting Rolando a job on it.

"I don't think it makes sense for me," Rolando responded in his most deferential tone.

"But why?" Mario seemed genuinely nonplused.

"I really like it here, taking care of the house, preparing the meals for the family and getting everything ready for you guys all summer long. I'm also not sure about how I'd feel on a boat. You know, I may get seasickness or something."

Mario knew damn well that Rolando enjoyed a simple and unchallenging life in Southampton. He paid Rolando far more than any other house manager in the Hamptons. What Mario didn't know was that Rolando had a lot going on in the Hamptons, operations that would come to an end if Rolando were shipped off to sea: his dope peddling and his kickbacks for work from the immigrants in the Hamptons. But Mario knew something else and it was time for him to share it with Rolando.

"Rolando, there's something I haven't told you," Mario began, uncomfortably. "I mean, you know about it, but you don't know that I know about it."

Mario took a deep breath and continued. "Josephine told Janice about ... an incident she says happened a few weeks ago with her daughter, Maria. I don't want to ... prejudge anything. I'd like to hear your side of the story."

Rolando shifted in his seat, broke off eye contact with Mario, and began to speak quickly without really saying anything.

Mario threw up his hands. "Whoa, slow down, my friend. I just want to hear your version of what happened."

How much did Mario know? Did Mario know they had had sex? Did he know they had gotten high together? Did he know that Rolando had been texting her regularly since, sending provocative photos, and explicitly offering his sexual services almost daily, always to be rebuffed?

"Well, we were cleaning the pool together, and it was really hot, and ... one thing... led to another."

"Exactly *what* led to *what*?"

"Well, you know, we sort of ended up... fooling around."

"Rolando, did you have sex with that girl?" Mario asked in the firmest tone Rolando had ever heard him use.

"Well ... kind of."

Mario was angry now. He wasn't to be toyed with by this immigrant house servant. "Look, you either had sex with her or you didn't. Which is it?" Mario's face reddened, his indignation on display in living color.

"Well, I guess we did."

"You *guess*? C'mon, man, I'm trying to help you here," Mario was resolute. "Okay, let me spell it all out for you. Josephine had a talk with Janice and told her that quite a lot occurred between you and her daughter. You insisted on getting Maria high and made her strip into a bikini and get into the pool with you. And then I was told that once she was totally inebriated, you brought her to your room and had sex with her. Is this true or not?"

Rolando hesitated. When he did reply, his voice was feeble, his excuses lame. "I didn't *make* her get high. She did it because she wanted to. And I didn't force her to put on her bathing suit. We both needed to do that, so we could scrub the algae off the inside of the pool." Rolando didn't respond to the last allegation – that he had taken the sixteen-year-old to his bed and screwed her.

"But did you offer her pot in the house? In *my* house?"

"No, it was by the pool," insisted Rolando, convinced there was some credible distinction between offering marijuana to a sixteen-year-old girl by the pool as opposed to inside the house.

"Rolando, between you and me, did you fuck that girl or not?" Mario was steaming, and his voice betrayed his anger.

"It's not like that. That makes it sound so violent and forceful."

Mario was done playing games.

"Janice wants me to fire you. Today. She doesn't think it's safe to have you around Roxanne and Jessica. And if I ever caught you offering them drugs, not only would I fire you, but I'd beat the crap out of you myself." Rolando was fully engaged now. His mind was flush with the night he had gotten high with Jessica Garramone and had also made out with her, feeling up her breasts. Blaming a family history of pedophilia was certainly not going to cut it with Mario if he ever found out about that night.

"You didn't answer me about having sex with her, so I'll take your silence as an admission that you did it. I don't want this to be any more embarrassing for either of us than it already is. And I don't want to hear any details. But let me spell this out for you. In New York State, this is statutory rape. And with statutory rape, there is no defense at all. If the girl was under 18, and you had sex, you would be found guilty. Period. So, if Josephine or Maria ever went to the cops and told them what happened, you'd be immediately arrested and would most probably be convicted and sent to prison for years. I wouldn't be too happy about it either. It would be all over the papers that my friend Rolando, who babysat my daughters, was a sexual predator."

Mario paused. Rolando jumped in. "But have you ever

seen Maria? She doesn't look sixteen. I swear she could pass for 21."

Mario stared at Rolando, momentarily stunned. It was the bad punchline to an old joke. Christ, Rolando, tell it to the judge. "You're not listening," Mario said finally. "Because she is, in fact, under 18, there is absolutely no defense to the crime of statutory rape. Even if she showed you a driver's license, a birth certificate, or a goddamn passport that said she is 21, it's still no defense. She could have a parade of priests and rabbis swear she's twenty-one and it would still be a crime. There is no defense. None. Unless you didn't actually do it."

Rolando began to understand the severity of what Mario was saying. He thought of all those texts he'd sent Maria. Had she kept them?

No, there was no way he could deny that they had sex. But why was Mario laying all this on him now? And why had he told him about the ship opportunity just that morning? Rolando was confused.

It didn't take long before Mario tied it all together for him.

"This morning, I told you about the ship because I thought you'd jump at it. Obviously, I was wrong. It's up to you, I'm not forcing you to take the job. I would never do that. But I am going to be forced to terminate your employment here because it seems that everything Janice told me is true. And please don't insult me by denying it. But I think I could convince Janice, and Josephine, to keep this matter quiet and not go to the authorities as long as you're not here anymore. And when I say not around here, I mean not in this house, on this block, or in the Hamptons at all. If I were to fire you, I'm sure you could get another job out here within a week. But if Janice or Josephine saw you around, they might just get angry enough to report you to the police.

"Look, we've all made mistakes," Mario continued. "You just happened to make a really stupid one. I like you. I really do. And I'm trying to help you here. You've been good to me and I've been good to you. If you take the boat gig, you'll get away from here and never have to face the music. On the ship, you can have a whole new beginning. But let me be clear with you Rolando. You're going to have to leave the Hamptons. I'll give you a week to make up your mind about the boat and two weeks to be gone. Janice and I have already spoken and we're going to tell the girls that you decided to go home to Panama. Of course, you'll tell them that, too.

Rolando's eyes filled up. He had been with the family for twelve years. He watched the girls grow up. He taught the girls to ride their bicycles, catch fireflies, bait hooks, and fly kites. He taught them how to bake. He listened when they cried over skinned knees, dead birds, and first loves. There were many times when Mario and Janice were away, and the girls were with Rolando for days or weeks on end. They were always such happy times.

He was happy that night he'd made out with Jessica. It seemed so natural. She was becoming a woman.

Oh, Christ. He knew Mario was right. He had a problem. He knew it. He was being fired for banging the housekeeper's daughter. What would have happened if he had gone further with

Jessica?

The weight of it all suddenly came crashing down on him and he cried. Not just a few stray tears or a whimpering exhalation, it was a full on, man-sized cry.

He was angry. Not with Mario or Janice or Josephine or Maria. He was angry at himself and his testosterone-fueled stupidity. For one afternoon, for one nice piece of ass, he had compromised his job and his life in this area he had called home for the past dozen years. He had been rash and reckless and would now have to pay for it.

It was gone – all of it, the house, the car, the friendships, the respect as one of the biggest fish in the pond, all of it.

Mario also wept. Rolando had been an ally, an additional male presence in a house full of perfumes, shoes, handbags and tampons. Rolando had undoubtedly covered up for Mario's indiscretions, even though Mario didn't know exactly which ones or when. But Janice insisted on having Rolando fired and Mario really had no choice.

"I'm sorry about this, my friend. I like you and that's why I brought up the whole boat thing. I think you have amazing talents and I'd like to help you. But it just can't be here."

"Thanks. I appreciate that," sniveled Rolando. And he really did.

"Get yourself together and we can all tell the girls tomorrow afternoon. Then, we can plan something really special for all of us next weekend to help you celebrate your return to Panama. Besides, I know some pheasants who are waiting for you." And with that, Mario arose and walked into the house to wait for Janice so he could tell her the deed was done.

# CHAPTER THIRTY-SEVEN

G illian English spent much of that summer in seclusion. Bouncing from job to job, and growing increasingly depressed about her 170-pound frame and unkempt appearance, Gillian had had enough. Widowed at such a young age, unable to provide Cara with the life she wanted for her, Gillian had every reason to check out. Like so many other middle-aged Manhattan divorcees and widows she knew, she could have climbed into a bottle of vodka, binge-watching Netflix.

She'd had an electrifying courtship and marriage with Mark, only to plummet into the deep despair when he left her so young. Every year, on September 11th, the horror of Mark's murder replayed in her head, and on television sets across the country. She knew she was losing her battle against the darkness. She had to fight it.

She knew she had the strength to be tough, she'd been tough before. She had worked hard to take her small company, CallPro, public, owing in part to the efforts of Mark and his colleagues at Goldman Sachs. She was part of a small fraternity of people on this planet who had promoted a small company all the way to the point of being listed on the NASDAQ. That chapter of her life left her with a great depth of skill and experience to draw from.

Now, at fifty-eight, Gillian had one last fight in her, and this was her year to go for it. On her doctor's advice, she was determined to lose the weight, adopt a healthy lifestyle, and learn how to eat right – whatever all that meant. Her closest friend, Diane Silverman, suggested the Pritikin Center in Miami, the country's finest all-inclusive weight-loss center. Diane had been there herself four years earlier, reinventing her approach to health consciousness.

After six weeks at Pritikin, Gillian lost sixteen pounds, but achieved so much more. By her eighth day, Gillian was off her beta blockers and diuretics in favor of an all-natural way of reducing her chronically high blood pressure. By the end of the second week on Pritikin's healthy eating plan, with her blood results being analyzed every seven days, Gillian's Crestor also found its way into the trash. She adopted a prudent exercise regime, not the hard-core diet of Pilates and spinning all her Manhattan friends preached, but too often ignored.

She listened attentively to all the lectures, attending three seminars a day led by dietitians, wellness experts, chefs, and physical therapists. She learned how to read labels, becoming fixated on the sodium content of foods. Sodium was the enemy, abetting her body's ability to retain unwanted water weight. Most importantly, Gillian tempered her alcohol intake, promising herself no more than one glass of wine a day, no matter what. She learned the technique of always having a glass of club soda with lime in her hand at a party, so she could satisfy her desire for social drinking without the negative repercussions.

By the end of her stay in Miami, Gillian had learned a whole new way of caring for herself and vowed to continue on this path and never to let health get away from her again.

Recapturing her physical well-being was only half of Gillian's new life. Back in New York by early August, while her prosperous comrades were golfing and sunning themselves in the Hamptons, Gillian took advantage of the dearth of competition in Manhattan and looked for a job. Her resume freshly dusted, she hit the pavement with vigor. Gillian called all her friends and wasn't shy about asking them for leads in the job market. Suddenly she was getting interviews for jobs that had eluded her over the past dozen years.

Unfortunately, none of the interviews panned out. Was she too old? Out of the job market too long? Whatever the reason, Gillian was not getting second interviews. One of her friends suggested that Gillian get involved as a director of DriveMe, a start-up, ride-sharing company. Gillian knew little about the ride-sharing business, but she thought a board position could punch up her resume with some new activity. It would give her relevancy in the current marketplace.

Jamie Einhorn, the CEO of DriveMe, took a liking to her at their first meeting, a two-and-a-half-hour lunch event at Balthazar, one of Jamie's favorite hangouts. A week later, Gillian was recommended for board service. This turned out to be the most fortuitous professional event of her life.

Gillian didn't know that DriveMe was preparing to go

public in the fall. The reason she breezed through the interview process was because of her experience as the CFO of CallPro. The CFO of DriveMe had just been diagnosed with cancer and resigned. The board had hurriedly hired a new CFO who, though exceptionally bright, lacked the gravitas needed to star on the road show that would have to be launched to take the company public. On the board level, the thinking was that Gillian's experience made her uniquely qualified to oversee the work of the new CFO through the rest of the financing and filing periods.

Her first-year board salary was a bit below market for the extraordinary amount of work she was being asked to perform, but her total compensation package included 100,000 fully vested shares, and options on another 300,000 shares. If the company was successful in its initial public offering, Gillian would make over $6 million in her first two years of board service.

Thanks to Pritikin and DriveMe, Gillian was all set to steer herself back into the left lane of her accident-prone life.

# CHAPTER THIRTY-EIGHT

Eva was having an early supper with Lorraine Williams at Ed's Chowder House, an upscale fish restaurant on West 63rd, across the street from Lincoln Center, where they had tickets for that evening's performance of *Aida*. Ascending the twelve white marble steps leading to the hostess station, Lorraine checked in, handing her beige Burberry raincoat to the coat check girl. As soon as she was handed the claim check, Lorraine heard a familiar voice behind her. "You always arrive before me. And I really thought I would beat you today," said Eva with a welcoming smile.

The two ladies embraced and were shown to their table. It was a tradition for them to meet at Ed's before attending the opera, but the ladies still studied the menus and read through them as if they had never been there before. Their waitress, a young, tall blonde trying a little too hard to look like Scarlett Johansson, stood by waiting expectantly for their order.

As she always did, Eva ordered the clam chowder as an appetizer while Lorraine ventured out from her normal fare and chose a half dozen raw Kumamoto oysters. For their entrées, Eva ordered the lobster rolls, excellent although quite pricey at $30 for two small rolls, while Lorraine indulged in the scallop ravioli, a highlight of the menu. After an unnecessarily lengthy conversation about which wine would pair best with their dishes, they settled on a bottle of Kim Crawford Sauvignon Blanc from Marlborough, New Zealand.

"You must be excited. You get your ship in a week, don't you?" Lorraine asked.

"Twelve days, actually. And it's not *my* ship, it's *our* ship. The money all gets wired out on the 15th, and I take possession on the 16th. Lorraine, I could never have done this without you, you know."

"Oh, don't be silly," Lorraine chirped, waving her off. "If you hadn't coerced me into indulging in your little fantasy, you would have found some other wealthy spinster to go in on it with you."

"You may be wealthy, but you're no spinster," Eva flattered. "Besides, I don't have a lot of other friends who can spare $100 million."

"I can't spare it either, my dear. I'm investing it – in you and in your dream. It sounds perfectly marvelous to me and I am probably as excited about it as you are." Lorraine's Canadian accent betrayed her roots, much as she tried to hide it. "We are doing something special to celebrate the launch, aren't we?"

When Karen Romanello had asked the same question, it seemed like a polite inquiry. But when Lorraine Williams asked it, it was much more. Eva thought quickly. "Of course, we are. Don't be silly. Karen Romanello is arranging it all."

"Good. I can't wait to hear all the details. And what about you? What are you up to?"

Eva Lampedusa had been up to nothing for the past two months. Nothing, that is, except raising the $270 million she needed for next week. The heavy lifting was done, commitments had been made and banked, and this was the first moment she could relax and enjoy a social date in months. The two ladies chatted about end of summer escapades, Labor Day weekend happenings, Fashion Week highlights. They laughed discovering they'd both attended the US Open on the same day as guests of Mercedes Benz without knowing that the other was there. And, of course, they talked about men.

But they kept going back to the ship, feeding off each other's excitement. Lorraine was tickled to know that she would be the owner of the stern luxury suite on the ninth deck, the one deck immediately above Eva's. "I can keep an eye on you from my room," she told Eva, with an all-knowing grin.

It frustrated Eva that Lorraine kept referring to the large luxury suites as rooms and the smaller ones as cabins. They were luxury suites, she reminded Loraine, repeatedly, but courteously. They plotted themes for parties, places to visit, and events to be sure to attend, including the Olympics, Carnival in Rio, Wimbledon, and trips to wine regions such as Napa Valley, Bordeaux, Piedmont, Cape Town, and Marlborough.

Through careful study and some advice from friends, Eva had set the itinerary for the first eight months of the ship's voyage. She was keen to get everyone on board, so they could establish committees to deal with various ship operations. Eva thought Marc Romanello would be a brilliant choice to head up the audit committee, and Harris Hirschfeld could run the membership group. Right now, Eva was wearing all those hats.

Eva, with the advice of her great friends who were yachting experts, had already hired most of the "marine team" as she called it, the captain and engineering staff who would be operating the ship when it launched. All had decades of experience in the cruise ship industry. Although she was adamant that her ship was anything but a cruise ship, those were the only ships at sea comparable to her vessel. Her ship would be among the ten largest privately-owned yachts in the world.

On the other side of the onboard organizational structure was the "hotel team" as she called it. They would deal with all the services for the suite owners – the concierge, the entertainment director, wellness center manager, and an executive chef. Under each of these were countless others, most of whom had worked in very high-end properties like the Four Seasons. Eva also took the advice of all her yachting friends and insisted that all her new staff had to have at least one year's experience at sea. She couldn't afford to bring people onto the team and then learn they were prone to seasickness or couldn't bear being away from home for protracted periods of time. They all had to have earned their experience on the world's oceans before they could be part of her team.

The senior most staff would rotate, four months on and four months off. Midlevel employees would work six-month shifts. And the lowest tier on the ship, consisting of mostly Filipinos, would work eight-month shifts.

"Why do they have to be Filipino?" inquired Lorraine.

"In the cruise-ship business, Filipinos are the largest single nationality employed in the crew – cargo ships, too. There's a strong maritime heritage in the Philippines, they are naturally drawn to the sea. It's their culture. Plus, English is the official language of the Philippines. That's a big advantage."

After trying to get Scarlet Johansson's attention for ten minutes, the women were finally able to order their desserts with just enough time to pay the check, hustle across the street to the legendary opera house, and deposit their coats in the cloak room. They took their seats just as the iconic and glamorous crystal chandeliers ascended into the ceiling, marking the beginning of the performance.

# CHAPTER THIRTY-NINE

The school year had begun, and Roxanne Garramone was immersed in preparation for the SATs. She found Hank Blaser's easy-going manner very comforting. The more frustrated Roxanne got during their sessions, the calmer Hank remained. He was steady and deliberative, cajoling Roxanne and reminding her of her excellent scores in her practice tests. Cara English had joined their sessions and was also religious in completing the exercises and practice tests Hank assigned.

The sessions alternated between Hank's apartment and the Garramones', which was like going from a Schwinn to a Bentley. The Garramones' apartment was ... well, perfect. It was an eight-room apartment in one of those celebrated pre-war buildings on Park Avenue coveted by the elite of Manhattan. Hank lived in a rear-facing apartment on the fourth floor of a walk up on West 76th Street, between Broadway and West End Avenue. It did face south and had large windows and stunningly ornate parquet inlaid floors from the late 1800s, but that was about all that could be said on the positive side for the apartment. Oh sure, the perky brunette real estate agent had described it as:

"A charming little starter apartment with a dishwasher, excellent light, great closet space, attractive hardwood floors, and a renovated bathroom." A better description might have been "a large walk-in closet that pretends to be a real apartment."

Up the four flights of narrow, mostly broken metal stairs through the center of the unair-conditioned building, was the door to Hank's apartment. Like most apartments in walk ups in New York, the three-inch thick steel door was burdened with four locks, two of which hadn't worked since the 1970s.

Inside there was a small butcher block table in a state of disrepair, with two white metallic Ikea chairs that didn't aesthetically fit with the table, or even the rest of the apartment. On the wall, just behind the full swing of the hideous door, was a four inch by twelve-inch piece of stained oak with four dulled brass hooks that served as the apartment's coat closet. A 48-inch LG television dominated the center of the apartment and appeared to be the only piece of furniture from the post-Nixon era. The couch was bachelor brown corduroy, with two navy blue throw pillows Hank had picked up at the Spence-Chapin thrift shop on East 92nd Street. The epidemiology of its many stains was better left uncontemplated.

The *attractive* hardwood floor was anything but, and Hank had obscured half of it with a floor covering typical of a young urban male – a maroon synthetic Oriental rug purchased at ABC Carpets, on West 15th Street for around $200, reasoning that it looked like an authentic Turkish carpet. It didn't. Three framed black and white photographs of lower Manhattan from the 1930s and a 2016 poster of Bernie Sanders comprised the artistic expression of the apartment.

The only illumination came from two standing floor lamps purchased on Etsy for $39 each, that stood on either side of the corduroy sofa. There was not even the slightest hint that Hank's girlfriend, Stephanie, had anything to do with the decorating of this man cave. Because she hadn't.

Roxanne and Cara thought the apartment was *cool*, as was everything about this sophisticated 28-year-old man. He was obviously extremely intelligent, but he used words like "fuck" and "cool," which the girls thought made him fucking cool. Unlike most of their friends who parroted the conservative, right wing propaganda of their wealthy parents, Hank leaned left and spoke reverently of socialist movements. They imagined that he smoked dope at night, surrounded by a cadre of other intellectual leftists. The girls were right, but he would never let them see the bong with the image of Che Guevara etched on its surface that he kept hidden in the back of his closet.

Often, Hank would be running around the East Side, so the tutoring sessions would be at the Garramones' apartment. One night, the girls finished a tutoring session and Hank was due to receive his bi-weekly check. But Janice was at the gym and Mario was at the office – or perhaps running around with Melanie Hunter. So Hank ambled across the park to his apartment on the West Side.

Hank and Stephanie were planning to go to the Sugarloaf Resort in Vermont for the weekend for some relaxation, tennis, and pumpkin picking, and Hank had been counting on that $3,600 check. He sent Janice a text message asking if she could please leave a check with the doorman for him to pick up the next morning. Janice felt terrible. She always prided herself on paying people on time. She hadn't seen Hank in almost a month and was anxious to get caught up on Roxanne's progress. She texted him back: "SO sorry. At the gym for yoga and workout. Can u stop by later for a check and chat? Around 7 tonite?"

Hank had already reached the West Side, so he changed into his khaki shorts and navy Cutter & Buck golf shirt and fetched Che from the back of the closet. But he was keen to get his check that night so, after his dinner of munchies disguised as comfort food at the Metro Diner on West 101st Street, he hopped a cab and traversed the park once again to pick up his check.

Janice had returned from the gym, sucked down her protein smoothie, showered, and donned her robe. She opened a bottle of Sancerre and poured herself a glass. She had planned to put on her Lululemon black pants and whatever shirt she could grab, but the doorbell had interrupted her. No worries, she thought to herself, this won't take long.

"I'm so sorry about the check, Hank. I had planned to leave it with Roxanne, but I was running late and ran out of the house without remembering to even write it," she explained, handing Hank the check. "If you have a few minutes, I'd love to hear how Rox is doing. Can you spare a second?" Having just accepted nearly $4,000 from her, Hank felt obligated. He was already high, and his girlfriend wouldn't be home for another hour. He hated sitting alone in his apartment when he was stoned. "Sure thing."

Janice reached into the Chippendale dining room hutch

and grabbed another crystal wine glass. "Care for a glass?" she asked, holding up the cold bottle of Sancerre.

"Sure thing," repeated Hank. Janice poured a glass for Hank, topping off her own glass while she was at it. Already feeling quite relaxed, she pulled out one of the antique dining room chairs and deposited herself on the faded burgundy velvet seat. Hank did the same. He gave Janice a detailed report on Roxanne's SAT preparation. Roxanne had near perfect scores on her practice reading and language tests. He even pulled out some tests from six years ago, reputed to be the toughest SATs ever administered, and Roxanne had scored 99-percent levels in every category.

Janice listened attentively, and without realizing it, her azure blue silk robe fell a bit open, exposing a tantalizing glimpse of the inner third of one of her ivory white breasts, outlined by her otherwise golden sun-baked skin. The pace of Hank's narrative changed. He meant to continue with a review of Roxanne's performance in the math portion of the practice tests, but his mouth wouldn't respond to what his mind wanted it to say. His glance dropped to Janice's bosom and it was in that moment that she felt newly appreciated as a woman. She and Mario had not been having much sex over the past year. Well, she hadn't. Mario certainly wasn't lacking in that department. But now, with this young Adonis staring at her breast, Janice felt sexually desirable once more, and she was loving the attention. She knew she couldn't reach down and pull her robe closed without causing embarrassment to them both. It was obvious – her breast was exposed, and Hank was staring at it. The unspoken conversation between them was thrilling.

Janice was feeling comfortable flirting with, and even teasing, Hank. She was confident it would go no further. Hank, on the other hand, had no idea what was going to happen. One of his few complaints about Stephanie was that her breasts were tiny and now he was face to breast with what he estimated were a perfect pair of 34Cs. They were exquisite and he was infatuated with them. And since he was stoned, his sense of propriety was fading. He just stared, almost totally paralyzed by the sexual tension.

Hank's glass was empty, Janice walked towards him to refill it. As she leaned down to pour, she was almost entirely exposed. Hanks eyes filled with those perfectly round, white, firm breasts so close to his mouth. What was she doing? Did she know they were so exposed? Was she doing this on purpose? Did she want him to do something? Hank ached to reach up and hold her, sexual energy coursed through his entire body. Did she know how aroused he was? Could she see the growing bulge in his shorts? Was she about to reach down and grab him, take him out of his pants, and beg him to make love to her? But then Janice sat down. And just like that, Hank thought, the moment was over.

But it wasn't. Janice's robe remained parted. She ran her fingers slowly along the edge of the robe but didn't close it. Instead, it remained even more open than it was before. Other than her nipples, Janice's breasts were almost entirely visible to Hank. His eyes took in her luscious legs that were even darker than the outside of her breasts. Those perfect breasts.

Hank knew that Janice had to be aware of what was

happening. As they made eye contact, it was impossible that she could have missed his eyes moving from her face to her breasts. He thought he detected a smile on Janice's face when she caught him looking down. She did. She smiled. But now what? What was he supposed to do? Had she intentionally arranged for them to be alone? He knew that Roxanne had gone out with Cara, but where was her sister? Where was that housekeeper, whatever her name was? And where was Mario?

A look of feigned embarrassment rolled across Janice's face. "I'm so embarrassed. You must think me so inappropriate." And before Hank knew what to say, Janice continued, "I can't believe I served you wine without any cheese or crackers." Janice ascended from her chair and walked into the kitchen, very much aware that Hank was following her gorgeous ass with his eyes. At that moment, she wished she were wearing her shorter robe so even more of her long brown legs would be exposed and he might even get a glimpse of the bottom of her cheeks. Hank couldn't see that Janice allowed a massive smile to illuminate her beautiful face. She was absolutely glowing, although she wasn't sure why. None of this had been planned, and she didn't know what she would do with it, but it felt so good. He was a 28-year-old stud who could have any woman he wanted, and she had him eating out of her hand.

"Shit," Hank heard Janice mutter from the kitchen.

"Are you okay?"

"Yeah, I was just trying to reach something but I can't quite get it." Hank was out of his chair and in the kitchen in a flash. He was thankful Janice was facing the cabinets so she couldn't see the bulge in his shorts, which he tried unsuccessfully to hide by walking with his hands in his pockets. When Janice turned around to face Hank, her robe had fallen open even more. It was a miracle the sash was still in place at all. "I'm trying to reach that cheese board, but I can't quite get it," Janice groused with a smiling pout. She turned her back to him once again and was on her tiptoes, now reaching up to a board that was almost out of her reach.

Hank stepped closer, and then even closer. Now he was against her. Firmly against her. He was pressing himself into Janice's backside, his erection thrusting firmly between her cheeks. He sighed, a low sigh of ache and relief. It felt so good. His hands were on her hips and he held her decisively in place. Then ever so slowly, he began to pulsate against Janice's ass. She turned around and smiled, put her arms around the top of his back pulling him against her. In an instant, they were locked in a long, passionate kiss. Any lingering doubts that might have remained were gone.

She reached down and grabbed him, making sure he was as hard as he appeared. She smiled. This was no longer teasing; the line had been crossed. She took his hand and gently suggested, "Follow me." They walked out of the kitchen, through the dining room, and into the bedroom. For the next hour, it was Janice who was the tutor.

# CHAPTER FORTY

Her partying weekend well behind her, Carly was entrenched in her investigative work for Harris.

"I'm on it, Harris," declared Carly as she sat in his office, which he seemed to require her to do more and more frequently over the past weeks. "Whoever shared the confidential law firm material with the US Attorney's office isn't going to elude us for long," she assured him.

These days, Carly was assuring Harris of anything and everything, just as long as she didn't have to sit in those damn Sam Rayburn chairs any more than absolutely necessary and get ogled like a well-worn *Sports Illustrated* swimsuit issue. Every time she was summoned to his majesty's lair, she felt his eyes burning through her blouse. Sheryl Sandberg's feminist catchphrase "lean in," took on a whole different meaning in Harris's office. Every time Carly would lean in, Harris would look down her blouse. Every time she walked out of Harris's office, she was keenly aware of his focused stare on the rhythmic striding of her perfectly sculpted ass. At first Carly enjoyed the attention. But by now, she was skeeved out.

Back in the safety of her own office, Carly immersed herself in her cyber investigation, with occasional detours down side rabbit holes. One such distraction was Marcia Coleman's social media presence, which continued to fascinate Carly. Marcia was so buttoned up at work. But, online! Every weekend Marcia was posting selfies in hot outfits: super short skirts, diaphanous blouses, once even a lace bustier worn as a top under a silk tuxedo jacket. More interesting to Carly, every weekend, Marcia's Instagram or Snap story was a photographic record of all her latest random hook-ups. Not much was left to the imagination among the mobile uploads of Marcia snuggling provocatively with one club hunk after another, usually with a joint or a Cosmo in hand.

It was all so ... intriguing.

Carly was much more cautious herself. Especially about men. She was still young and inexperienced and a paralegal, but her instincts had only betrayed her once, and that was when she was still a kid and she married a man who hadn't yet sowed his wild oats. That would be the last time she'd let a man hurt her like that, she vowed.

So Marcia's kind of chance-taking – this lack of inhibition that unfolded every weekend on Marcia's social media – was intriguing to Carly.

Carly told Marcia about her assignment for Harris, but never mentioned her cyber-spying on Marcia herself. It really wasn't that big a deal, was it? OK, so maybe she felt a twinge of guilt. As a result, she over-compensated by confiding in Marcia more of the details of her secret investigation for Harris than she probably should have. She divulged to Marcia that confidential law- firm materials about the US v. Boeing case had been revealed to the US Attorney's office. Still, she kept to herself the connection to the EuroHoldings situation. There were some things that just didn't need to be revealed, she reasoned.

So, she shared secrets with Marcia. And kept secrets from Marcia.

Marcia was shocked to hear about the leak and huddled with Carly to consider the potential suspects in Bergman Troutman who could have been the culprit. Every few days they'd sit together, compare theories, and land on a new suspect. Then, they'd rip their new theory apart and be back to zero. It was exciting, feeding off each other's energy, sharing confidences, sharing secrets. They spent more and more time together.

Soon, more of the personal crept into their intimacies. Marcia slowly revealed a few nuggets of her nocturnal life to Carly. Carly pretended not to know, which just heightened her fascination with Marcia. She was excited that Marcia felt close enough to confide in her, and excited that Marcia didn't know how much she already knew about Marcia.

Exciting, and confusing.

"Carly, you should come out with me some night," Marcia suggested one day, trying very hard to make it sound like a spontaneous idea and not something she'd been thinking about for weeks. "I have a lot of fun – imagine how much fun we could have together!"

Carly wanted to. She'd been hoping this moment would come, that Marcia would invite her into her secret life. She wanted to, badly. Not just to let go, to drink and dance and tease and flirt, but to deepen this closeness with Marcia. It was so compelling ...

An image filled her head. A young, firm man. Beautiful in a perfectly fitted dark suit, flashing a big, mischievous smile at her and Marcia. The three of them at the bar, the dance music pounding. Marcia leans in to whisper something in his ear, he laughs. Marcia then nibbles playfully on his ear, gently licking it with her tongue. He puts his arm around Marcia's waist, pulling her closer. She slips her hand under his shirt, her nails grazing his chest. Carly does the same. Their hands meet, touching under his black silk shirt...

She felt light headed.

She shook it off, clearing the image from her head.

She enjoyed partying occasionally, but never forgot her father's stern admonition when she started at Hinkle Morris back in Wichita: "You don't shit where you eat." That was good advice in Wichita, but even better in New York City where there were millions of lovers available to her and she didn't need to share her personal sexual exploits with her co-workers.

Still, she needed Marcia's friendship. It was complicated.

Gradually, Carly opened up about her simple Midwestern upbringing and the way she had been scorned by Tommy Sugar at such a young age. Marcia listened attentively, captivated by Carly's tales of waking up before dawn on her grandmother's farm to milk the cows and collect the eggs from the chicken coops.

"There were days in the summer when it was hot. I mean seriously hot. I'd spend a month on my grandparents' farm every summer and I had to take sandwiches to the farmhands outside the brick red, rickety barn. That was one of my little jobs, bringing the farmhands their lunch. Believe me, there were a lot of dirty jobs on a farm − feeding the hogs was no fun − but I looked forward to this one. Some of these boys ..." her voice trailed off as Marcia giggled. Carly warmed to the game she was playing. "I mean, some of these boys were ... well, all that fresh air and manual labor. It does wonders for a young man's physique. They'd take off their shirts, and the beads of sweat would be glistening on their hard chests, their little waists squeezed into tight Wranglers. Sometimes I'd make sure to unbutton the top of my blouse before I went over there, and I'd wear my best lace bra."

Carly knew all too well of Marcia's sex life. She felt a delicious, warm shiver of power and control, knowing she was arousing Marcia with her own totally fictitious story. "Their muscles would get so sore after a long morning of hard work in the middle of God's country. There was one boy, Teddy. He was so strong, beautiful eyes. I'd tell him, 'Teddy if you're a good boy I'll give you a back rub, work out those knots in your back.' I'd dig my thumbs deep into his back, pressing out the knots. He was so grateful..."

As a girl who had grown up in Farmingdale, New York, a middle-class bedroom community on Long Island, Marcia was mesmerized. She had never met a farmboy. Marcia was riveted.

Carly arched an eyebrow at Marcia, then smacked her on the leg. "It wasn't like that! Well, maybe a little." Carly could be a pretty good storyteller, especially with an appreciative audience.

Marcia loved it nevertheless, all these tales of life on the farm, even if they weren't true. The truth was most of the guys on her grandparents' farm were slobs. Overstuffed, white rolls of fat – they were more Michelin Man than *GQ* model.

At least once a week, they went out for lunch, usually at Sushi Yamura, their favorite Japanese restaurant near the office. The purpose of these off-campus meals was usually to gossip and, more often than not, the two ladies had a target or two to dissect and snigger over. Quite frequently, it was Harris, as Marcia educated Carly about his pathological affinity for anything in a skirt. "I think if he went to an Irish funeral, he'd get the hots for the bagpipe player," Marcia snickered.

None of this particularly shocked Carly, but she was surprised at the tolerance of Harris's partners, allowing his shenanigans to continue unchecked.

"When you generate as much revenue for the firm as Harris does, your partners tend to look the other way," Marcia explained, rolling her eyes. "If his partners forced him out of the firm today, he'd have tons of offers from other firms tomorrow. No, there's no way they'd force him out unless he fucked a goat on the conference- room table."

"That's reassuring," replied Carly sarcastically. "What about all those training sessions on sexual conduct we have to attend. Don't the partners get those lectures, too?"

"You're such a hayseed," laughed Marcia. "They don't mean shit to guys like Harris."

"But I see all the partners at them. They have to attend too, right?" asked Carly, hinting Marcia was mistaken.

"It's all CYA so the firm can check off that box with its malpractice-insurance carrier. If someone sues the firm for sexual harassment, the firm has a built-in defense: the guy was a rogue employee because the management did its part, the firm had a sexual-harassment policy, and all employees are properly trained on it. It's good business, that's all."

Marcia was avuncular with the younger Carly telling her – as so many other lawyers back in Kansas had – that she'd make an excellent lawyer and should consider attending law school. The two became closer every day. Eventually, they did get together for drinks after work a few times (after all, Carly told herself, what was unusual about that?), and even went shopping together for makeup and accessories.

Marcia offered to take Carly to some of the shops Marcia frequented for her more *adventurous* party clothes. And lingerie. Carly just laughed and shook her head. Although she wanted to indulge, she just couldn't bring herself to do it in front of Marcia, a co-worker, even if she was a friend.

One Tuesday at lunch, the ladies finally made plans to get together that Friday evening and go dancing in Fat Cat, a club in the West Village. As the week progressed, Carly grew more excited about their date, planning and replanning what to wear, thinking about it at night in bed. She'd wake up every morning, smiling at the thought that Friday was almost here. Throughout the week, Carly pressed Marcia for advice on how she should style her makeup and hair.

"Why don't you come over to my apartment Friday night before we go out?" Marcia offered. "You can meet Melanie, my roommate. She's great, you'll love her. We'll order in some Chinese, open a bottle of wine and play some music to get inspired for our girls' night out. I'll help you with your makeup, but honestly Carl' lemme tell you, if I looked like you, I wouldn't be worrying about makeup."

Carly blushed. She had wanted to make girlfriends in New York, but never envisioned that Marcia would be one of them, or that they'd feel this close so soon. It was all so heady, her image of Marcia – from the prim and proper New York lawyer she met her first day at Bergman Troutman to the fearless party girl, exposed on social media for all the world to see: club hopping, sexy, daring, enjoying the attention of handsome men without shame, without caution. And now they were friends, close friends, and Carly was invited into Marcia's exciting world.

Carly dutifully appeared at Marcia's apartment with a bottle of white zinfandel in one hand and her makeup kit in a Nike sports bag in the other. Marcia greeted Carly with a bear hug and kisses on both cheeks. The reception felt perfectly natural to Carly, but she definitely recognized that this was the first time they had hugged. Marcia ushered Carly into her all-white living room. "Gold Digger" by Kanye was blasting through the Bose speakers. The irony of the song made Carly smile. Marcia disappeared into the kitchen to fetch a corkscrew and glasses, as well as some cheese and crackers and olive tapenade she had picked up from the Korean deli downstairs.

"Okay, kiddo!" Marcia laughed, raising her glass. "Here's to a great evening – wherever it leads us."

Carly laughed, too. Then downed her glass in one gulp.

"Whoa! You must be awfully thirsty," she teased, pouring Carly another. "But take it easy, it's gonna be a long night."

Carly touched her hand to her lips, a little embarrassed. "I guess so! But it's good wine." Marcia smiled, delighted as Carly rolled her eyes in a self-deprecating way Marcia had never seen before.

A tall, blonde woman with a sensational body materialized in the living room doorframe. Marcia and Carly were seated on the couch, so she looked even taller than her lanky five feet, ten inches.

"Oh, Carly, this is my roommate, Melanie Hunter. Mel, this is Carly, my friend from work I was telling you about."

"Nice to meet you. I hear you're from Kansas," Melanie smiled warmly.

"Yes. Well, someone has to be." Why did I say that? Carly thought. She suddenly felt herself trying a little too hard. "Where are you from?"

"Chapel Hill," Melanie replied in an unmistakable southern accent. Her voice was as warm as her smile.

Another glass materialized and the three young women relaxed. Within moments they were having a grand time exchanging thoughts on music, designers, clubs, food, and men – lots and lots of men.

It didn't take long before the zinfandel was finished, and Marcia produced a sauvignon blanc from the kitchen. The conversation became more relaxed, eventually turning to office gossip about Harris. It was obvious that Marcia had already filled Melanie in about Harris and his addiction to women.

"You're so beautiful, Carly. I'm surprised he hasn't hit on you yet," laughed Melanie.

"Oh, he has," Marcia assured her as Carly laughed and nodded.

"He has? How'd that go?" Melanie leaned in, her knees almost touching Carly's.

"Carly's no dummy," Marcia replied, answering on Carly's behalf. "She's been playing him like a country fiddle. Like one of her farmhands back in Kansas."

The girls laughed.

"How about you? Do you have a lot of that where you work – older guys hitting on younger women?" Carly asked Melanie.

Melanie and Marcia looked at each other and giggled.

"Funny you should ask," Marcia blurted out. "Tell her, Mel."

"Well, I'm kinda seeing my boss," explained Melanie, her voice lowering, unsuccessfully attempting to soften the impact. The gossip level had just been ratcheted up a notch and Marcia laughed and slapped Mel on the shoulder.

Seeing the two of them smiling, Carly smiled as well. "Well, is he nice? Good looking? Rich? You can't just say you're dating your boss and leave me hanging."

"Oh yes, all of those," answered Melanie.

"But ...?" Marcia chimed in, arching an eyebrow.

"But ..." Melanie shrugged, nodding her head. "But he's married."

"Oh, and how's *that* gonna work out?" Carly chided

Melanie.

"We'll see. I know, I know ... But, for now, it's perfect for me. It's all good. Mario, that's his name, is the number two guy at the bank, and if all goes the way it's supposed to go, he'll be the CEO by the end of the year."

"That sounds good for him, but how about you?" asked Carly while Marcia excused herself to go to the bathroom.

"Well, he has this major client, EuroHoldings, that I'm helping him with. They're already a huge client of the bank, but if these deals Mario is working on come through, I'll be the junior banker on all the deals, complete with a very nice raise. Plus," she leaned in conspiratorially, "he's great in bed."

Carly was dumfounded. As soon as Melanie had uttered the words "EuroHoldings," Carly had lost focus on anything else she had said. EuroHoldings. That was the other company being investigated by the US Attorney's office and being compared to the Boeing investigation as Harris had explained to her. That was the connection she had been tasked to uncover. Carly almost shivered visibly. There was no way this was the leak – no way, she rationalized. It had to be a pure coincidence that these two roommates worked for men with connections to these two cases. But could it be? Damn, Carly cursed the fact she had already consumed two generous glasses of wine because she wasn't able to think quite straight or put the pieces together. But there was something here, she sensed, and she would figure it out when she was sober.

"Hey, what'd I miss?" Marcia said, playfully bopping back to the beat of Kanye's "Through the Wire."

"Boring business stuff, nothing sexy. Well," Melanie laughed, "maybe a little sexy. I was just telling Carly about Mario and our EuroHoldings deals." Marcia shrugged, she'd already heard all of Melanie's accounts of her trips with Mario and their plans for her "special assistant" relationship. She had never really focused on the client's name or any of the details of the deals they were working on. In fact, Marcia didn't ever remember hearing the name EuroHoldings. She just wanted her roommate to be happy. The fact that Melanie's relationship with Mario insured that she'd be able to pay her share of the rent was good, too.

Feeling nicely buzzed, Marcia felt the pull to join in on true confessions time.

"Carly, do you remember when you asked me how the acquisition of that small boutique law firm could affect my future?"

"Yes, and you said it wouldn't because none of the new associates were in the same potential partnership class year as you." Given her present state of dizziness, Carly was impressed that she was able to remember the conversation at all, let alone the details.

"Well, yesterday Harris called me into his office for a discussion about my future."

"Uh oh. That's never a good thing," interrupted Melanie. "Why didn't you tell me?"

"Because I'm not sure there's anything to tell yet. Although I was right that there is no one from my class year in the new group up for partner this year, there are two people from the year ahead of me and two people from the year behind me."

"So what? They've only just arrived at the firm and you've been there for years," blurted Carly.

"Well, here's the thing – when the partners in the new group decided to leave their old firm and join Bergman Troutman, some of the associates didn't want to make the move. The two associates who are now in front of me were up for partner this year at their old firm and would have made it – *if* they had stayed there. So when the big defection was announced, the old firm was so pissed at the guys leaving they went to the senior associates and promised them an accelerated partnership track if they would stay. But the senior partners going to Bergman desperately wanted to take those associates with them."

"Why was that such a big deal to them?" Carly asked.

"It's like this – the partners make the rain and bring in the business, but the associates are the real brains behind getting everything done. The partners knew, without the associates they'd be out on their asses in a year."

"So what?" inquired Melanie, confused.

"So what is that Harris was forced to promise those two associates they'd be made partner at Bergman *this* year or the whole deal would have fallen apart. I'm up next year and then the other two guys the year after me. Harris has power, but there is no way he can make more than two or maybe three partners within a six- or seven-year period. You get it? The numbers don't add up."

"Wait a minute – did he fire you?" Melanie was getting angry. It was hard to tell if she was pissed that Marcia had been mistreated, or that something so dramatic had happened and Marcia hadn't filled her in on it.

"No, not at all. We had a really good discussion. Harris is super connected with all his clients, including a bunch of the top companies in the United States. He told me he'd like to advocate for me as a potential assistant general counsel to several of those companies."

"So ... he's firing you." quipped Carly.

"No! I've always wanted to go in house, not become a partner at the firm. When you make partner, the workload just gets heavier, but an in-house lawyer makes good money, gets terrific benefits, has less work, and gets to leave the office at 6, not 10. There are tons of perks, too. Usually you get plenty of stock options which can end up turning into seriously huge money," explained Marcia. She wasn't defensive at all, this was all very carefully thought out.

"So where's he going to park you? Someplace where you can't tell people what a pig he is?" asked Melanie.

"No, he was really nice about it. He told me to give it some thought and think of specific companies I'm interested in. He also said he has some ideas of his own, but he wants to flesh them out."

"I'll bet he does..." Carly cut in. Melanie and Marcia giggled. "What do you think he has in mind?"

"I don't know. But I'm telling you, he was really cool about it. He genuinely felt bad about the position he was in because of this new group at the firm," Marcia continued. "Anyway, that's all there is to tell right now. When another shoe drops, I promise you'll be the first people to know."

"But . . . right now we have more important things to attend to! March!"

They stumbled, laughing and whooping, into Marcia's bedroom, having a wonderful time trying on outfits for the evening and applying makeup, fake nails and hair extensions. Like little girls playing dress up. All part of the heady game of giving the men they'd meet tonight a taste of anything but who they really were.

But Carly couldn't quite concentrate. EuroHoldings. That was precisely the company Boeing was comparing itself to in Bergman Troutman's internal analytical documents and the same name the Assistant US Attorney, Steve Krotz, had told Harris about at that cocktail party. No way was this a coincidence, Carly told herself, no way.

# CHAPTER FORTY-ONE

A s she sat back and evaluated her progress, Eva congratulated herself on her amazing job of defining her vision, organizing a syndicate, and collecting the funds so she could pay the Sheik and Mitsubishi Marine – all in only a few months. In a week, the ship would be launched for sea trials and when that was complete, Eva and her posse would take formal delivery and move in.

With all the ingredients in the bowl, the time was right to mix them together and enjoy the fruits of her recipe.

All the owners of the newly-minted Lampedusa yacht were invited to attend a get-to-know-each-other party in the Imperial Ballroom on the 11th floor of the New York Athletic Club. Eva had overseen the decorations herself, and had enlisted Eddie, the restaurant captain, to concoct a nautical theme and spare no expense. The formal grey-silk tablecloths had been removed and replaced with blue ones adorned with small white sailboats. The centerpieces were small white wooden schooners filled with blue morning glories and white roses. Each table held a simple brass cylinder with a lid shaped like a ship's wheel. The beige curtains had been pulled open, exposing polished, brass-trimmed floor-to-ceiling windows with million-dollar views of Central Park.

For this special night, the satin ties of the curtains were replaced with white nautical rope. Small globes adorned each table and a large map of the world hung on the room's only windowless wall. The ship's new captain was present and had outlined the map in red marker to show the course of the ship's first eight months at sea.

On that same wall was an organizational chart of the onboard team, each member pictured wearing his crisply ironed white uniform. The totality of the effect and what it signified was not lost on anyone. Eddie told Eva that this was one of the grandest parties he had ever had the privilege of organizing.

Eva's greatest consideration went into constructing the seating chart for this glorious event. She had spent a long weekend with the Romanellos at their Westport home as she and Karen, with occasional input from Marc, tried to figure out who would be best seated next to whom. Marc was glad to be involved in the planning, it helped him get through his grieving over the Yankees' recent failure to make the postseason.

The challenge was, as Marc reiterated time and again, that only Eva knew the personalities of the all the invitees. And even at that, there were still four owners who were friends of friends whom Eva had never even met. Over a glass of port after their roasted lamb chops, Eva had become quite relaxed and shared with Marc and Karen the predilections of some of the owners, especially those who were notoriously lecherous. Those men probably shouldn't be seated next to anyone's beautiful wife.

More careful discussion was spent on the size and arrangement of the banquet tables than at the Paris Peace Accords to end the Vietnam War. Karen shook her head at the silliness of the minutia at play in the discussion, but Marc reveled in it. When Marc was at Citibank and they'd organize holiday parties for the managing directors, Marc always played the role of the *de facto* social chairman. He'd always thrived on making everything just so and he became more invested with Eva's ship every day. They might not have the largest luxury suite on the ship, but he and Karen were the only couple who were planning to live on the ship full time. Marc was only too happy to invest the time upfront to define the parameters of the social intercourse among the owners. He reasoned that it was far better to create a governance structure he wanted than to fight uphill against a model somebody else would impose on the owners.

Eva finally divulged that six of the top officers and executive staff from the ship would be in attendance at the New York Athletic Club event. The multimillionaire owners would be entrusting their journey, lives, and fate to people whom they had never met. These investors were all control freaks to some extent and were all anxious to see what they were getting into. So it made sense to have the senior officers present.

Captain Paulo Pugliese was the Italian skipper who would be the most decorated man in the room. A seasoned mariner with eighteen years of experience and two wives astern, Captain Paulo looked like he had stepped right out of central casting – complete with military bearing, and perfect white hair.

As the captain of the vessel, he would be the highest-ranking officer on the ship, responsible for the entire operation. That entitled this handsomely bearded, 6'3 seafarer to wear a crisp white dress uniform with four black-and-gold epaulets on each shoulder, identifying his position on the top of the food chain. Captain Paulo would be seated at Eva's table, along with Richard Winchester, the British general manager who would bear responsibility for all elements of the hospitality side of the operation. Richard had been employed by the Ritz-Carlton hotel chain for two decades, rising to the position of general manager of the Ritz's property in Tyson's Corner, Virginia. Then, Richard took to the seas and served as the general manager of the *Joy*, the largest ship in the Norwegian Cruise Lines fleet.

Rounding out the table would be Marc, Karen, and Lorraine Williams. Eva insisted that Marc and Karen sit with her and that it was only right that Lorraine be seated at the head table since she was the largest investor.

Four other members of the ship's team were invited to the party. Having spent six years as the Cruise Director on the Reflection, the largest ship in the Celebrity cruise line, Elaine Dwyer jumped at the opportunity to be the ship's Entertainment Director, responsible for identifying and hiring upscale onboard entertainment, including cultural lecturers, musicians, and the occasional scientist or professor who would add intellectual gravitas to this community of knowledge seekers. No comedians nor jugglers need apply. Elaine was an attractive, though not comely, 38-year-old brunette who enjoyed men's company but had never enjoyed it enough to commit herself to matrimony. Maybe because she was equally fond of women.

Candy Podeski had been a sales manager for Four Seasons Residence Clubs for the past six years, selling glorified time shares to the uber-wealthy. When Eva and Richard Winchester were searching for someone who could sell luxury residences on their floating condominium, Candy seemed like a good fit. At 34 and naturally radiant, Candy had the quintessential sales personality, along with perfect teeth and comely cleavage, none of which she was shy about. Eva knew she'd be a hit with the men, but how would women buyers receive her?

But in the end, even Eva became smitten with Candy's infectious smile and passion to sell. This woman, Eva had concluded, could sell dry ice to wet Eskimos. Hopefully, it would take Candy no time to fill the remaining luxury suites and get the visitor flats up to one hundred percent occupancy on a regular basis. And that was important.

Steve Draper was the ship's Security Officer, an amusing Popeye-like character. He grew up in the sleepy suburb of North Tonawanda, a few miles north of Buffalo. A heralded player on his high school football team, Steve enrolled in Niagara Community College intending to be a gridiron star, albeit on a small stage. He had all the athletic ability, but none of the grade-point average. When he was eventually declared academically ineligible pursuant to NCAA regulations, he decided that spending four more years in the frozen tundra of Western New York studying physical education was not his calling.

At nineteen, Steve followed his father's footsteps, enlisting in the Marine Corps. The senior Mr. Draper had left the

Corps and become a Buffalo police officer in the 1970s. Steve admired his father's commitment to law enforcement and so he volunteered for MP duty. When he left the service after eight years, Steve bounced around private security details in the Buffalo area, at one point rising to the position of director of security at a Niagara Falls Indian casino.

But cold weather and Steve just were not meant for each other and the two-hundred-and-eighty-pound, heavily tattooed former linebacker became a security officer on the Norwegian Cruise Line *Joy*, where he met Richard Winchester. When Richard was tapped to be the general manager of Eva's ship, he immediately asked Steve to join his team.

The final member of the team invited to join the kickoff event was the ship's engineer, Chad Stonington, a tall Australian. Chad possessed a stoic personality and was far from the ideal conversationalist socially, but Eva wanted him there to show the owners, and the Captain, the importance of his role on the ship. As Chief Engineer, Chad was the second highest-ranking officer on the vessel. Besides, some of the male owners on the ship were frustrated childhood model builders and engineers themselves. They'd love to hear Chad's recounting of all the operational aspects of the ship.

# CHAPTER FORTY-TWO

T he guests started arriving at the Imperial Ballroom of the NYAC. The ship's General Manager, Entertainment Director, and Sales Director were each sporting blue blazers with grey pants, or skirt, a light-blue shirt and blue-and-white striped rep ties. They looked like an older version of Andover seniors attending their convocation. The Captain, Chief Engineer, and Security Officer all donned their dress-white uniforms, with the Captain looking most impressive and striking a formidable station of obvious importance.

Four staff waiters circled the room, deftly supplying glasses of pink champagne and red and white wine. Marc had pushed for nametags in order to make the meet-and-greet process more user-friendly, but Eva rejected that suggestion – this was to be more like a cocktail party in one's home because, after all, the ship would be their home at sea.

Eva was the common thread among all the attendees, so she made sure to position herself near enough to the fourteen-foot door that she could spy each person as they entered. When Eva greeted guests, it was not the classic New York air-kiss greeting.

Eva was real, and people appreciated her for that. She greeted everyone with a warm hug and a kiss solidly planted on the cheek, *one* cheek. None of this pseudo-European two-cheek kissing. Marc and Karen stood close by, serving as first lieutenants to Admiral Eva. Marc was totally obsessed with the details of the meeting and had worked diligently to make sure everything went off flawlessly.

Karen enjoyed seeing Marc more engaged in launching the ship than he had been with anything since he left Citibank. He needed a hobby. For a while last summer she worried that, with no job to occupy him, he might find himself socializing with Westport's Blonde Bobs. It was no accident Karen had buried Marc with so many administrative tasks for the launch and governance of the ship. A busy Marc would be a faithful Marc.

Eva was apprehensive about having so many massive egos in one room. Particularly Mario and Harris. They both were big personalities with sharp elbows, climbers in the world of New York business headlines, and big skirt chasers. She winced at the thought of all the mischief and embarrassment those two testosterone-overdosed idiots could cause aboard the ship.

The cocktail hour proceeded exactly as planned. People chatted with each other, anxious to get to know the other crazy travelers who had signed on to this ride. To make introductions easier, and lessen any "first-date anxiety," Eva had circulated a list of all the owners in advance. Everyone had already Googled everyone else, so they walked into the room with a certain amount of virtual familiarity with each other. They were all impressed at the troupe Eva had assembled: successful, adventurous and, hopefully, fun.

After loosening up with a few cocktails, everyone took their seats, buzzing and chatting happily. Mario and Janice Garramone sat at the head table alongside Liam and Danielle Perlmutter, Don Bickford, and his wife Donna.

Harris and Becky Hirschfeld, along with Oliver and Heidi Rasmussen, Carmine Scantello, Cindy Miller, and the Security Officer, were at the last table. Eva took pains to keep Mario and Harris as far apart as possible. There just wasn't enough room for them *and* their opinions of themselves to be shoehorned into a small space.

The waiters served appetizers of foie-gras terrine and enormous shrimp platters. Things were going swimmingly at the head table – Eva and Lorraine Williams had been friends for many years and, of course, Marc and Karen Romanello were part of the inner nucleus of the organization. The Captain, General Manager, and Chief Engineer added color and livened things up with charming tales of their life on the sea.

At the second table, the peacocks presented themselves. At seventy years of age, a successful cardiologist and entrepreneur, Liam Perlmutter fashioned himself the master of the table. Dr. Perlmutter considered himself the most successful man in the room. Lorraine and Eva may have been wealthier, but they lacked the necessary chromosomal composition necessary to challenge his unspoken assertion of male dominance.

Mario Garramone was no wallflower either. Just two years Liam's junior, he was only a few months away from his coronation as CEO of New York Savings and Guaranty and he made sure everyone knew that. His conceit would not allow him to assume a subordinate posture to another male peacock. He was proud of his arm candy, Janice, the most dazzling woman. He also loved that she was able to hold her own in any discussion of finance or economics and could make even those dry subjects sparkle.

Compared to Mario and Liam, Don Bickford was downright demure. He was just as successful in his field – hedge funds – as they were in theirs, but he had a quiet self confidence that, for all their wealth and status, eluded them. Don smiled across the table at his wife, Donna, enjoying her company as always, content. She was a mainstay among the Blonde Bobs of Westport. Donna glanced over at Janice Garramone and felt a pang of self-consciousness – she knew she wasn't quite in the same league.

Elaine Dwyer, the affable and charming Entertainment Director, sat to Mario's left, keeping him alert and engaged throughout the dinner. From their own table, Eva and Karen glanced over at Mario on occasion to see if he was paying more attention to Elaine than he was to his own wife – he was.

They had been careful to seat Candy Podeski, the Sales Director, directly across the table from Mario. Candy was stunning, and her blue blazer was tailored perfectly to accentuate the contours of her ample bosom. Eva had toyed with the idea of seating Candy next to Mario, but wisely decided against it. No point risking the whole enterprise collapsing under the weight of Mario's womanizing on the first night.

He certainly was enjoying Candy's sensual presence

though. He let his mind wander – the possibilities were wonderful. He allowed his head to fill with images of Candy ...

At home later that night, Janice was so happy. Mario devoured her with a hunger he hadn't shown in years. So seating Candy at that table had served a noble purpose after all. Furthermore, although neither Mario nor Janice was aware of it, while Mario enjoyed ogling Candy, Candy was ogling Janice, letting her mind wander through that bisexual side of herself few knew existed.

At the final table, Harris Hirschfeld held court. He dominated the conversation so completely it was hard to notice that he and Becky were barely speaking. Within moments, Harris made sure everyone at the table knew he was the largest rainmaker at the most prestigious firm in New York. He could barely contain his excitement.

Like so many other dinners before tonight, Becky longed to scream that it was her, not Harris, who had all the family money. It was *her* annual $100,000 contribution to the Metropolitan Opera that had earned them their prestigious Patrons status. The Hirschfeld Endowment, offered to one leading neuroscientist each year by the Alzheimer's Association, was *her* doing not Harris's. But she didn't scream. There was no room to scream anyway, Harris was sucking up all the oxygen in the room. So she just sat there, not saying a word.

Amazingly, Harris had some competition at the table. He made the error of taking a breath, and Oliver Rasmussen pounced on the opportunity. Loud and bombastic, Oliver regaled everyone with his experience as the head of First National Bank in South

Africa and his numerous connections with world leaders. At one point, when the waiter referred to him as Mr. Rasmussen, Oliver corrected him, "It's actually Dr. Rasmussen." He was damn proud of that Ph.D. and never let anyone forget it – even if it was only honorary and only conferred after he donated the South African equivalent of $80 million to his alma mater, the University of Cape Town.

Although Oliver was just as pompous and long-winded as Harris, he had a certain jovial charm that Harris had never been able to develop. So despite all his oafishness and bluster, everyone loved Oliver. The only thing his dinner companions were always perturbed by was Oliver's tendency to spit when he spoke, and even more so when he ate. It was not at all uncommon for a piece of cheese, or whatever Oliver had just stuffed into his mouth, to fly as far as five feet as he blathered on. Such misadventures caused more embarrassment to the receiver, as she would have to subtly dab the buckshot off her face, only to get sprayed again. His wife, Heidi, was quiet and unassuming, tolerant of his off-color humor. Around Oliver, it was impossible to get a word in, but Heidi was fine with that. While Oliver was enthralling his tablemates, Heidi struck up an enchanting conversation with her seatmate, Cindy Miller, and they became fast friends by the end of dinner. And although neither Eva nor Karen had met Carmine Scantello before that evening, their instincts were on the money, seating him next to Steve Draper, the Security Director. The testosterone-fueled match up of a career security expert and a construction developer from Brooklyn was a natural. These two blowhards were entertaining, providing some comedy relief for Becky Hirschfeld.

Eva asked Captain Pugliese to make some introductory remarks, which he was only too happy to do. Most seafarers who have served as captain on a cruise line are blessed with, or necessarily develop, a sense of dramatic flair and a gift of spoken charisma. They are often asked to dine with the occupants of the ship's most expensive suites and are called upon to be fascinating and alluring. Captain Pugliese was no exception. In his majestic dress whites – bedazzled with the gold trimmings and brocade commensurate with his rank – and fine Italian accent, he rose to speak.

"I first would like to thank the owners of this magnificent vessel – yes, Eva, but of course, all of you – for this grand opportunity. And, I thank you for recognizing the wisdom of that sage, old nautical saying 'a very new ship needs a very old Captain...'" They all laughed appreciatively. Like a seasoned entertainer, he held for the laugh.

"Looking out at this wonderful assemblage, I know this ship is in very good hands..."

Deftly, he spoke a few words about each member of the crew assembled at the dinner. He spoke eloquently about the scores of crew not present, whose job it would be to attend to the seamanship of the mighty vessel and all the creature comforts desired by the owners.

"This ship, this powerful vessel, will carry a full-time crew of fifteen engineers to regulate the mighty machines, pulling up to 8200 horsepower. Man's triumph over the seas, yes, but at the same time we know that we must be wise stewards of nature's incredible bounty, for we share this world at sea with all the amazing, vibrant forms of aquatic life. With that responsibility foremost in our minds, the ship will consume lightweight NGO fuel, which burns cleaner than the diesel fuel used by cargo ships."

There was much nodding and murmuring appreciatively, even though most of them had no idea what he was talking about. But apparently this was some kind of fuel that killed less fish, so that was good.

The captain continued, "While running at ten knots, which I anticipate will be our fairly normal cruising speed, we will burn approximately 35,000 liters of fuel a day and that will enable us to cover 241 nautical miles in twenty-four hours. Before you all pull out your calculators, let me help you. If you were to perform all the necessary conversions, you would conclude that the ship – your ship – will burn approximately 8,200 US gallons of fuel per day which amounts to 385 gallons an hour."

They all appreciated the enormity of the venture. Many of them also silently contemplated the amount of condo association fees they would pay to keep this floating gas guzzler moving in the right direction.

Captain Pugliese continued explaining the way seawater would be converted into drinking water at a rate of 500 metric tons of water a day. As his discourse unfolded, Eva marveled at his natural skill of conveying just enough factual material to keep the owners' attention but stopping just short of overburdening them with minutia.

Winding up with comforting assurances that his security

detail was armed with the kind of long-range weapons Captain Phillips would have coveted, he again thanked them all for the opportunity and reclaimed his seat.

Eva leaned over to him. "That was perfect," she whispered.

Perfectly on cue, the waiters swooped in, attending to each of the participants, placing their platters of Dover sole or New York sirloin before them. The burble of the room grew in volume as everyone commented on Captain Pugliese's remarks and opened up to share their own stories of how they knew Eva and why they wanted to be part of this adventure.

Eva's relationship with so many people in the room served as a tacit recommendation of their social and financial bona fides. Everyone could dispense with the traditional Manhattan cross-examination performed at such functions, designed to determine societal status. In ordinary circumstances, two simple questions would reveal everything you needed to know about a person's ranking in the New York hierarchy. "Where do you work?" and "Where do you live?" Armed with a title and a zip code, Google and Zillow would provide the rest.

The young people even adopted the practice, retreating to bathrooms in clubs and doing their due diligence on their smart phones. It was a simple 21st century ritual before exchanging phone numbers or swapping saliva. But none of that was necessary tonight. This was one of the most exclusive clubs in the world – Eva's boating community. They all knew they were rich, and Eva's approval spoke to their social standing. There were thousands of millionaires around the country, but you really wouldn't want to spend months traveling with most of those arrogant bastards. Not us, they each assured themselves, we're the cool kids.

Soon it was Eva's turn to speak. She knew she needed to captivate everyone's attention, impart a degree of seriousness, share some levity, and most importantly, reassure everyone that this was a decision they should be proud of. In a flowing chartreuse and lime green satin Etro dress – baring just enough cleavage to keep the men engaged but not make the women uncomfortable – Eva rose. The room grew hushed. Eva, the consummate trial lawyer, began.

"I appreciate each and every one of you for the commitment you've made to this exciting and adventurous new nautical community. More importantly, I want *you* to take a moment to appreciate *yourselves*. Each of you has worked hard to achieve a unique level of wealth and status. Not one of you is a trust-fund baby. You know what it means to work hard to succeed. No one here tonight is unidimensional or uninspiring. Quite frankly, if you were, I would've left you home." A wave of subdued laughter rolled across the room.

Eva took a few minutes to formally introduce the Chief Engineer, General Manager, Entertainment Director, Sales Director, and Security Officer. "There are two other original employees – 'original' because we'll be going from this core group to over a hundred employees in a matter of days – first our General Counsel, Marcia Coleman. She couldn't be here tonight, she's at a wedding in Atlanta. Though it's not her wedding, so she probably could have been here!"

Eva smiled. It was an ad-lib, and it worked, getting a nice laugh.

"She comes to us courtesy of Harris Hirschfeld and is in her ninth year at Bergman Troutman. Harris says she's one of the brightest young lawyers he's ever had. I've met her and he's right, she's very impressive. In fact, I wish I had hired her before Harris's firm did. She specializes in contracts and entertainment law. And with this eclectic group, entertainment is probably just the right word."

Everyone giggled. Having outsourced his precious associate – so he could continue to stalk her, with her now even more beholden to him – Harris smiled more than most.

"The second employee wears a white uniform, but does not have any epaulets, gold braiding, shiny shoes, or medals on his chest. Knowing some of the folks in the room the way I do, I'm guessing you'll be just as interested in interacting with him than with the boys on the bridge. Thanks to the efforts of Mario Garramone, we have been able to secure the service of an outstanding Executive Chef, Rolando Carew. Rolando worked for Mario's family for twelve years and we were lucky enough to convince him to join our floating paradise. Mario and Janice were kind enough to invite a few of us over to sample Rolando's talents and, all I can say is – start buying pants with larger waistlines." The room was filled with polite laughter. Not as big a laugh as the wedding ad-lib.

"I've known some of you for decades, and only met some of you tonight," Eva continued, her gaze moving from Lorraine and Liam to Carmine and Cindy. "You are my colleagues, my clients, my friends. Some of you may even have been closer to me than just friends," she added with a wink that launched a thousand concerns.

An awkward laugh peppered the room. Eva didn't seem to register that the joke hadn't landed. Many of the women looked around. Janice Garramone, Danielle Perlmutter, Becky Hirschfeld and Heidi Rasmussen all had credible reasons to suspect their own faithless spouses. Each of their husbands had been caught in any number of affairs. Why had Eva interjected that little tidbit, they each wondered?

Karen Romanello felt particularly uncomfortable the moment the words left Eva's lips. She had always suspected Marc had slept with Eva before she and Marc had met, and this rogue allusion sealed the deal for her. It was all in the past, right? Who really cared, she concluded – or she convinced herself she had concluded.

"Tonight, we are all shipmates," Eva continued, "adventurers who will explore the globe together. With the help of our esteemed captain and his hand-picked crew, together we'll see all the world and visit our favorite cities like Venice, Hong Kong, London, and Singapore. We'll explore civilizations that we have only read about in books. Places like Borneo, Komodo Island, Easter Island, the Solomon Islands, Namibia, the Northwest Passage, and even Antarctica are within reach. We'll enjoy a lot of fascinating voyages together, and I know we'll have a great deal of fun. We'll have challenges along the way, that's for sure; but if we remember that we're here to have fun and enjoy the experience, and use a little respect and common courtesy with one another, this will be an amazing journey.

"Fortunately, we are not limited by funds, and our only restraints are those we impose on ourselves if we lack imagination. Our concierge staff and Entertainment Director have been expressly prohibited from saying 'no' to any and all requests." She glanced at the voluptuous Candy Podeski and corrected herself. "Well…"

Eva looked up, raising her eyebrow. Big laugh. She'd recovered from the "closer than friends" misfire. "Any *appropriate* request. That means that you can have anything you want, as long as you can dream it – and won't get us arrested for it." Small applause break. Not bad Eva, she thought.

"Now, we can't get everywhere in the first year, so we're going to have an itinerary committee to plan our adventures a year ahead. That way, you can all plan your air travel and lives in concert with your business schedules. And I know many of you have such busy dating lives." Eva smiled as she stared directly at her friend Lorraine. "We wouldn't want to interfere with those plans, now would we?"

"Now I think it's time we finally slapped a name on the bow of this vessel, what do you all think?" Eva was sounding like a fine litigator, appealing to a jury's sense of getting personally involved in the decision as she reached her crescendo.

"You may have noticed that in the center of each table, there is a small brass canister with a lid that resembles the wheel from a mighty sailing ship. Under each of your dinner plates was a small piece of paper. Now that the plates have been cleared, you can see those papers." Oliver Rasmussen was mumbling and searching frantically for his, fearing his paper might have been cleared with his plate. Eva noticed and scolded, "Oliver, don't worry, I'll give you another one. But you must promise to write in English, not South African. We just can't understand the way you speak." Oliver was puzzled for a second, before everyone erupted in the most boisterous laughter so far. Red-faced, Oliver shook his head.

"I am going to give you a collaborative assignment. Each table is to come up with one name for the ship, write it down, and place it in that little cylinder. After dessert, Captain Pugliese will come around and collect the three names and read them aloud. Then we will take our first vote as a community. We're going to name our ship *tonight!*"

With that Eva, returned to her seat and the buzz among the tables grew to its highest level of the evening. Laughter, prodding, insults and shouting could be heard from every table as the new owners of one of the largest private yachts in the world set about naming the place they would be calling their floating home. Eva had been masterful in how she had structured the entire evening. Cocktails and 90 minutes of mixing and mingling had served to loosen everyone up a bit. The speeches, appetizer, entrée and dessert courses had been generously spaced out, and now people were truly engaged with one another.

Once the chocolate soufflés, mixed berries, and key lime pie had been thoroughly enjoyed, Captain Pugliese solemnly fulfilled his obligation and collected the three pieces of paper with the names for the vessel. Striding gallantly to the center of the room, he prepared to read each one aloud. Eva asked that one person from each table stand and defend the proposed name in two sentences or less. She was keen to see just who would emerge as spokesmen; she had no doubt that the women would be shunted in favor of their male counterparts.

Captain Pugliese slowed his pace, lending an added air of theatre to the proceedings. Holding the first piece of paper in his right hand, he shared its contents: "The Traveler." From the second table, Mario Garramone rose slowly. Without prepared notes, he elucidated, "That's what we'll be doing, away from our terrestrial homes, traveling. So we thought it would make sense to name the ship after ourselves." People nodded, raised their eyebrows and were generally appreciative of the effort. A few "Not bad," and "I like it" comments could be heard from the other tables.

Captain Pugliese slowly read the second name aloud, "The Explorer." Scarcely a moment before the words had left the captain's mouth, Harris was on his feet. In Eva's presence, he was not about to be upstaged. "Explorers, that's what we'll be. Banded together like the great explorers who proceeded us on the high seas – Ernest Shackleton, Christopher Columbus, Marco Polo, James Cook, and the lot." Eva, Lorraine, Marc, and Karen remained absolutely stoic. There was nothing to be gained by rolling their eyes. Harris continued. "Tonight, we are tenderfoots, yeomen sailors out to discover our vessel and sail the seven seas. And Eva, thank you for introducing all of us to each other, and to your masterful vision. Once aboard, the true exploration will begin as we visit remote and exotic parts of this wonderful planet we call Earth. With the name Explorer firmly emblazoned on our hull ..."

Harris was now six sentences into his two-sentence defense, with no end in sight. Eva was trying to figure out a polite way to interrupt the peripatetic colloquy without causing Harris undue embarrassment, when she saw Captain Pugliese rise to his feet again. "Terrific suggestion, Harris. Makes great sense to me." Nicely done, thought Eva. This captain is a real captain – deftly taking control and not allowing anyone to run afoul of the spoken directives.

"The third name is 'Paradise,'" boomed Captain Pugliese, as Harris sheepishly folded his legs beneath his chair. From the first table, Karen Romanello rose. Marc had actually put forth the name and intended to present it to the group but when he saw his wife move to stand, he knew better than to upstage her. "I just, we just, thought that since what we're seeking to achieve is a state of paradise, Paradise would be an appropriate name. It's our itinerary and our objective." She sat down. Nothing more needed to be said and Karen was not particularly comfortable speaking in public, especially before this group of egos. Around the room there was appreciative nodding: the name was attractive in its simplicity.

Eva regained her feet. "So there you have it. Those sound like three pretty good ideas to me. In the ideal world, we could take a few weeks to mull this over and, with all the lawyers and smart people in this room, come up with several other drafts and iterations." Giggles again. "But we don't have that luxury. I am being told by the shipyard they would like to proceed with the painting of the name on the bow this weekend. And we need to order stationary, pens, robes, menus, and all kinds of things with the name of our enchanted vessel. So this won't be the most deliberative process, but it will be the most democratic. I am going to ask Richard, our GM, to rip up some sheets of paper and hand them out. Each owner gets one and the name with the most votes wins. This is going to be simple; one luxury suite, one vote. And for you married couples, you'll need to come to a compromise quickly. That's where Lorraine, Carmine, Cindy and I have it easy."

For most, this was not a major deliberative process. But being the type-A gunners they were, Mario Garramone and Harris Hirschfeld hurriedly lobbied their tables. It was a competition, a joust, a match, and they had to win. At Mario's table, Liam Perlmutter was happy to go along with The Traveler. It was nice, but more importantly, Danielle liked it. Whenever Liam could please his wife without it costing him six figures in jewelry, he was only too happy to do so. The Bickfords were overwhelmed by Mario's tenacity so they swiftly acceded to support his efforts so he would shut up. What they told Mario they would vote for and what they actually wrote down, however, may have been two entirely separate things.

Harris was no less indefatigable in his efforts campaigning for The Explorer, but he was having a tougher time, encountering significant verbal resistance at his table. Carmine Scantello and Oliver Rasmussen, themselves loudmouths, resented Harris's forceful tactics. Carmine and Oliver may have been in favor of The Explorer, and may actually have voted for it, but they, too, wanted to be heard – and different – and loud. As

Harris, Carmine, and Oliver shouted each other down, everyone else in the hall enjoyed the show.

At Eva's table, there was barely any discussion. They had all loved Karen's suggestion of Paradise. Marc was not about to interfere with his wife's proposal, not if he wanted to have sex again before Christmas – and that was months off.

Richard Winchester glided from table to table collecting the ten scraps of papers. He looked at Eva and opened his shoulders, thrusting his palms forward as if to ask what now?

"Why don't you just read them all out loud, Richard?" Eva suggested, hoping against hope there would be no tie. "Even better, why don't you count them yourself and just announce the winner? That might save some embarrassment for anyone who promised to vote one way and voted another," she explained, as she smiled at Mario and Harris. That possibility hadn't occurred to them. But what troubled them more than their failure to take that into account was the fact that Eva was one step ahead of them.

Standing by the bell captain's station in front of one of the tall windows overlooking Central Park, the setting sun illuminating the festive collage of yellow and orange leaves, Richard read the names to himself, counted them a second time, and cleared his throat.

"Welcome to Paradise."

"Yesss!" Marc whooped, his voice clearly discernible in the room's initial silence. Eva led the applause, and everyone joined in. Captain Pugliese stood up, raised his glass, and toasted, "To Paradise, the finest ship on the sea."

"To Paradise," everyone chanted in unison.

"Well, I look forward to seeing all of you in Spain next week," Eva exclaimed.

She said nothing more. She looked around the room, watching her shipmates. They drank, they laughed. Eva sat down, feeling a little light headed.

She was happy. Her vision had been realized.

# Acknowledgments

The most daunting task of the entire book-writing endeavor might be the drafting of this section. Not for fear of writing the wrong thing, but for fear of leaving out someone critical to the enterprise, or to my efforts. Accordingly, I have instead opted to be succinct. And to those who feel offended as a result of their exclusion, my apologies.

Many people have influenced my life, but none more than my parents. I have addressed them in the Dedication but because I know they are both anxiously looking down on me to make sure I don't generate any missteps; they should consider this another shout out.

My children have inspired me perhaps more than anything in life. Part of that was pure selfishness. I wanted so badly for them to succeed that I set my own bar impossibly high and spent my entire adult life trying to set an example for them. Often, I cleared the bar, but most of the time it was because of the push their influence had on me. I was never surprised, though, when they set their own bars higher than mine, and cleared them.

My son, Alex, has always been a forgiving and calming influence in my life. He saw me study for bar exams, prepare for hearings and trials, and strive to reach excellence in a career that demanded nothing less. He was always there to lend an encouraging ear, to inspire me to work harder, and to tell me not to stress more than necessary. His steadfast and principled approach to life is beyond admirable and he has influenced me in ways he will never know.

My daughter, Nicole, has always been the wind beneath my wings. On occasion, she is a full-blown hurricane. Nicole's assertive approach to life, always wanting to know why we can't do bigger and better things, will serve her well. As I watched her clear so many challenges in her own life, I became motivated to do more of the same in mine. In her first 25 years, she has already accomplished great things and has unknowingly driven me further than she could ever imagine.

I am a product of my education. As a creative writer, I was taught by the finest teachers one could imagine. I am forever in debt to the educators at St. David's School and Collegiate School in New York, who molded my writing style and cheered my creativity.

Lynn Krominga was a constant source of inspiration throughout the writing process. Besides being my traveling companion and supporter, she played the roles of best friend, proofreader, and fiction checker.

I have known Susan Konig since we were children playing together on the streets of Manhattan in the early 1970s. Alas, it was inevitable that I would select her publishing company,

Willow Street Press, to bring this project home. Susan's guidance, assistance, support, and professionalism have been invaluable throughout the entire editing and publication process.

I would also be remiss if I did not thank Susan's husband, Dave, for all his behind-the-scenes work on this book, especially his very direct editorial style.

Vicki Iovine, whose creative-writing accomplishments and successes are distinctively impressive, was a source of friendship, good ideas, and reinforcement at the right times.

From Fresno to Fairfield, from Casablanca to Corfu, Tami Orloff kept me motivated, sane, and joyful. Her passion for all things has no equal.

Many other friends and family members, too numerous to mention individually, have been inspirational to me throughout the writing process. When I was inclined to abandon the project, they encouraged me to forge forward. They proofread drafts, offered substantive comments, and provided general reinforcement. Without that assistance, you wouldn't be reading this.

And finally, I note my heartfelt appreciation for my fellow travelers aboard The World. Together, we have enjoyed fascinating experiences and called upon some unique places on this beautiful planet. I would have liked to include some of you in this novel, but since it involves only wholly fictional characters and events, I was unable to do so!

# About the Author

**Peter Antonucci** was a commercial litigator in the New York City offices of two of the largest law firms in the world before retiring from the active practice of law at age 52 to sail around the globe on a megayacht and write books. He has visited over 100 countries, traveled to Antarctica three consecutive years, and holds a Guinness Book of World Records certificate for having been a part-owner and passenger of a boat that traveled to 78°43'-99.7" S, 163° 41' 42.1" W in 2017, the southernmost point ever reached by a vessel, surpassing the previous records set by Amundsen, Shackleton, Ross, Scott, and Hillary, his heroes of Antarctic exploration.

Made in the USA
Monee, IL
29 May 2024

59097135R00204